"Do you remember the last time we spent the night together?" he asked.

"I've never spent a night with you," Pip said indignantly.

"I was referring to the night in the Broadhurst hayloft when we were children," John Henry reminded her. "Don't you recall? We were caught in the most ferocious storm."

"Oh, yes . . ." Pip said, a reluctant smile on her lips. "I do remember. We were playing out in the woods when the storm hit, and the cow barn was the only shelter within reach."

"Exactly. The wind nearly blew us over as we ran for cover." He laughed softly. "I remember both of us stripping down and diving under the hay for warmth."

Oh, she *did* remember. Despite their fear, it had been a wonderful night, John Henry holding her protectively throughout. She'd never given a moment's thought to their nakedness—all she'd cared about was sharing his warmth, feeling safe in his arms. Now his face loomed only inches from hers, far too close for comfort. She sat up abruptly, holding the covers tightly against her. "This isn't a hayloft," she said, "and no storm is raging outside."

"No, we're not in a hayloft, and we're not children, but I do hope one thing hasn't changed."

"What is that?" She turned to look at him. John Henry's eyes burned into hers. The pit of her stomach felt hollow. His body was clothed in a nightshirt, but the expression on his face was completely naked.

"I hope we still have trust between us," he said quietly.

The Sound of Snow

"*The Sound of Snow* is as lovely a story as its name.
It is a timeless tale of the miracle of true love, which
conquers all, heals all, and makes all new again
Add interesting characters, unexpected plot twists,
and a touch of the supernatural, and the result
is a memorable, feel-good read."
—*All About Romance*

"KATHERINE KINGSLEY HAS DONE IT AGAIN.
The Sound of Snow is a true gem . . . a sheer delight. Guy
is possibly one of the best heroes I've read in years and
you won't want to miss *The Sound of Snow*.
I treasured every word."
—*The BookNook*

Call Down the Moon

"FASCINATING . . .
an 'A' all the way!"
—*Atlanta Journal Constitution*

"Katherine Kingsley's magic touch once more provides an
emotional story that combines enchantment and the
wonder of love. . . . A beautiful and uplifting story—
the kind that makes readers sigh with pleasure and smile
through their tears. Tender, sweet, joyous, sensual and
poignant, this novel is simply wonderful."
—*Romantic Times*

Books by Katherine Kingsley

In the Wake of the Wind

Once Upon a Dream

Call Down the Moon

The Sound of Snow

In the Presence of Angels

Lilies on the Lake

KATHERINE KINGSLEY

Lilies on the Lake

A Dell Book

Published by
Dell Publishing
a division of
Random House, Inc.
1540 Broadway
New York, New York 10036

This is a work of fiction. Names, characters, places, and incidents either are the product of the author's imagination or are used fictitiously. Any resemblance to actual persons, living or dead, events, or locales is entirely coincidental.

Dell® is a registered trademark of Random House, Inc., and the colophon is a trademark of Random House, Inc.

ISBN: 0-440-23602-9

Manufactured in the United States of America

Published simultaneously in Canada

August 2001
10 9 8 7 6 5 4 3 2 1
OPM

In loving memory of Melinda Helfer
Who contributed so much to the romance genre, and whose
deep and abiding love for the Regency genre inspired us all.
You shall be sorely missed, dear friend.

Acknowledgments

With much love and many thanks to Jane Wood-ward and Jan Hiland, who were kind enough to read and comment, hug me, wipe away tears, and when necessary beat me about the head and shoulders during the course of writing this book.

I also owe thanks to my many dear friends in Mykonos, who pick up the pieces when I arrive right after finishing the manuscript—this is not a pretty picture, and they are very good to me.

My editor, Wendy McCurdy, was an angel, taking this book on nothing but faith (and probably prayer). Bless you.

As always, I thank you, the readers. I truly enjoy hearing from you (and please be patient if you don't hear back from me for an extended period of time—see above). You can write me at P.O. Box 37, Wolcott, CO 81655, e-mail me at katherinekingsley@yahoo.com, or visit my Web page at http://ourworld.compuserve.com/homepages/kkingsley.

Happy reading!

Katherine

Now folds the lily all her sweetness up,
And slips into the bosom of the lake:
So fold thyself, my dearest, thou, and slip
Into my bosom and be lost in me.

ALFRED, LORD TENNYSON
THE PRINCESS

1

October 16, 1835
Alexandria, Egypt

 $\mathcal{P}$ ip Merriem leaned on the railing of the ship, gazing out over the brilliant blue sea as the port of Alexandria came into sight. She released a deep, contented sigh. Finally. She was finally approaching the place she'd fought so long to see. Even as a child she'd dreamed of going to Egypt, and now here she was, about to embark on the adventure of her life.

Granted, her life was only twenty-seven years long, and although a great many people considered her over the hill, practically middle-aged and a spinster to boot, she felt as if she had just begun to live in this moment. Everything else had been nothing more than preparation—all her studies, her steadfast insistence on retaining her independence, the battles with her family merely steps on her path to her goal.

She brushed a blowing lock of auburn hair off her face and closed her eyes for a moment, savoring her hard-won victory, but she quickly opened them again so as not to miss a second of the miraculous sight before her. An amused smile flashed over her face as she considered that in the end, she really had to thank Isabel Bryson, of all people, for making that victory possible. The thought struck her as ironic, since Isabel had spent the entire journey confined to her cabin, suffering from seasickness. She wondered if Isabel was going to make a suitable traveling companion, given her performance to date. There were greater hardships yet to face, and she could only pray that Isabel would prove to be of stronger mettle than she had shown thus far.

Still, if Isabel hadn't presented herself as the perfect chaperon, Pip wouldn't have been standing there gazing at the coast of Egypt. Poor but educated, Isabel had been the straw that broke the camel's back. Pip's family had been forced to capitulate to her wishes, since she'd finally managed to produce the ideal person to accompany her. Isabel was plain, sober, not given to flights of fancy, and eminently respectable, even though she was as old and unmarried as Pip.

Turning to her friend, who still looked slightly green about the gills even though they were in calm waters, Pip grinned, her sapphire eyes sparkling. "What do you think?" she asked. "Doesn't the sight before you surpass everything you imagined in your wildest dreams? I certainly never expected the light to be quite so brilliant, or the sun so bright, or the buildings so impossibly white. Isn't it *glorious*?"

Isabel glanced at her with no trace of the enthusiasm she had shown back in Norfolk when she'd accepted the job of paid companion on Pip's wild adventure. "Oh, Portia, it is . . . it *is* lovely," she replied in a flat voice. "Forgive me if my eagerness doesn't match yours, but I shall not feel comfortable until we are off this awful ship and on steady ground. I am sure that I will recover my composure then."

"I'm sorry that you have endured such difficulties. If I had known that you would be so badly affected by sea travel, I would never have suggested you make the journey at all." She bit her lip, then laughed. "Although in all honesty I have to say I cannot regret that I did."

To Pip's surprise, Isabel suddenly burst into tears, sobs racking her body. Bewildered, Pip drew Isabel into her arms and attempted to comfort her. "What is it, my dear? What causes you such distress? We shall be docked in no time at all, and once we reach Cairo you will be so much more comfortable. Shepheard's Hotel is said to be all that is luxurious."

"Portia . . . Portia, my dear friend, I have not been entirely honest with you," Isabel mumbled into the embroidered handkerchief Pip had pressed into her hand. She looked up at Pip with anguished eyes, the brown of her irises blurred by fresh tears.

"Not—not been honest with me?" Alarmed, Pip ended the embrace and took a step back, intently examining

Isabel's face, the freckles standing out against her pale skin. "I don't understand. You said that you shared my fascination with Egyptology, that you wished for nothing more than to accompany me. Has the seasickness made you so ill that you wish yourself back in England?"

"No! Oh, no, anything but that," Isabel cried, screwing the handkerchief into a tight knot. "I had to get away, and when you made your proposal—well, it seemed like the perfect solution." She dropped her gaze to the deck, her shoulders hunched in misery. "There is no going back, at least not at present." She sighed heavily. "I have made my bed, I must lie in it, and God will make His judgment upon me."

A prickle of alarm ran down Pip's spine. Isabel's distress was clearly caused by more than severe mal de mer. "I don't understand you," she said, frowning. "What could God possibly judge you for? You are all that is good and kind, Isabel. If God is going to judge anyone, I shall be His target, for I have been nothing but disobedient and headstrong my entire life—you know how often I've flown in the face of my family's wishes."

Isabel said nothing.

Pip attempted a smile and continued. "Most recently, for example, I refused the offer of the Duke of Worcestershire, a considerable honor at my advanced age, according to my grandfather. I, on the other hand, felt that marrying a complete bore with an overinflated opinion of his own worth would have been a considerable dishonor to me."

"At least someone offered for you, and certainly not

for the first time," Isabel said, blowing her nose loudly into a linen handkerchief. "I have never been offered for by anyone, ever, and I'm not foolish enough to delude myself as to the reason why. Unlike you, I am not attractive in any way, and I have no dowry to offer. But oh, Portia, I *did* think I had finally found love and would at last be happy and looked after and have my own house and—and—"

Another flood of tears overwhelmed her, and she fell back into Pip's arms.

"My dear Isabel," Pip said, when her companion finally regained her senses, "you never made mention of a gentleman suitor. Did someone lead you on and then disappoint you? Who was the blackguard?" Her blood boiled at the thought.

Isabel refused to meet her gaze. "I cannot speak his name," she whispered. "I made a fool of myself and what transpired is no one's fault but my own."

"Never mind, my dear. I think I understand," Pip murmured, her heart breaking for her old friend. She knew that Isabel's greatest wish had always been to marry, though her chances of making a suitable match were slim, given her unfortunate situation.

Pip had met Isabel during their second Season in London, when they had been drawn together by a mutual interest in academics, which none of the other debutantes, and certainly not the young dandies, shared.

Pip hadn't given two shakes about Isabel's plain features or her lack of fortune. She enjoyed conversing intelligently on a number of subjects they both enjoyed, so she had championed Isabel, taking a deep pleasure in forcing the idiots of society to accept into their midst a girl whom they otherwise would have shunned.

That the social elite accepted Isabel only to please Pip, who had somehow become the toast of the *ton*, made her revile the members of polite society all the more.

Nothing had changed in the years that followed. Oddly, the more Pip defied society's strictures, the more she was admired, being hailed as an "original." Isabel hadn't been so lucky. They shared a love of knowledge and a dedication to furthering their education, but what was deemed endearingly eccentric in Pip was condemned in Isabel. All of this because Pip was considered a beauty, and Isabel anything but. Of course, it didn't hurt that Pip was also the stepdaughter of the Marquess of Alconleigh and had an independent fortune of her own. That by itself was enough to put a mist into a man's eyes when it came to his interpretation of beauty.

Pip released Isabel and took her trembling hands, squeezing them gently. "Let us forget about this ridiculous person who has caused you such distress. If indeed he is what sent you away from England, then we shall have your heart healed in no time at all. Just think, Isabel, of what awaits us. All of Egypt is about to be spread at our feet, and you will find yourself so transported that you will be able to think of nothing else."

"Nothing else," Isabel said, her red-rimmed eyes finally meeting Pip's. "I wish that were so, but I fear that is not the case. I have lied to you mightily, and you will be right to condemn me, even cast me off, for my abominable deceit, which I can no longer hide. Or at least not for much longer." She released Pip's hands and laid a palm over her belly. "Do you understand now the nature of my transgression, why I have been so ill?"

Pip stared at her in horror as a hundred thoughts, a hundred concerns, rushed through her mind. Isabel, *pregnant*? Her condition changed everything.

Pip's bright, wonderful dream collapsed beneath her. As the great noise of the dropping anchor sounded, she couldn't help thinking that her dream had been only within footsteps of realization.

She wanted to scream her rage to the world, but instead she silently took Isabel by the hand and led her down below, all the while trying desperately to think of how she was going to deal with the catastrophe that had befallen them.

February 17, 1836
Luxor, Egypt

"Portia—oh, Portia, for the love of God, deliver me of this child!" Isabel writhed in agony, her eyes wild with fear, her body covered with sweat as she strained against her burden. Twelve hours she'd been like this, with no sign of progress, and Pip had no idea what to do to help her.

Biting her lip hard, she sponged Isabel's pale face and neck with a cold cloth as she tried to reassure her. The stifling heat outside didn't help, but Pip wasn't thinking about that. She was praying desperately that their dragoman, Hassad, would return with help of some kind.

The *dahabeeyah*—the flat-bottomed houseboat that had served as their home for the last four months—bobbed gently on the waters of the Nile, the crew doing its best to ignore Isabel's pitiful cries. Pip didn't expect anything else. The men did their appointed tasks graciously and well, but delivering a foreign woman's baby was not among them.

They'd moored miles and miles upriver from Cairo, where a European doctor could have been found, but Pip couldn't have anticipated the possibility that Isabel would go into labor six weeks early. Instead of turning back as she could have, Pip lingered to sketch the temple of Medinet Abou at Thebes and to have another look at the amazing excavations in Karnak.

She and Isabel had become so close in the last months that Pip felt as if they were more sisters than friends, linked not only by the bond of Isabel's growing baby but by their shared adventures. To Pip's surprise and relief, once Isabel recovered from her sickness, she was a firm Egyptology enthusiast, traveling out to various sites and helping Pip catalog their experiences and impressions. Only in the last week had Isabel found herself unable to venture out as her pregnancy became more advanced, the heat depleting her strength.

Pip thought nothing of continuing her work, since Isabel was content to stay on the houseboat and rest. If only Pip had known how fragile Isabel really had been. If only . . . But "if only" did no good now.

Cursing herself for her ignorance, she tried to focus on the task at hand. Surely in the small village Hassad would find a midwife, or at least a woman who had experience with delivering babies. Of course, Pip thought grimly, even if Hassad found someone, there was no guarantee that the woman would observe any standards of hygiene. She'd never seen such filth as existed in the local villages, or such disregard for even the most rudimentary sanitation.

Pip pushed her damp curls out of her eyes and pulled back the single sheet that covered Isabel's swollen belly to see if there was any sign that the child was coming. She steeled herself not to cry out at the sight of bright red bloodstains on Isabel's nightdress and the bedding beneath her. Pip didn't know much about childbirth, but she was sure that a copious amount of blood wasn't a good sign.

"Be strong," she murmured. "For the baby's sake you have to be strong. Everything will be all right, you'll see." But as reassuring as her words might have sounded to Isabel, Pip's icy fear was turning her bones to water.

February 17, 1836
Karnak, Egypt

Thoroughly fed up, John Henry Lovell gave his donkey another hard kick in the flanks. The donkey, behaving as ill-tempered as John Henry felt, continued to drag its feet in the midmorning heat, stopping every two minutes to forage. John Henry had nearly to pulverize him in the loin to move on.

John Henry knew he should have given in to the equally ill-tempered Egyptian who'd rented him the beast and taken the higher-priced animal, but he hated being exploited. Absolutely nothing had gone right in the last month. He'd broken his long journey from India to England so that he could conduct some important business, but naturally his business contact had been unexpectedly called away to Damascus and wasn't expected to return until March.

John Henry wouldn't have minded, since he'd planned to travel in any case, but he hadn't counted on the European academics. Full of their own importance, they spent their time carting off irreplaceable antiquities that would end up in foreign museums or private drawing rooms. They called this activity scholarship; John Henry called it rape.

Equally boring were the women in their entourage, who had no knowledge of or even interest in Egypt, beyond trying to create a social setting identical to the one they'd had at home. He'd seen enough of that in India and had been no less disgusted by the colonial attitude particular to the British. Take over a country and impress upon it one's own social values, reduce its native people to serfs—that was the order of the day. The British Empire ruled, and to hell with the consequences on the local people and their heritage.

To his immense relief, the two temples that he'd come specifically to see finally loomed into sight, and he dismounted and tied the donkey's reins over a conveniently placed outcropping of rock. He removed the saddlebags that contained his lunch and water, slung them over his shoulder, and proceeded toward the temples, happy for the peace and privacy.

Settling in the shade of a small hill, leaning back against a large rock, he pulled out one of his water bottles. He drank thirstily, then poured the remainder over his dark hair and his shoulders and shook his head vigorously, flinging droplets in every direction.

Cooler, he cupped a hand above his eyes and took in the magnificent sight in front of him. He didn't have any difficulty in traveling back thousands of years, picturing the people coming to worship in the great temple of Amun.

After a time, he unpacked his simple lunch of bread, cheese, and olives and ate slowly, his thoughts wandering back over his ten years in India, then turning forward to England and what he might find upon his return. How strange it would seem.

He felt joy at the thought of seeing his family again, as well as the beloved countryside of Dorset so often revisited in his mind. At the same time he wondered if he, such a different man now, would see either in the same way as before. So much had happened over the years. His life had taken so many unexpected twists and turns since his departure at the inexperienced age of twenty that he couldn't help but wonder if England would feel the same to him.

He stopped trying to work out the imponderable and gave in to the seductive tug of sleep.

A voice rattling away in Arabic woke him and he sat up in alarm. Directly before him stood an Egyptian, dressed in a keffiyeh, arms flying as he pressed home his point.

"*Yellah. Imshi,*" John Henry replied in his scant Arabic. He'd become accustomed to the persistence of the local people who begged for *baksheesh.* "Go on, then," he added in English for good effect. "Go away. Scat. Take yourself off."

"You are the *effendi* Lovell?" the man asked earnestly, switching to English. "I have been sent by the man known as Hale, he who works for the good of the people. He said you would be here and be able to help."

John Henry sat up straighter. George Hale wouldn't send for him unless he had a damned good reason. A missionary who had lived in these parts for the last five years, George Hale was an exception to the rule of European interlopers. He had also become a friend whom John Henry admired for his unceasing work for the local people. John Henry had unexpectedly encountered the man two weeks before and had so enjoyed his company that he'd spent many nights in his camp.

"What is it?" he asked. "Did Reverend Hale say?"

"Yes, *effendi.* He said that you know about the

birthing of children. My young mistress, she is having her child, but it is too early, and the *effendi* Hale, he is with the family of a dying child and cannot be spared. He said you would help."

John Henry stood and brushed himself off. Attending the birth of a premature baby was not his idea of a good time, but he'd spent the first nineteen years of his life as a farmer's son, and so was conversant with the rudiments, at least in animals. That, and a smattering of knowledge of Ayurvedic medicine he'd picked up in India, might be of some help.

"Where is your mistress?" he asked.

"We stay on a *dahabeehyah*," the Egyptian answered, his weathered face reflecting his relief. "The river is not so far from here. Can you come now?"

John Henry packed up his saddlebags. "How long has your mistress been laboring?"

"I do not know exactly. My other mistress summoned me this morning and sent me for help, but no one in the village wanted to touch a *ferengi*, you understand."

John Henry nodded as he started toward his donkey. So the two women were Europeans, not that he could understand what a pregnant European woman was doing floating up the Nile, especially in such a remote location. Nor did it sound as if there were a husband around. The situation seemed highly suspicious to him.

"My mistress, she has the flaming hair, you see. My people consider this a sign of the devil, and to have two mistresses with the same hair, it is a double evil eye—I do not believe this, for they are good women, but for my people . . ." He shrugged.

John Henry frowned. Red hair did not bring to mind happy memories. Indeed, the last time he'd laid eyes on a redhead, his life had been shattered. Shattered enough, anyway, to cause him to leave England and make his way in a country as far away as he could reasonably manage. He forced the thought of Pip from his mind, which was not difficult after years of training, and focused on the task ahead.

An hour later, he boarded the *dahabeehyah* and looked around. The boat appeared well appointed and comfortable, with plump, colorful cushions lining the seats of the outside salon and a clean cloth on the dining-room table. No sign of poverty here. The boat itself was in good repair, the wood and brass gleaming. He turned to the man he now knew to be called Hassad.

"Show me where I can clean my hands, then take me to your mistress," he said.

Hassad bowed, took him to a place to wash, then led him below, and gestured to a cabin.

John Henry drew a deep breath and knocked.

"Enter! For the love of God, enter," a woman cried, and John Henry pushed the door open. The scene that met his eyes nearly caused him to gasp. The smell of blood was thick in the hot air. A young woman lay on the bed, white as a sheet, although the sheets themselves were stained a deep red. Her hands were curled loosely around her swollen belly, and the delicate skin of her closed eyes was as blue as her lips.

John Henry bit his bottom lip hard, trying to stifle

the nausea that suddenly overcame him. He'd never been particularly bothered by blood, save for the one time that Pip had jumped off a haystack and nearly bled to death from a cut to her foot delivered by a hidden scythe, but this time the blood didn't trouble him. He had seen death enough times to know that it was imminent in this case, and he didn't have the skill or knowledge to prevent it.

The redhead who bent over the laboring woman looked up as he walked toward the bed, her blue eyes wide with fear. She turned to face him. "Thank God," she whispered. "Are you a doctor?"

John Henry could only stare. Like a ghost from the past, the woman about whom he'd just been thinking stood before him, her tousled auburn hair falling about her shoulders, her face damp with perspiration.

"Pip?" he croaked, his parched throat barely getting the word out. "What the devil—? What are you doing here?"

She stared in return, as stunned as he was. "John Henry? Can it be? But this is impossible. . . ."

He gave one quick nod of his head, then put everything else out of his mind—his shock and disbelief, the surge of emotion that somehow managed to combine love, resentment, and confusion. "Never mind. Tell me quickly. What has happened here?" As he spoke he pulled the sheet aside. He'd never seen so much blood.

"I—I don't know," Pip whispered. "She just . . . started bleeding like that. I don't know how to stop it, John Henry. Isabel had six weeks yet to go and was in perfect health. But late last night her pains started and she's had no respite. What strength she had is nearly gone and I can't seem to reach her. She doesn't respond to anything, and the baby—I don't know what to do about the baby."

He looked up at her, taking in her red-rimmed eyes, her obvious exhaustion and dismay. In that moment he made a decision. Isabel was lost, that much was clear, but the child might still be saved.

"Call Hassad. Have him bring me a sharp knife."

Pip inhaled sharply, her face paling. "No . . . Oh, no, John Henry."

"It's the only way, Pip. If the child has a chance at all, this is it. Your friend is in God's hands now. Let us not consign both of them to His care if we can help it."

Pip blinked, then slowly walked to the door and issued instructions to Hassad, who stood just outside. Returning to the bedside, Pip picked up Isabel's hand and kissed it softly, then held it close against her heart. "I love you," she murmured. "I swear to love your child and to do everything I can to see to its well-being. Forgive us for what we are about to do. Forgive me for not looking after you better. Go with God, my dearest. Be safe and well in His arms."

She took a deep breath, then laid Isabel's hand back on her chest. Standing straight, she bowed her head and stood silently for a long moment. Then she looked John Henry squarely in the eyes. "Do what you must," she said. "I will help you if I can."

Despite the old and deep anger he held toward her, John Henry could not help but admire Pip for her courage. She reminded him of the wild, steadfast young girl he'd once known and loved, not of the flighty, self-centered young woman he'd last met, with her airs and graces and condescension that had ripped out his heart and all his hopes along with it.

He turned abruptly, unable to meet her steady gaze for a moment longer. "I think it might be best if you go elsewhere," he said. "This is not the place for you."

"No. I will be here for Isabel until the last."

John Henry didn't bother to argue. There'd never been any point in arguing with Pip anyway. If she chose to stay, that was her decision. God only knew, he hated the prospect of what he had to do.

Hassad came into the room, a large bowl of steaming water in hand, towels slung over his arm, and a long, sharp knife resting across the top of the bowl. Solemnly, he laid the items on the table next to the bed. John Henry had a strong feeling that Hassad would rather have been anywhere else.

Pip looked at Hassad as he walked out, his head bowed, then she took the armful of towels and began to lay them out around Isabel.

Neither one spoke, each mentally preparing for the grim task.

When all was ready, John Henry drew a deep breath. "Pip," he said quietly, "I don't know if the child is still alive, but I swear to you I will do my best to bring it safely into this world. I helped my father do this surgery on the farm once or twice. No harm can come to Isabel now. She is in God's hands."

Pip nodded. "I trust you," she whispered.

He'd never thought to hear those words from her again.

"Thank you. I think you should look away. This won't be a pleasant sight."

Pip drew Isabel into her arms and buried her face against Isabel's damp hair with a choked cry.

Taking the knife in his right hand, John Henry said a quick prayer and then drew the knife down Isabel's swollen belly, careful not to cut too deeply. Once he'd exposed the womb, he reached down, took hold of the tiny infant's body, and gently pulled it from its mother.

To his immense relief, the child shuddered in his arms, then weakly flailed its arms and legs, giving out a faint mewl of protest at being removed from its cozy nest. John Henry stared down in amazement at the newborn, perfect in every miniature detail, his little mouth pursed, his fists clenched and waving about as if he were trying to find the boundaries of this new world.

"It's a boy, Pip," he exclaimed. "A beautiful little boy."

Pip slowly sat up, and John Henry reached down with one hand and swiftly threw a towel over Isabel's open wound to spare Pip the sight.

"A boy?" she said faintly, turning to look at him, her face drained of color. "He's alive?"

"Very much so," John Henry said as the infant began to cry in earnest, "or at least for the moment. He's very small."

Pip peered down at the baby. "Oh, my," she breathed,

awe written all over her face. "Oh, my goodness. He is beautiful, isn't he?"

Then she turned to Isabel and stroked her still face. "You have a son, my darling. You must wake up now and take him in your arms. Come, it's all over now. Wake up, Isabel. You have to wake up!"

Recognizing the note of panic in Pip's voice, John Henry quickly tied and cut the umbilical cord, then prepared to hand Pip the infant. "Wrap him warmly," he said, doing his best to sound calm. "He needs you now."

Pip grabbed a clean towel and took the baby into her arms, but her gaze was focused on Isabel's white face. "John Henry?" Her voice shook. "Is she . . . ?" She was unable to form the words.

"Yes," he answered quietly, knowing that Isabel had gone before he'd made the incision. "She is at peace now. But she has left you a part of herself, Pip, and she would want you to be thinking of him now."

Pip didn't answer, clutching the wailing baby to her breast, her body rocking with silent sobs.

Since he could think of nothing comforting to say, John Henry decided to keep his peace. Pip had never taken comfort easily but found her way in her own time, and she would in this case too. He couldn't imagine she'd changed that much.

Eventually, she raised a tear-stained face and regarded him gravely. "Thank you," she mumbled. "Thank you for saving Isabel's child, even if you couldn't save her."

"She was past anyone's help. I doubt if the best doctor in the world could have made a difference, Pip. The baby's placenta was in the wrong place, at the mouth of the womb, which is why she bled so heavily. It happens."

"Yes," she said. "It happens." She wiped her eyes with the back of her hand. "I have so much to think about, what to do next."

"I know the subject must be very difficult for you, Pip, especially given the circumstances, but the first thing we must do is see to Isabel's burial this evening. The heat is a huge factor and—well. You understand."

"Yes, of course. I'd—I'd like to see her buried near the river. She so enjoyed the sunset from the bank." Pip wiped her eyes again.

"I'll arrange everything," he said. "Also, a wet nurse must be found for the child. He cannot go without milk for long."

"Hassad might be able to help." She looked down at the infant in her arms, gently rocking him.

He'd finally quieted, but John Henry knew that he would soon be hungry. "I have a better idea," he said, thinking of his missionary friend. "Take the baby to your quarters, Pip, and let me clean up in here. Then I'll make all the arrangements."

She nodded. "I cannot think what gift of God brought you here in this time of need, John Henry, but I am truly grateful."

"We'll talk about that later," he replied, anxious to get on with the details. When the time was right, he and Pip would have a long talk. A very long talk, whether she liked it or not. He strongly suspected that once she recovered from her shock, she would revert to the impossible girl she'd always been, independent to the last and unwilling to listen to anyone's reasoning but her own.

In any case, he needed time to think through the immediate situation. Pip had managed to get herself into a very large mess, and John Henry had a sinking feeling that he was the only person who could get her out if it.

That evening at sundown, Pip stood beside the shallow grave that had been scratched in the unforgiving ground of Egypt. She watched, her heart aching as the burial crew laid Isabel's simple coffin in the trench and began to shovel earth over it.

Each hollow thud of dirt falling on the lid of the coffin pounded home her sense of guilt. Isabel's death was her fault. If only she hadn't delayed . . . if only she'd known . . .

Pip covered her face with her hand, choking back tears as Hassad intoned the last of the Islamic prayers over the grave. The deep pain in her heart spoke only of remorse and regret. She waited for the others to walk some distance away, then knelt by the grave and said the Anglican prayers for the dispatching of the soul, which Isabel would have understood. The offering gave Pip comfort.

At dusk, as streaks of red and purple and gold slashed across the darkening sky, Pip finally rose and turned away, leaving behind a piece of her heart that would stay with Isabel always. She took a deep breath before facing her waiting companions, then glanced at John Henry, who stood off to one side, observing the proceedings.

She still felt dazed by her old friend's sudden appearance earlier in the day, just after she had prayed for help. She'd always known that God worked in mysterious ways, but He had truly surprised her this time.

At their last meeting, she'd considered John Henry no more than a provincial boy, an unsophisticated farmer's son with no prospects. Now, ten years later, he had miraculously appeared in Egypt, calmly stepping in and taking control of the horrifying situation. His cool head and courage had kept Isabel's death from becoming a double tragedy. Not one of Pip's acquaintances would have considered trying to save the unborn child, and the thought gave her a newfound respect for the man she wasn't at all sure she knew any longer.

Pip suddenly became aware that the object of her thoughts had turned his dark, piercing gaze in her direction as though seeing for the first time the woman she had become. The instant their eyes met, Pip realized how much their positions had changed. The enigmatic eyes of this tall, broad-shouldered stranger held none of the adoration John Henry had always accorded her from the time they were children growing up together in Dorset.

In the past he had given silent homage to her higher social standing and education, even while taking the lead in their childhood escapades. The man before her today seemed to take stock of her character and find her wanting.

She looked away in confusion, thinking that he had certainly matured. A natural, masculine confidence emanated from him. She couldn't help wondering what had happened to change him so much—even his speech had lost its Dorset accent and taken on the tones of an English gentleman.

She imagined she would find out soon enough, for John Henry had made himself very clear. They would talk; and when they did, she would have a lot of explaining to do, rather than the other way around.

Pip wasn't looking forward to the experience.

They ate a late dinner on the top deck of the *da-habeehyah*, barely speaking of anything beyond the most rudimentary subjects. Pip's deep grief kept her from anything more challenging, and John Henry seemed lost in his thoughts. She thought she might be able to slip off to bed without further conversation, but when John Henry put down his knife and fork and rested his forearms on the table, fixing her with a penetrating gaze, she knew she'd been mistaken.

"So, Pip," he said, his voice neutral but his expression determined. "Just what the devil are you doing here, and what in the name of God has been going on? The truth, if you please."

Pip looked down at the table, then out across the

Nile. "I don't know what you mean," she replied, stalling.

"You know exactly what I mean. Isabel Bryson, God rest her soul, is dead, you've been landed with her newborn child, and I'd like to know just how all of this came about. What do your parents think about this?"

Pip was most uncomfortable at the mention of her mother and stepfather, who would be horrified if they knew anything of her present circumstances. She looked back at him. "They know I'm somewhere in Egypt but not my exact location. I haven't known myself from day to day where I would be."

"But what were you doing here in the back of beyond, with a heavily pregnant woman and no medical facilities anywhere to be found? Why don't you start there?"

Pip drew herself up. "I don't see how this is any of your business."

"You made it my business," he pointed out curtly. "I think that entitles me to an explanation. Shall we begin again, and this time please answer my questions without your usual evasions. I find them not only tedious but a waste of my time."

Pip flinched. That air of command she'd earlier admired was proving to be a problem. "Very well. If you must know, Isabel Bryson was my friend. We—we met in Cairo after her husband had been called away to Istanbul on business. I offered to look after her." She smiled in what she hoped was a disarming fashion. "Since I had already planned to travel up the Nile and needed a companion, I invited her to come along with me so that she might escape the heat of Cairo. Of course, neither of us expected her to go into labor so early."

John Henry narrowed his eyes. "Are you telling me you were in Cairo without a companion?"

"Unfortunately, the companion who had traveled with me from England became ill and had to return," she said, thinking fast. There. He had no way of knowing the truth, and her explanation sounded perfectly plausible. "As for what I'm doing in Egypt, I came to see the ruins like everyone else who is here. I've been studying Egyptology for years."

"Hmm. That much I do believe. You always were a scholar at heart, although the last time I saw you I thought you had a budding career ahead as an idle and capricious member of the *ton* and some fop's future wife. Happily, you seem to have avoided that particular pitfall—or am I mistaken?" He regarded her in a particularly biting manner. "Perhaps you married after all, but decided the arrangement didn't suit you and bolted. Nothing much would surprise me."

Pip was shocked. She'd never imagined her old friend was capable of such meanness. "How dare you!" she cried, anger rising swiftly. "I would never do such a terrible thing as leave my husband. Even if I loathed him, I couldn't possibly disgrace my family in such a manner. Just who do you think you are to speak to me like this?"

"Oh, I know precisely who I am, Pip. You made my position very clear at our last meeting. I'm not fit to lick your boots, as I recall. I can imagine your distress that I'm not keeping my place, but much has changed since then."

"I can see that," she snapped, uncomfortable at the memory of her ill-considered words ten years before. "I never before found you to be rude and boorish."

"No. That was your forte. I learned from a master."

Pip felt as if she'd been slapped, and her eyes welled with tears. "I—am sorry for what I said," she muttered. "I was young and thoughtless, and if I hurt your feelings, please accept my apology." Apologies did not come easily to her, and the words stuck in her throat.

"On the contrary," he said calmly, folding his hands together. "You opened my eyes. Perhaps I should thank you, for your rebuff inadvertently sent me down a path I might otherwise not have taken."

"What path was that?" she asked, hoping to change the subject. "Where have you been all this time, and what are *you* doing in Egypt? This is the last place I expected to find you."

"Like you, I came to see the sights and also conduct some business on my way back from India, which is where I've been living for the last ten years. But never mind that." He folded his napkin and tossed it onto the table. "Let us return to the subject of Isabel Bryson. To be honest, I find your story a bit far-fetched. I would appreciate something that more closely approximates the truth. If you choose not to tell me, I'm sure Hassad will be happy to oblige."

Pip opened her mouth, then closed it again. John

Henry had learned well over the years how to play cat and mouse, and he had her cornered. The problem was that she was not accustomed to being the mouse in their relationship.

Chewing on her bottom lip, she considered her options. Maybe, just maybe, if she told him the whole story, he would offer his assistance. She didn't see how she was going to manage on her own at this point, and two heads were supposed to be better than one.

John Henry wasn't in a position to go back to England and spread the story about, for who would listen to him? He didn't have the ear of anyone in polite society. But if she appealed directly to their old friendship, maybe he *would* continue to help her. But was he to be trusted with Isabel's secret?

John Henry leaned forward. "You can trust me, Pip, you must know that."

She nearly jumped out of her chair, feeling as if he'd read her mind. "If I do tell you the truth, do you swear to keep it to yourself?" she asked, regarding him intently.

"I just told you as much." A faint smile crossed his face. "We were childhood co-conspirators, after all. When did I ever betray you?"

It was I who betrayed you, she thought miserably. "Never," she said. "You were always the best of friends."

"You needn't try to placate me." He looked down at his hands. "I am merely offering my services. All I ask is that you tell me everything that led up to this moment. I will do what I can."

"That is fair enough. Very well, John Henry. I will tell you the full truth, but keep in mind that for Isabel's sake, everything I say you must keep in confidence."

He fixed his gaze on her. "If you're waiting for a vow of silence, I've already given it to you."

Pip had to force herself not to look away. She wished with all her heart that John Henry hadn't grown into such a fine-looking man. The promise had always been there, but she'd never paid much attention to it. He'd always been just John Henry, her friend. Now she found his presence unsettling. She wasn't accustomed to noticing men's physiques, but John Henry emanated a powerful masculinity that was hard to ignore. Whatever he'd been doing in India must have involved serious physical labor, for his muscles were well developed, his shoulders and chest broad, his waist narrow, and what she'd seen of the rest of him, now thankfully hidden by the table, wasn't lacking in strength.

"Pip?" He rested his square chin on one hand. "Why are you regarding me in such a peculiar fashion?"

She colored furiously, embarrassed to have been caught staring. "Sorry," she said. "I was just wondering where to start."

"At the beginning would be sensible. When and how did you really meet Isabel Bryson? I very much doubt you adopted a pregnant woman in Cairo and chose to haul her off up the Nile."

"No, I didn't," she replied. "I met Isabel in London when we were both eighteen. We became friends, sharing many of the same interests."

"Let me guess. Men and marriage—would that be close?"

Pip glared at him. "No, not even remotely. Isabel and I talked about history and literature and other subjects of that nature. She also had a fascination with ancient Egypt."

"I see. So the two of you suddenly decided years later that going haring off to indulge your mutual captivation was a brilliant idea."

She nodded. "The idea was actually mine, one I'd had for some time, but Isabel took a great deal of persuading. She—she tended toward a more cautious nature than I possess."

John Henry snorted. "Perhaps *sensible* would be a better word. I cannot believe that her husband thought this a good idea."

"She wasn't married."

"Ah," John Henry said, leaning back in his chair. "Let me see . . . Isabel believed a prolonged trip away from England a good solution for her unfortunate condition, and you thought her unfortunate condition a perfect solution to solve the problem of the needed companion."

"No—it wasn't like that at all, I swear. Whatever you might think of me, I would never do such a terrible thing. I had no idea of Isabel's condition. Indeed, she came to me and said she'd changed her mind and was willing to undertake the journey." Pip rubbed her hands across her face, forcing back tears. "I didn't know that she was with child until we were sailing into

Alexandria. I was appalled to hear the news, but there was nothing I could do at that point."

John Henry shot her a sharp look, then nodded. "What did you do next?"

Pip sighed. "We kept the pregnancy a secret, of course, deciding that it was best to hire the *dahabee-hyah* and vanish for a few months, then return to a remote part of Cairo when Isabel's time was near, under assumed names. There was a risk that we'd be found out, but it was the best plan I could think of."

This time she could not hold back her tears and bent over, her remorse nearly suffocating her. "I made such a mess of everything. I didn't ever think that Isabel would go into labor so early, but I should have. I *should* have."

"You cannot be faulted for Isabel's lack of judgment in not initially telling you the truth," John Henry said quietly, pulling a handkerchief from his pocket and handing it to her. "I understand her reason, but it was foolish, as was your decision to take on the entire responsibility. No matter her shame, she'd have been better off returning to her family."

Pip sat up straight. "You do not know anything about her family," she shot back, ignoring the hot tears streaming down her cheeks. "Believe me, they would not have understood, and Isabel would have found herself out on the streets without a penny. Isabel's father is a self-righteous country squire, and a more tedious, moralizing man I have yet to meet. Her mother is no better—she saw Isabel as no more than a slave at her beck and call."

Pip slowly shook her head, drying her eyes on the handkerchief, which smelled of fresh air and something more elusive but nice. "No. The solution we found was the only one that made any sense."

"If the solution made so much sense, what did you plan to do with the child once it appeared? Clearly Isabel couldn't have kept him if she was to retain any respectability. Answer me that, Pip. How did this grand plan of yours include the future of this child?"

Pip would very much have liked to kick John Henry in the shins at that moment, but knew she couldn't afford to incur his wrath if she was to enlist his aid. "We planned to have him adopted," she said. "We thought we might find a sympathetic missionary family on our travels."

John Henry scratched his cheek. "And what is your grand plan now?"

Pip's cheeks went hot. "I don't have one," she finally admitted. "I haven't had time to think properly. The one thing I do know is that I cannot give him up. I owe that much to Isabel."

John Henry stared at her as if she were mad. "You must be joking. What are you going to do with an infant? Surely you don't think you can take him back to England with you?"

"What else am I to do?" she replied, knowing she could never pull off such a deception. "I can't abandon him now. How could I? In any case, I made a vow to Isabel and I'm not going to break my promise," she added stubbornly.

"Pip . . . surely you realize that no one would believe

he wasn't yours, no matter what story you made up. You must think of your position, your reputation."

"I don't give two figs about my position *or* my reputation. I only care about that tiny boy who hasn't a soul in this world other than me who cares about him!"

"Perhaps, but surely you care about the position and reputation of your mother and stepfather. There would be whispers and innuendoes, you know that, and you don't want to expose your family to that. It's all well and fine for you to ruin yourself, but to put their good name in peril seems going too far."

"I don't see why you care," Pip retorted belligerently, even though she knew he had a good point, and one she was deeply concerned about. "It's not as if you have any deep love for them."

"As it happens, I have," he said, his voice softening. "I owe the marquess a good deal and I don't want to see him hurt. On top of that, I've always been very fond of your mother, who was nothing but good to me and my family. If you cannot understand my concern for you, at least try to see that I would be loath to see them subjected to scandal of any sort."

Pip buried her face in her hands, knowing he was right. She would be subjecting her family to the worst sort of gossip, and although she truly didn't mind for herself, she minded terribly that they would inevitably be tainted by her actions.

"Please help me," she said in desperation. "I truly don't know what to do next, but I cannot hand this child over to strangers and walk away."

"I understand," he said gently. "I no more want to see that innocent little boy be put into uncaring hands than you do. There's something about helping to bring a new life into this world that leaves one with an overwhelming sense of responsibility for that life."

"Then you really do understand," Pip exclaimed with infinite relief. "And you will help me now?"

"Let me sleep on it," John Henry replied. "I confess that I'm exhausted. If you don't mind, may I shelter here for the night? I know I'll put you in a compromising position, but quite honestly, I don't know if I have the energy to make my way back to my own camp at this late hour."

"By all means," Pip said, relieved to know that John Henry would be close at hand. "Take the cabin that is first on the right. We will speak again in the morning. I imagine the night will be a long one, given that the baby has no more than a cloth of goat's milk to suckle on."

"That he is suckling at all is a good sign. Pip . . ." He hesitated for a moment, running his fingers through his dark hair. "We have talked about his future, but I must warn you that it's possible he won't survive. He is very small and his birth was difficult."

"I know," she said. "But I have every faith that his spirit is strong. He will survive, you shall see."

John Henry smiled. "In that case, you had better give him a name."

Pip grinned in return. "Peter. I'll call him Peter, after the saint. Look at the obstacles he overcame and all the good he did the world as a result."

John Henry's smile widened, carving deep lines along the sides of his mouth. "It is a good, strong name. He will wear it well. Good night, Pip."

"Good night," she said, rising. "Do not let your sleep be disturbed by young Peter, for I cannot imagine he will be quiet much longer."

"Once my head hits the pillow I'll be out cold. I wish you good luck with our small friend."

"If I'm to be his mother, I might as well start right now," she replied, heading for the stairs. Tomorrow. They'd work everything out tomorrow. John Henry would find a solution. She'd always been able to count on him.

Despite his exhaustion, John Henry tossed and turned the entire night through, trying to make sense of his jumbled thoughts. Pip had always had a talent for trouble. In this instance, she'd managed to exert that talent to its fullest. The future of an innocent child lay at stake.

The other problem, just as troublesome, was his state of confusion. For the majority of his life he'd loved Pip. After years of concerted effort, he thought he'd finally managed to dislodge her from his mind and his heart. But walking into that godforsaken room yesterday and seeing her had brought it all back in one great painful rush. He'd done what was necessary, never anticipating the aftermath of his decision.

Every instinct told him to come to her aid one more time. He couldn't abandon her—that was out of the question. He'd done his best to use his old, familiar resentment to protect himself, but that hadn't worked. Pip's pain and remorse over Isabel's death cut too close to the bone, opened avenues that ran straight to his gut, avenues he thought he'd long since redirected.

Which left him precisely nowhere but back at the obvious and only solution to his quandary, as much as he'd tried to avoid it. Shoving the thin sheet aside in frustration, he swung his feet out of the bed and padded over to the open window. He stared out across the moonlit river.

If he was to keep Pip's and little Peter's lives intact, he would have to become the sacrificial lamb. He didn't know what Pip would make of his decision, but he'd have to convince her of the sense of his rash plan.

As reluctant as he was to lay his neck on the block, he owed a large debt of gratitude to Pip's stepfather, and John Henry was not one to neglect his obligations, no matter what the consequences to himself.

3

Little Peter had kept Pip up most of the night, so
she'd finally taken him from his makeshift cradle,
which was nothing more than a basket cushioned with
towels. She tucked him up beside her in her bed,
where he slept fitfully between bouts of suckling on
the goat's-milk cloth.

Looking down at this tiny scrap of humanity, his
skin so pale and thin that she could see the blue veins
running beneath it, she wondered at the miracle he
was. Her heart ached for his vulnerability, his complete
helplessness in the world. Motherless, and to all intents fatherless, this dear little being had no one but
her to see to his needs, to love him.

And she did love him, she realized with a sudden
jolt. She loved him as if he were her own flesh and

blood. Tears started to Pip's eyes as she stroked his downy head. Picking up one minuscule hand, she marveled at its perfection. His fingers curled with surprising strength around hers, and he gave a little hiccup.

She gazed down at his miniature pink fingernails, like the smallest and most translucent of seashells.

Gently lifting him in her arms, she rested him on her raised knees and looked at him, her heart swelling with love. He gazed back at her, his eyes examining her face intently, as if he knew she was his mother now.

"I *am* your mother, sweet boy," she whispered. "I will guard and protect you, never fear. I will kiss your grazed knees and soothe away your tears, and whatever life deals out to you, I will be there always to love and guide you. This is my promise to you."

His little brow crinkled and he flailed his fists, his eyes never leaving her face.

Pip couldn't help laughing. "You are a wonder, my darling, a true wonder. I don't think I understood how much until now. I will always love your mother and I regret her death with all my heart, but you will remind me of her every single day."

She kissed the top of his head. "But here you are, my little boy, and I couldn't be happier. I must say, you made your entrance in a most dramatic fashion. I do hope you don't plan to carry on being so flamboyant. We could all use a little peace."

Peter yawned and shoved one fist into his mouth, his eyes closing.

Pip tenderly laid him next to her and curled up around him protectively, his tiny form held like a boat in the safe harbor of her body.

As her eyes closed, she couldn't help but worry that he wasn't getting enough nutrition, but nothing could be done about that until a wet nurse was found. Hassad was none too hopeful on that score, but Pip prayed that he would succeed. For the moment, goat's milk would have to do.

Stifling a yawn, Pip made her way up to the top deck. She cupped one hand over her forehead, the bright sunlight hurting her eyes. Pip spotted John Henry, who had ensconced himself in a chair at the table and was drinking coffee, his gaze fixed on the river.

"Ah, there you are," he said, rising and pulling out a chair for her at the table. "How does our small friend fare this morning?"

"He is finally sleeping peacefully," she said, taking her seat. "And yourself? Did you sleep soundly?" She observed that John Henry looked as tired as she felt.

He shrugged one shoulder. "I had much on my mind." He offered her the basket of toasted bread and pushed the butter and jam toward her. "You probably did as poorly, if the dark circles under your eyes are anything to go by."

She attempted a smile. "Peter did not give me much time for thought." That wasn't entirely true, but when Peter had dozed, she hadn't been able to think of anything but what the future held for him and for her.

"John Henry," she said impulsively, "do you think if I go back to England with Peter and say that he is the child of missionaries who died from illness, I might be believed?"

John Henry ran a hand over his face. "Pip," he replied, dropping his hand and looking at her with exasperation, "perhaps in a better world you might be, but people, especially those in your social position, always jump to the worst possible conclusion. You, an unmarried female, left for the back of nowhere in a rather abrupt fashion, and now you think to return home with an infant—a white infant, no less—and you expect everyone to believe such a story?"

She shook her head. "I realize the scenario sounds ludicrous. What else am I to say, though?"

He fiddled with his butter knife, turning it over and over in his fingers. "I believe a visit to the Reverend Hale today would be in order. He's the missionary who had me summoned to help Isabel—did you not speak to him about this problem?"

"We arrived only two days ago. I wouldn't have known that a missionary would even be in such a remote location."

"That's fair enough. Still, here he is, and he might have some thoughts on the matter, possibly even a solution." He looked at her. "In the brief time I've known George Hale, I've found him to be a man of broad thinking, which will be necessary in this case. I do not think he will pass judgment, since his business is to find solutions, not to create more problems. Will you come with me?"

Pip frowned. "Do you mean I have to tell him the full truth? For the sake of the baby, I confided in you, but more than that seems like a betrayal of Isabel's confidence."

"He's a minister," John Henry pointed out. "We have to trust someone, and if you truly do care both about Peter's future and keeping Isabel's secret, then George Hale is the man to help. *Please* stop being so hardheaded and have a modicum of faith in my judgment, even if it does go against the grain."

Crushing her napkin into a ball in her lap, Pip told herself that John Henry really was trying to help and she had, after all, dragged him into her disaster. He'd gotten her out of scrapes before, so why should she doubt him now?

"Do you have any better ideas?" he asked, lazily peeling an orange. "If you have, now is the time to voice them."

Pip shoved her forehead onto her palm in frustration. "You know I haven't. I already told you that," she said, with a sincere desire to wrap her hands around his strong, muscular throat and strangle him.

"Very well," she said, making her decision. "We will go to the Reverend Hale, and I pray that he can be trusted."

John Henry popped a segment of orange into his mouth. "Good. We'll leave as soon as you can organize yourself. What about Peter?"

"What about him?" Pip retorted, annoyed by John Henry's casual attitude to her crisis.

"Peter can't come with us, not in this heat. Someone

needs to look after him, and I saw Hassad leave some time ago to try to track down a nurse."

"I'll ask Mohammed to keep an eye on him. He's the cook—he ought to be able to work out what to do with a baby and goat's milk on a flannel."

"Mmm. A little *baksheesh* might be in order. I assume you're in funds?"

"My funds are none of your concern, but paying a bribe to Mohammed will not be a problem. I shall go and have a word with him and then change my clothes. How far is Reverend Hale from here?"

"An hour's ride. Do you have a donkey at your disposal?"

"Naturally," Pip said, wondering how she was going to manage to stay awake and upright that long. She wanted nothing more in that moment than her bed, a cold cloth on her forehead, and the oblivion of sleep. "I assume you have your own donkey. There is no way in heaven that two of us will fit on mine."

John Henry didn't bother to reply. "Excellent," he said instead. "I hope you haven't turned into one of those exasperating females who takes hours to prepare herself to venture outside."

Pip couldn't help grinning as memories of their many escapades flooded through her, all the times she'd escaped through her bedroom window and down the thick ivy vine on a moment's notice, hearing the sharp sound of stones against her window followed by John Henry's whispered command.

"When have I *ever* taken more than a moment to pull myself together?"

He regarded her intently. "Never, as I remember. But that was long ago, Pip. I no longer know you, any better than you know me. The last time I saw you, your behavior had altered considerably, if you remember."

Pip flushed, regretting again the cavalier way she'd treated him all those years ago. She'd been testing her newfound wings, trying to impress him with her fancy dress and polished manners. She'd forgotten in the first flush of exhilaration that John Henry might not appreciate the change in her. He had remained the simple farm boy, and she had gone off to become a marquess's stepdaughter, even though her basic nature had never changed. She supposed she hadn't given him the chance to find that out.

She couldn't help but wonder why he was now so willing to help her. He could easily have walked away after delivering Peter. More interesting was what he'd said about owing a debt to her stepfather, Will, and her mother, although she couldn't imagine what it could be.

"Don't just sit there daydreaming," he said, breaking into her thoughts. "We need to be off before the sun becomes too hot."

"I'll be back in a moment." She dashed downstairs to instruct Mohammed in the care and feeding of Peter. Though looking thoroughly alarmed at the prospect, Mohammed agreed.

"Whatever the lady wishes," he said, looking everywhere but at her. She could only imagine what he was thinking, but the money she left on the kitchen counter went a long way toward helping him keep his tongue in check.

That task accomplished, she looked in on the infant and found him still sound asleep. She ran one finger down his fragile cheek, the skin thin, the veins visible beneath it. "Hold on, little one," she whispered, her heart swelling with a protective love. "We'll work something out. I will let no harm befall you."

She dragged out her hat and long scarf, then ran back up the stairs. There John Henry was leaning against the railing, looking thoroughly bored.

"What are you waiting for? I thought you were in a hurry."

He turned abruptly. Soon they were on the dusty road to Reverend Hale's house.

Pip had to force herself not to laugh at the sight of John Henry's long legs dangling over the sides of his fat donkey, especially since his donkey looked as displeased with the arrangement as John Henry did. Another two inches and John Henry would have been walking the beast along, rather than the other way around.

He kept kicking the donkey's flanks, but the animal didn't alter his plodding pace one iota. She wasn't sure she'd ever seen a donkey's ears laid flat back against his head.

"Have you tried speaking to him in Arabic?" she offered helpfully.

He glared at her. "Whether I address him in Arabic, English, or Hindi isn't going to make the slightest difference."

"Perhaps you need to change your choice of mount?"

"Don't you think you should be worrying about other things? This—this *creature* is the least of our problems." He gave the donkey another swift kick and flapped his reins.

"Might I suggest that we change mounts? I might be a bit easier a burden for him to carry." She didn't want to add that she'd always had a way with animals, especially those of the equine species. "You did mention that time was of the essence."

John Henry pulled the donkey to an abrupt halt, not difficult since it was going at a snail's pace and only too happy to stop. "Fine," he snapped. "You try, and see how you get on with him."

Pip happily dismounted. "His name?" she inquired.

"Abdullah," he said, pushing the reins into her outstretched hand.

Pip moved to Abdullah's head and gently stroked his nose. "Now, then," she murmured in Arabic. "I know you're hot and tired, but we have important business to accomplish. I promise you a nice, long, cold drink of water when we arrive at our destination, and I very much appreciate your cooperation in the meantime. I'm sure you're a lovely boy who's been underappreciated and most likely even abused," she added, stroking his muzzle again. "Let's get on with it, shall we?"

Abdullah looked up at her with moist, glowing eyes and snorted lovingly into her hand.

"Good," she said, moving around to his side and mounting. "Let's go, my darling."

Abdullah set off at a brisk trot, his head high, his ears pricked eagerly forward. Pip didn't risk looking over at John Henry. She knew she'd laugh so hard that she'd fall off Abdullah. Maybe not that much had changed, after all.

Forty-five minutes later they arrived at a village, if it could be called that. Filth littered the dry streets, and small children ran nearly naked, unwashed and unkempt. The houses were no more than mud huts, hastily built and destined to be just as hastily destroyed when the rains came. That was the way of life, the way it had always been and the way it would stay, regardless of the Reverend Hale's best efforts.

Pip glanced around, ignoring the children who crowded around them, hands outstretched for money or food. She had only one thing on her mind—finding the Reverend Hale.

"This way." John Henry pointed to a tent on the far side of the village. "Let's pray he is in."

Pip prayed fervently. God had not smiled down on her for some time, she thought.

To her relief a slender, blond man no more than thirty years of age appeared from the tent as he heard them approach. Much to her surprise, he was dressed in the loose flowing kaftan and headdress customary to the Egyptians.

He blinked in the sudden assault of sunshine, then smiled broadly as he recognized John Henry. "Ah," he said, striding forward. "I trust you received my message in a timely fashion? Did all go well, then?"

John Henry swung down off his donkey and shook

Hale's hand. "Not as well as I might have wished. Allow me to present Miss Portia Merriem," he said, gesturing toward Pip, who had also dismounted. "She is an old and trusted friend from England and was also friend to the woman you summoned me to help."

Reverend Hale nodded at her in acknowledgment and then looked back at John Henry. "You speak in the past tense, my friend. Do you come to ask me to conduct a burial service?"

"No. That we did last night. The situation I put before you is more complicated and delicate. Might we go inside and discuss the matter?"

George Hale inclined his head and stepped back, at the same time gesturing to two men who had appeared out of nowhere. "Take the donkeys and water them," he said in proficient Arabic. "Give them shade and food when that is done." He switched back to English. "Miss Merriem, I have little to offer in the way of refreshment, but perhaps you will take some mint tea."

"Thank you." She moved gratefully inside the tent, out of the sweltering sun, leaving the two men in deep conversation. She liked the Reverend Hale, who appeared to be practical and thoroughly adapted to the local customs.

Her eyes slowly adjusted to the dim light, and she took in her surroundings. A simple cot neatly made up stood in one corner, and a table off to one side held a pile of books. In the Arab tradition, he'd fashioned a seating area of large pillows along one side of the tent with a low table in the middle.

Pip's respect for him grew as she absorbed the

environment he'd created—one that was familiar and comfortable for the people he'd come to minister to.

A few minutes later Hale entered the tent, followed by John Henry.

"Miss Merriem," Hale said. "I am sorry for your loss. John Henry gave me the briefest of details. Please do not blame yourself for what could not have been avoided."

Pip bowed her head, fighting back tears. "Thank you for your kind words, but I cannot help feeling that if I'd taken Isabel straight back to England when I learned of her pregnancy, she would not have died."

"A natural part of grief is looking to ourselves for blame. You must remember that we are in God's hands. As I said, your friend would have died in any case. Thanks to John Henry's quick action, at least her baby survived. We must think of the child now."

Pip wiped her eyes, then looked up. "Yes. That is why we've come. I—that is, Isabel and I—thought to turn him over to a European family, but I cannot give him up now. Not now, not after everything."

"I understand," George Hale said, bending over a small stove and putting a pot of water on to boil. "The question becomes how you can keep him without creating a stigma for both of you. Unfortunately, England is harsh in the matter of illegitimate children." He straightened and fixed her with his brilliant blue eyes. "I have an idea, but I do not know if you will find it readily acceptable."

Pip's heart quickened. "An idea? One that would allow me to keep Peter?"

"Yes. One that would allow the world to believe you to be Peter's mother, but in an acceptable fashion."

Pip frowned. "How is that possible? I am not married, and that is the only way that Peter would be accepted as legitimate."

"Precisely," Reverend Hale said, pouring the boiling water into a pot filled with tea leaves and mint. "You must be married."

Pip stared at him in disbelief. "Married? But to whom? I'd have to have been married at least seven months, and in any case I cannot think of a single candidate—unless you are offering yourself up as a husband," she added dryly.

He laughed. "No. That was not my idea. I would make a most unsuitable husband, and my life's work is here, not back in England."

Pip slowly shook her head, completely baffled. *Marriage?* The idea was preposterous. Surely he meant a sham marriage—that had to be it. She forced a smile. "I think you must be funning with me, Reverend. I could no more pretend to be married than I could pretend to be a—a Turk."

He handed her and John Henry steaming glasses, looking amused. "I was not suggesting a pretense of either sort. I refer to a real marriage. I have someone in mind who would do very nicely, providing you agree."

"But—but who would agree to such a deception?"

"An old and trusted friend of yours. John Henry, to be precise."

"*John Henry?*" she gasped in horror. "You cannot possibly be serious." Her gaze flew to John Henry, only to find him looking at her, arms crossed, his face perfectly still but his eyes piercing hers in a highly disconcerting manner.

"Why do you look so appalled?" he asked, his voice lazy. "Do you think me so beneath your regard that the very thought sickens you?"

"No—no, not at all," she said, trying to catch her breath. "I just never . . . the thought never occurred to me." She put down her glass, her hands shaking. "Why would you make such a sacrifice?" she asked, her voice as shaky as she felt. "You don't even like me. You've made that clear enough. I cannot imagine that you would want to take on such a responsibility, never mind such a dangerous charade." She sank down onto one of the cushions, her head spinning.

"You, my dear Pip, are begging the question. If you want a way out of your dilemma, I am prepared to offer it. If, on the other hand, you find the idea so repulsive, then you are on your own. I will vanish back out of your life and you can carry on without any further interference from me." He picked up his tea and took a sip, his gaze never leaving her face.

"But—I don't understand." She tried desperately to think clearly. "You can't be doing this for my sake alone. What is the advantage for you? You must want something, or you would never agree to shackle yourself to me and an infant that isn't even yours." She looked at him hard. "Do you want money, is that it?"

He lowered his gaze, stroking his thumb over his chin. "Let us just call this an arrangement. I offer my name to you and Peter, and in return you give me something that I would not otherwise obtain. That seems fair enough."

Pip felt the bottom drop out of her stomach. John Henry wanted to advance himself through her? That he could be so coldhearted sickened her to the depths of her being, bringing back memories of her late father, who had married not for position but certainly for money. Love had not entered into the equation.

She never would have imagined in a million years that John Henry could be so callous as to take advantage of her troubles. Still, what option did she have? Peter's future lay at stake, and John Henry had presented the only possible solution. She squeezed her eyes shut, covering them with one hand, trying to reason it out logically but getting nowhere.

She'd always sworn she'd never marry without love, but Peter's birth and Isabel's death had changed all that. John Henry felt nothing for her but contempt, that much was clear. What sort of a union would they have? On the other hand, what sort of life would Peter have if she didn't consent? He had to be considered above anyone else.

Pip swallowed against the tight, dry knot in her throat. "Very well, then," she whispered hoarsely, the last of her life's dreams and ambitions crumbling to dust with each word. "I will marry you for Peter's sake. I cannot see that I have any choice."

He looked back up at her, his eyes shuttered so that she could not read their expression. "Just so that we understand each other, let me reiterate that I am not coercing you. You make this choice of your own free will. I expect none of the usual things that a wife would offer her husband, if that is what worries you."

Pip's cheeks flamed. His words cut deep, and for some unfathomable reason she felt disappointed and humiliated at the same time. So John Henry found her unattractive, did he? Fine. She didn't give a fig. She'd consented to the marriage for only one reason—to protect little Peter and keep him with her. John Henry could go hang for all she cared.

"That suits me," she replied coldly. "I expect nothing of you, either, other than that you keep your end of the bargain. I will go my own way and you will go yours once this is done."

"No," he said, his tone adamant. "That is not part of the agreement. We will live together as man and wife, at least as far as the world is concerned. I have no intention of creating a scandal when we've gone this far to avoid one." He released a long breath. "On top of that, Peter needs a father, as every child does. I will be that father to him, and he need never know the truth of the matter. As I told you last night, I feel a sense of responsibility toward him, and part of that responsibility is seeing that he doesn't suffer for other people's mistakes. He deserves the best start in life we can provide for him, and if this is the only way to make that happen, so be it."

Pip blinked, feeling like a child who had just been soundly chastised.

Every child deserved a father. She'd last seen hers at the age of three, when he'd gone dashing off to the war to become a soldier; a few years later he'd been killed at Waterloo. Even though she had no memory of him, she'd missed having a male presence in her life. And then Will had come along, married her mother, and filled the gap in her heart. He had changed her life completely, giving her a sense of security and love that had been missing all those difficult years when they'd been financially struggling. Will had made them into a real family, and Peter deserved the same. If John Henry was prepared to love Peter, if not her, she had no reason to complain.

"You are right, of course," she said in a low voice. "Peter deserves whatever security we can give him. I agree to your terms."

"George?" John Henry said, pulling himself away from the supporting pole he'd been leaning against and standing straight. He was so tall that his head reached the top of the tent. "Will you marry us?"

Reverend Hale gave them both a long, considering look. "Yes. Yes, I think I will. I do believe that marriage might suit the two of you once you've come to your senses." He went to the table and picked up his prayer book. "If you'll just stand here in front of me and join hands, we'll begin."

Pip moved to the spot Reverend Hale indicated, her back stiffening as John Henry came to her side and took her hand in his. Its warmth and firmness sent a shiver down her spine, but she did her best to ignore her physical response to his touch.

Reverend Hale smiled at them, cleared his throat, and began:

"Dearly beloved, we are gathered here in the sight of God to join together this man and woman . . ."

4

$\mathcal{B}$y the time they'd emerged from the tent the sun blazed like a furnace, heat shimmering off the ground. Pip would have accepted Reverend Hale's invitation to stay until late afternoon, when the journey would have been more comfortable, but she desperately wanted to get back to Peter.

Reverend Hale had agreed to come to the boat and baptize the infant that evening at Pip's insistence. She mounted Abdullah, fully aware of the irony of the situation: Peter's survival was by no means guaranteed, and should he die, she would still be shackled to John Henry by the vows they'd just exchanged. Those could not be undone.

She shot a surreptitious glance at John Henry, who appeared unperturbed by what had just transpired between them. Her head was spinning at the thought that they were now married, bound together for the rest of their lives.

After half an hour she shifted uncomfortably, the combination of heat, lack of sleep, and delayed shock causing her to feel faint. Running her hand over her forehead, she willed herself to stay upright.

"Pip?" John Henry's voice seemed to come from a distance, and she opened her eyes, trying to clear her head. "Pip, are you feeling unwell?" he asked, his voice edged with concern.

"Fine," she murmured. "I'm just fine. Just . . . just tired, that's all."

"Let's stop and rest. A little food and water in the shade will do you good."

"No—I must get back to Peter," she said. "He needs me."

"That may be so, but you'll be of no use to him if you arrive overheated and exhausted. You look very pale. I think we should stop, find some shade. Mohammed can manage a bit longer without you."

Pip opened her mouth to object, but the words never came out. The last thing she registered was the peculiar thought that the sun had been obliging enough to extinguish itself.

John Henry breathed a huge sigh of relief when Pip finally stirred in her bed. He'd nearly fainted himself when she'd slid off the donkey's back and landed in a heap on the hard-packed earth. For one horrible moment he'd thought she might have broken her neck, for she lay still and unmoving, unresponsive to his voice and his touch.

Quickly realizing that her neck remained in one piece, and cursing himself for failing to see her fragility, he'd scooped her up and practically beaten his donkey into a gallop in his desperation to get her safely back to the *dahabeehyah* and out of the punishing sun.

For the following hour he'd done nothing but berate himself as Pip lay still and white, cursing himself for his unkindness to her, for practically forcing her into a marriage that she clearly didn't desire. The bitter truth was that she wanted nothing to do with him, accepting him only for the sake of the child.

Although he couldn't help feeling deeply hurt, he decided to let her think what she wanted. He would stand by his agreement and to hell with his feelings. His only hope was in time she would come to accept him for himself.

The problem was that when he'd spoken his marriage vows, he'd meant them. He hadn't realized how deep his feelings ran until he'd actually voiced the words and the shock had nearly knocked him over. He still loved her with all his heart, and that heart had come close to breaking, for he knew that she felt no affection for him.

Pip's eyelids fluttered, then opened. She gazed at him blearily, though the sapphire blue of her eyes was as brilliant as ever. "John Henry?" she whispered. "What happened? Where am I?"

"In your own bed," he said gently, wanting nothing more than to stroke her auburn hair. "You gave me the devil of a shock out there, falling off Abdullah and landing in a heap, but all's well now."

"Oh . . . I remember," she said, her brow furrowed. "The sun. The sun was so hot. I'm—I'm sorry."

"Don't be silly. Here, drink some water." He held out a glass.

Pip raised her head and drank thirstily. "Thank you. How is Peter?" She rested her head back against the pillow and regarded him anxiously.

"Thriving, according to Mohammed. He's milking the goat again. Peter's appetite is as healthy as he is."

Dear God, but she was beautiful. He wished he could take her into his arms and drink in her smell, feel the softness of her skin, but that might very well never happen. He would have to learn to live with that.

After all, he told himself firmly, he'd lived with the knowledge that she would never be his for more years than he cared to remember. Now that she actually was, even though in name only, she was still as far away as the moon.

He imagined that what he'd once perceived as torture had taken on an entirely new face and the true agony was just beginning.

Rising from the side of her bed, he said, "I'll leave you now. We need to talk, Pip, but we'll do that when you're feeling better. Rest. I will see to Peter."

She nodded. "Thank you. What is the time?"

He glanced out the window. "My guess would be

about two o'clock. Reverend Hale won't be here for another few hours, so take all the time you need. Peter needs you feeling well and strong." *And so do I,* he thought.

Pip sat at her dressing table, brushing her hair. She winced when she encountered the bump on the back of her head, incurred, no doubt, when she'd fallen off Abdullah. The painful bump was the least of her worries. Her abrupt and unexpected marriage to John Henry occupied all her thoughts.

She had no earthly idea how she was going to explain her behavior to her parents, or anyone else for that matter. She couldn't even explain it to herself, save that she'd acted in Peter's best interest.

Moaning with frustration, she dropped her face into her hands. How had she managed to complicate her life so thoroughly? Only two days ago she'd been looking forward to the future, once she and Isabel had resolved the problem of what to do with the baby.

Now Isabel was gone, and she was not only a mother but a married woman. Even worse than being married, she'd married a man who cared nothing for her and whose motives were highly suspect, despite his high-minded words about fatherhood and responsibility.

She raised her head and scowled at her reflection in the mirror, her face showing the strain of the last twenty-four hours. This was *not* what she'd planned her life to be. She'd wanted only to be a scholar of sorts, to travel the world and record her impressions for posterity and her own satisfaction, even thinking in her more ambitious moments that she might present her papers and sketches to the British Museum, perhaps even give a lecture or two.

All those hopes and aspirations had gone up in smoke.

Resting her cheek on her hand, she sighed. She certainly didn't resent Peter's appearance in her life, as unplanned as that was. What distressed her was that John Henry was using her difficulties to advance his position in life. His ambition had been perfectly clear to her.

She wrapped her fingers around the handle of the silver hairbrush as if it were John Henry's throat. In one swift movement she threw the brush across the room, watching it hit the corner of the bed, skid off the carpet, slide across the bare wood floor, and come to rest against the wall.

Feeling not one bit better, she quickly put up her hair, pinning it fast, then marched out the door, determined not to let John Henry shake her equilibrium again. She was a grown woman with a mind of her own. She was also the mother of a newborn who was about to be baptized, and she wanted the occasion to be a happy one. Civility would be the order of the day.

Straightening her shoulders, she hurried down the corridor to attend to little Peter, thankful for the baby clothes she and Isabel had spent the last months sewing.

————

Holding the baby in her arms, Pip gazed lovingly down at him as Reverend Hale came to the end of the prayers. "Name this child," he said.

"Peter," Pip replied, a smile wreathing her face.

"Peter Henry," John Henry added. "For my father."

She shot him a dark look. "Peter *Charles* Henry. For my grandfather."

"Very well." John Henry ran his finger over Peter's silky head. "Peter Charles Henry it is. A fine name for a fine boy."

Reverend Hale looked at them, amusement dancing in his eyes, then produced a vial of holy water from his robes and poured a handful over the baby's head.

Peter squirmed in protest, bunched his fists, scrunched up his face, and proceeded to howl.

"I baptize thee in the name of the Father, and of the Son, and of the Holy Ghost. Amen." Reverend Hale shook hands with Pip and John Henry. "Congratulations. Your son has a fine pair of lungs, a good sign. If you will now join me in the Lord's Prayer?"

They bowed their heads and intoned the words along with Reverend Hale. Pip shivered involuntarily. They'd just taken their first step as a family and she felt a peculiar sense of connection that she couldn't define. She wasn't at all sure that she wanted to feel connected to John Henry in any way other than the obvious. She ascribed the sensation to the emotion of the moment.

Her new husband looked over at her, a broad smile on his face. "Well, that makes Peter official in the eyes of the Lord, although I can't help but feel that he was God-given, a miracle in his own right."

Pip nodded, at a complete loss. John Henry had just put her thoughts into words. "He is a miracle," she whispered, her throat suddenly tight.

"May I hold him?" he asked, reaching out.

She reluctantly handed him the small bundle.

"Hello there, Peter Charles Henry," he murmured, planting a tender kiss on the baby's brow. "I'm your papa now. Did you know that? I hope you think the arrangement as fine as I do."

Peter gazed up at him, his eyes fixed on John Henry's face as if he were concentrating on his words.

Pip couldn't help smiling. If nothing else, John Henry appeared to have the makings of a good father. She knew he'd been raised in a loving family and that his bond with his own father was strong. Perhaps this arrangement wouldn't be such a disaster after all.

"I have a surprise for you, a christening present," Reverend Hale said. "I'll be back in a moment."

Pip watched in astonishment as he appeared a few minutes later, a young Arab woman in tow, her gaze lowered, her veil pulled loosely around the lower portion of her face. "This is Aafteh," he said. "She is willing to be wet nurse to your son. I had the deuce of a time persuading her family to part with her, but she lost her own infant only two days ago, and since her husband died of a fever last December, she has become a burden. To put the matter bluntly, the family needs the money."

Pip's knees went weak with relief at this unexpected

stroke of good fortune for Peter, although her heart went out to Aafteh, whose gaze had already traveled hungrily, if surreptitiously, to Peter. "Thank you, Reverend," she said, meaning the words with all her heart. "Aafteh will make an enormous difference."

"She is a good girl and will cause you no trouble. Fortunately your Arabic is good, Mrs. Lovell, so you should have no problem communicating."

"George, you truly are a miracle worker," John Henry exclaimed. "I don't know how we can ever thank you enough or repay you for all you have done this day."

"I need no thanks, and you can repay me by giving this child and each other full and happy lives," he replied. "One thing: Aafteh believes this child to be yours. I told her this for safety's sake, and when I arrived I took the precaution of telling the crew that they are not to inform her otherwise—or anyone else, for that matter." He raised an eyebrow. "You are fortunate, Mrs. Lovell, that you have your crew's complete loyalty."

"They are good men," she said, moved nearly to tears.

"You will have to stay here and keep to yourself for some time to come, naturally. Peter is very small, and by the time he is ready to make his appearance to the world at large, he should look like a baby born at term. I doubt anyone will have any questions. No one knows exactly when you were married, seeing as you've both been out of civilization's eye for a time, and only those of us here know when Peter was born."

He gestured to Aafteh, who'd been standing off to one side, and spoke to her rapidly in Arabic. "She'll take Peter now and feed him. As for myself, I must take my leave of you. I have work that awaits me. I suggest that you travel farther up the Nile—the more remote the location, the better, just to be safe."

"That is sound advice," John Henry said. "There's no point courting questions."

"Just so. I'd also suggest that Mrs. Lovell stay out of sight as much as possible for the next few weeks."

Pip nodded, understanding his meaning. She was supposed to be heavily pregnant; in her slim state, she couldn't risk being seen by any Europeans.

They said their farewells and saw Reverend Hale off the boat, then returned to the upper deck. Pip, exhausted, sank into the comfort of a cushioned chair, grateful that Aafteh had taken Peter into her care and would give him the nourishment he so badly needed. She wished she could perform the task herself, but she was no more capable of supplying milk to an infant than of flying to the moon. At least she was his mother now, and that was all that mattered.

John Henry took a spot nearby, his face reflecting his own exhaustion. "So," he said, after a few minutes of silence. "That's done. Heavens, but we've had a day of it. How are you, Pip?"

"Hungry."

He chuckled. "Some things never change. Would you like me to ask Mohammed to prepare an early dinner?"

"That would be wonderful. I know I slept the

afternoon away, but I want nothing more than some food in my stomach, and my bed."

"I'll go speak to him directly." He vanished below, leaving Pip to the quiet of the evening and some much-needed solitude.

She gazed out over the river, watching the spectacular colors of the sunset shift and change as the rosy sky deepened toward night, the lowering sun shimmering like a thousand stars on the water's surface. A felucca, white sail furled against its tall mast, drifted past, the boatman silhouetted at the helm, his shadow dark and still.

She let the magic of the Nile, of Egypt itself, slip over her, hypnotically soothing, as was the gentle rocking of the boat. Past and present fused into one, the ancient culture of three thousand years before seeming no more than a breath away.

In the distance the voices of shepherds calling their flocks in for the night rang out faintly, every now and then punctuated by a camel's snort or a donkey's bray.

The life's pulse of Egypt echoed in her heart. This was the land of the pharaohs, the center of civilization at one time, its mysteries reflected in the pyramids, the temples, the artifacts and friezes that documented its extraordinary history. As connected as she felt to the land, she was only an observer, someone who merely passed through, no more important than a single grain of sand that blew over the vast desert.

She couldn't help but think that Peter, tiny as he was, had more claim over this country than she did. He'd been born here on its river, known for millennia as the river of life. Egypt's air was the first he'd breathed, its brilliant sun the first his eyes had seen, the milk he drank coming from its goats and now one of its people. Here was his genesis, no matter what came next. Peter would always have Egypt as part of his heritage, and she couldn't help but be grateful for the gift that had been given him.

Pip didn't realize that she'd drifted off until she felt a hand on her shoulder. "What is it?" she asked in alarm, rubbing her hands over her face, only to see John Henry bending over her.

"Is it Peter? Is he all right?" The fear that she might lose him hovered over her constantly. She still couldn't believe that such a tiny being could survive in a world as harsh as the one he'd been born into, despite all her romantic musings.

"He is as healthy as a horse, having taken a long and hearty meal. He's sleeping with both fists clenched by the sides of his face, looking supremely satisfied with himself. Aafteh looks equally satisfied, although I couldn't confirm that with words, my Arabic being so sketchy. I said 'good?' and she said 'yes' and that was the extent of it, although she hovers over him like a brood hen protecting her chick."

Pip breathed a sigh of relief. "That's good news. At least he's taken to her milk with no trouble."

"Quite frankly, I would imagine that Aafteh is as relieved as Peter is. She must have been suffering dreadfully from congestion, and he from the taste of goat's milk, not to mention the cloth in which it was delivered."

Pip frowned. "What do you mean by congestion? Aafteh isn't suffering from any sort of ailment, is she? Oh—John Henry! If she is, we must remove Peter from her immediately." She jumped to her feet. "How could you be so irresponsible? You know what infection is like over here."

He took her by her shoulders and pushed her back down into the chair. "Don't be absurd. Aafteh is perfectly healthy. If she weren't, George never would have brought her to us. I was referring to her breasts."

Pip stared at him, shocked that John Henry would be so crude. "How—how could you say such a thing?" she demanded in indignation. "You are are positively indecent!"

John Henry folded his arms across his chest and looked down at her, his head tilted to one side. "My. Haven't you become a spinsterish prude. Tell me, Pip, is it my mention of the word *breast* that so outrages you, or the thought that they exist at all? You do possess a pair yourself, if you've noticed."

She exploded. "That is enough! You may have been raised on a farm, John Henry, but I advise you to show more decency, or, to use an expression more familiar to you, I shall have your guts for garters."

He regarded her quizzically. "Is that so? Do you know, I find this an odd conversation, given that you spent a number of years on a farm as well. Do you remember what happened when a cow or ewe went without milking? Do you remember what sort of pain she suffered, the lowing or bleating we'd hear and how we'd go tearing out to remedy the situation?"

Pip looked away, remembering all too well how happy they'd once been on Broadhurst Farm, how well they'd worked together, each knowing the other's thoughts without having to speak them aloud.

"I see you do recollect that much, at any rate. Let me inform you, my dear, that human physiology works in the same manner." He pulled up a chair next to hers and turned to face her. "In the interest of your education, which you are so apparently keen on, I will verse you in the process of a lactating human mother. She experiences the same pain as any animal would should she go without relief, and Aafteh has gone two full days without benefit of having a child nurse from her. Peter might not be her own, but he certainly has the ability to draw milk from her swollen breasts— forgive my use of the dreaded word."

Pip felt like a complete fool. "Yes. Yes, of course."

"You were never slow to take my meaning. At least be grateful that Aafteh has milk aplenty and that Peter has the appetite and inclination to take it from her. I may be only a farm boy, but I do know this much— survival depends on nourishment, wherever it comes from."

Pip colored hotly. John Henry had made his point and made it with his usual efficiency. "I realize that," she said, rubbing her eyes with her knuckles. "Please, John Henry, I'm too tired to argue. We're in this predicament together, so we might as well make the best of it."

"I don't consider this a predicament. A challenge, perhaps, but challenges are meant to be overcome." He leaned back in his chair and stretched out his long legs, the strong muscles of his thighs straining against the cloth of his trousers.

Pip quickly looked away. She still hadn't adjusted to his commanding masculinity and cursed herself for not being able to ignore it or the peculiar feelings that stirred in her whenever she did notice. Unfortunately, that was more often than she liked.

She looked up at the brilliant stars in the moonless night sky. A challenge . . . well, maybe he had a point. The first challenge was to get through the next weeks together in the confinement of a boat without killing each other.

John Henry read her mind. "You needn't worry, Pip," he said. "I'll keep out of your way. I have plenty to keep me busy, and in any case, I have to go back to Cairo shortly to see to some business."

"Go back to Cairo? But—but you can't leave us just like that."

He laughed. "Missing me already, are you? Don't worry. You'll be perfectly safe with Hassad looking after you. I trust him completely—he's already proved himself to be more than competent."

"Yes, but what about Peter? You said yourself that he is fragile. What if something should happen?"

"I wouldn't dream of leaving until I feel sure that Peter is out of any danger, but I truly do have business that cannot be ignored indefinitely."

Pip wondered anew what sort of business John Henry was involved in. Before she could ask, he said, "I'm negotiating some trade routes and this sort of thing is best done face-to-face. You've spent enough time with Arabs to understand."

"Yes, of course," she said, astonished to learn that John Henry knew anything about trade routes, let alone how to negotiate them with an Arab. "Just because we're married, you're not shackled to me."

"Did I say I felt shackled, Pip? I don't recall expressing that sentiment." He leaned forward, regarding her intently. "You might have a different idea about our marriage than I, but I assure you, I intend to be a proper husband to you. I thought I'd made myself perfectly clear on that point."

Pip's mouth fell open. "But that's not what you said. You *said* that you didn't expect the usual—the usual things." She colored furiously. This topic was even more uncomfortable than breasts. "Surely you don't expect . . . *you* know."

"Oh. So we're back to that, are we?" John Henry didn't look the least bit perturbed. "You're worried that I'm going to assault you in your bed?"

Pip didn't know where to look or what to say. Jumping overboard and drowning suddenly presented enormous appeal, only she was too strong a swimmer for that tactic to be of any use. "Isn't that what proper husbands usually do?" she finally retorted.

He studied her as if she were a bug fixed on the end of an entomologist's pin. "Is that what you *think* proper husbands do? No wonder you never married."

"That is *not* why I never married. I just never found anyone I wanted to marry. You can hardly fault me for that."

"No," he said, with a look of satisfaction she didn't begin to understand. "I wouldn't think of faulting you for listening to your own heart. Indeed, I am happy you chose that course, given all the opportunities that must have come your way."

She shrugged one shoulder. "I had my share of proposals."

"Mmm. I can imagine. Tell me something, Pip. Did anyone actually kiss you when he was offering himself up?"

"Naturally," she said quickly, not wanting John Henry to think her inexperienced. She'd suffered her share of stolen kisses but found the process tedious, like having a piece of dry parchment planted on her mouth, or worse, a rather wet affair that made her think of a wriggling worm. That revolting experience had been delivered by Brewster Jenkins and was not one she had any inclination to repeat. "I had all manner of men kiss me."

He folded his arms across his chest. "Is that so? How very fortunate for you. I'm sure you made them all dance on the end of a string for the opportunity."

"I did not," she replied in indignation. "I rebuffed each and every one." She couldn't help the smile that tugged at the corners of her mouth. "The experience was not unlike swatting flies."

John Henry burst into laughter. "I see. Or at least I think I see. Well, Pip. You shan't have to swat at me." He wiped his eyes with the back of his hand. "I have no intention of forcing myself on you. I take no pleasure in imposing myself where I'm not wanted. Maybe . . ."

He started to laugh again, then composed himself. "Oh, dear. Maybe when I'm old and gray you'll finally decide to take mercy on me, and the shock will be so great that I'll die on the spot and you'll finally be rid of me."

Pip's expression softened. "Maybe, and only if you're very, very lucky." Oh, he did remind her of the old John Henry. At least his sense of humor hadn't changed—it had just become more sophisticated.

5

April 18, 1836
Norfolk, England

Carefully folding Pip's letter, her hands shaking, Louisa, Marchioness of Alconleigh, slowly put it on her desk and stood, trying to collect her frantic thoughts. She didn't know what to make of her daughter's news. Louisa had had misgivings about Pip's going off to Egypt, but she had trusted Pip's judgment and common sense, even though her daughter was prone to disregard society's dictates about the way young women should conduct their lives.

She was now beginning to have her doubts about that common sense. Rubbing her hands over her face, she tried to hold back tears. Then she picked up the letter again and went swiftly out of the study to find Will. Maybe he could make sense of Pip's actions, for she surely couldn't.

She found him in the stables, giving instructions to the head groom. "Will, excuse me for interrupting, but I must speak with you on a matter of some urgency."

Will turned and regarded her with an inquiring smile. "Don't tell me—it's the twins again. What mischief this time?"

"For once it's not the twins." She took his arm and pulled him outside.

"*Not* the twins?" he said dryly. "How remarkable."

"Yes, James and Kate have actually given me a peaceful morning. No, the news is from Pip."

His face lit up. "Pip? Thank goodness—we haven't heard in months. How is she? What does she say?" His pleasure slowly changed to alarm as he took in his wife's pale face. "Wait . . . you said the matter was urgent. She's not in any kind of trouble, is she?"

Louisa didn't know how to reply. Will had been the best of fathers to Pip, even though he'd only become a part of her life when she was eight. He adored her every bit as much as he did his own four children and Louisa was reluctant to upset him with Pip's latest eccentric act.

"Louisa? Come, sweetheart, do not keep me in suspense. Does she need money, is that it?" He frowned. "She can't possibly have run through her grandfather's fortune already."

"No, nothing like that. Here. I think you'd best read her letter for yourself." She handed it to him.

Will unfolded the neatly-written pages and scanned the contents. When he looked up at Louisa, the amused expression on his face was the last thing she expected to see.

"So," he said. "She's gone and married John Henry." He roared with laughter. "Oh, this is too good to be true."

Louisa was shocked by his reaction. "Will! How can you take this so lightly? She's going to have his child, for heaven's sake."

"That, my dear wife, is a natural consequence of marriage. You of all people should know that."

"And that, my dear husband, is not the point. What on earth was she thinking? According to this, she married him shortly after her arrival in Egypt—and she hadn't even laid eyes on him for ten years, for heaven's sake. What would possess her to marry him when she's refused every suitor who's asked for her hand, insisting that she didn't have any interest in marriage?"

"Has the thought occurred to you that she might love him?" Will shook his head, still grinning broadly.

"*Love* him? Will, what has gotten into you?" Louisa could hardly believe her ears.

"Nothing at all. You seem to be forgetting that those two were inseparable as children. Pip always used to say that she intended to marry John Henry."

"But that was when she was only a little girl," Louisa said, baffled. "She barely mentioned his name after we left Broadhurst Farm, or at least not in any serious fashion. I just don't understand this. I had such hopes for her."

Will caught her hands in his. "Louisa, listen to me. What is done is done, and there is nothing you or I can do about it now—not that I'd be inclined to change a thing. I think John Henry might be just the man for Pip."

He led her to a bench under a large lime tree and drew her down next to him. "They suit each other, and Pip is not one to marry lightly or without good reason, after she's resisted this long. Can you not be happy for her?"

"I suppose so," Louisa said reluctantly. "I'm more concerned about John Henry's motives. After all, what can he offer her? He comes from an entirely different world. Does he expect her to support him?" She looked up at Will, unable to disguise her anxiety. "I thought Val had married me for love, when all he wanted was my money. John Henry doesn't even have the social standing Val had. How well does that bode for Pip's future?"

Will examined her face. "My darling, John Henry is much stronger than you're giving him credit for. He has deeply ingrained moral fiber as well as a healthy respect for himself, both of which Val lacked. John Henry has also loved Pip for many years." He hesitated. "And there is something else. . . . Perhaps I should have told you at the time, but I promised John Henry to keep our bargain to ourselves."

"What bargain?" Will had never kept secrets from Louisa, or at least not since they'd married, and he'd promised he never would again. "What bargain?" she repeated, her throat growing tight with apprehension. "What did you do, Will?"

Will shifted on the bench, looking acutely uncomfortable. "Nothing nefarious, if that's what you're thinking."

"If you must know, that's exactly what I'm thinking." She looked off across the emerald-green fields.

She couldn't help comparing them in her mind's eye to the dry, parched earth of Egypt that had become Pip's current home.

"I just helped John Henry on his way. Pip behaved rather badly toward him the last time she went to Broadhurst, and as you know, John Henry, who felt deeply bruised, decided that he wished to leave the country, to make his way in the world. He came to me to ask my opinion about his options and I offered a suggestion or two, that's all."

Louisa narrowed her eyes. "What sort of suggestions?" she asked suspiciously. Will's heart was as kind as they came and many people had reason to be grateful to him, but she hoped that he hadn't done anything too ill-advised.

"Well . . . I've always thought John Henry a fine young man, so I thought he might prosper in India. I lent him a certain sum of money to help him get started, along with some references. He paid me back long ago," he added quickly.

"I see," Louisa said, idly watching a swallow sweep under the stable eaves to her nest. "You were the reason John Henry went all the way to India."

"Yes," Will replied, watching the swallow with the same apparent fascination. "As it happens."

"Yet you didn't see fit to tell me this."

"As I told you, I promised him that I would keep my silence. His pride would allow nothing less, and that I understood." Will inserted one finger into the collar of his shirt and tugged as if it were suddenly too tight. "I'm deeply sorry if you feel that I kept an important truth from you, but quite honestly, I never thought that John Henry's success or failure would have an effect on any of us. The matter was between John Henry and myself."

Louisa thought his words over before she spoke. She knew well enough that Will's own young struggles would make him sympathetic to John Henry's plight, and she also understood Will's deep commitment to keeping his promises. She couldn't really fault him for his silence, especially if he had thought his actions would never affect their family. Family meant everything to Will. "What else haven't you told me?" she asked.

"Only what John Henry asked me to keep to myself," he said with a smile. "But it is good news. John Henry has made a large fortune of his own."

"John Henry made a fortune?" she repeated, astonished. "But—how? He started with next to nothing."

"True, but he is nothing if not resourceful, and he did very well with his business dealings. Also, he managed to endear himself to a maharaja, whose son and heir he rescued from drowning."

"A maharaja." Louisa felt slightly dazed.

"Yes," he said. "This particular maharaja happens to have a large sphere of influence, and he used it on John Henry's behalf in order to express his appreciation." Will paused. "It happens that the maharaja was involved in some very tricky negotiations with our government, and part of his expression of appreciation was to grant some large concessions, for which the British government naturally felt very grateful. John Henry acted as intermediary."

Louisa pressed a hand against her mouth, stifling a laugh. "I see. Just how grateful were they?"

"Grateful enough to create John Henry a Knight of the Realm."

"Do you mean to say . . . do you mean that our new son-in-law is now styled Sir John Henry Lovell?" she said in disbelief, her laughter overflowing. She nearly doubled over in mirth at the irony. "I don't believe it. John Henry, our tenant farmer's son, a knight?"

"Absolute truth, I swear. The man is considered a hero in India. The interesting aspect is that he's embarrassed about the entire episode, feeling that he only did what anyone would have done if he saw a small boy being swept away by the river. He had no idea who the boy was until after the fact, and even then expected no reward, despite having risked his life. I think that in itself speaks to John Henry's character, don't you agree?"

Louisa nodded slowly. "Indeed it does. He wrote you about all of this?"

"He did, although he considerably downplayed his part. I had to do but a little digging to find out the truth of the matter. He hasn't even told his parents, and I wouldn't be surprised if Pip has no idea either."

The swallow swooped back out from the eaves and headed off toward the trees to the west. Louisa watched until it disappeared. She imagined the swallow had a nest of fledglings to nurture. Pip may have left their own nest some time before, but Louisa felt no less protective of her.

Given what Will had just told her about John Henry, he would let no harm befall her, at least as far as he could. However, one last point troubled her deeply, and she addressed it now.

"About poor Isabel," she said, her brow furrowing. "Pip says she died of a sudden fever. Will . . . who is to say that something of the same nature might not happen to Pip? She is in a fragile condition, after all. Why does she not come home to us now? Anything might happen, and she says she does not know when she expects to return."

Will took her hand. "We have to trust in God that Pip will be well. She knows what she is doing, Louisa. She must have her reasons for staying on."

"I pray you are right. I don't know if I could bear losing her. She is my firstborn child," she said, choking back a sob.

Will gathered his wife close in his arms. "And to all intents and purposes, mine as well. Try not to worry, my darling. Pip will return to us safely, and her child as well. They are both truly in God's hands, and I do not believe He will allow any harm to befall them." He kissed the top of her head. "Let us go back to our twins, who don't have the sense to stay in one piece from one moment to the next. We'll be lucky if they haven't managed to burn the house down in our absence. At least Gabriel and Frances are off at school and we don't have to worry about them for the moment."

Louisa allowed Will to guide her away, but her mind was no more settled than it had been before. Something was wrong. Every instinct told her that Pip had not told the full truth in her letter and that trouble was in the air.

She could only pray that Will was right, that God would look after Pip and her unborn child.

April 18, 1836
Abu Simbal, Egypt

The heat increased with each passing week as they traveled along the Nile. Pip spent most of her time in the shade of the canopy on the upper deck, chafing against her confinement. To her amazement, little Peter seemed oblivious to the soaring temperatures, thriving in Aafteh's care and growing like a weed. For that she was grateful. She loved him more each day, reveling in his every achievement, every gurgle and smile he bestowed on her like a little piece of sunshine. He'd captivated them all, from Mohammed to Hassad, both of whom treated Peter as if he were their own.

John Henry, on the other hand, had vanished off to Cairo weeks before, and she hadn't heard a word since. She worried that he'd been kidnapped by a desert tribe and was being held for ransom, or that he'd been killed in a raid. Or that he'd decided to renege on the marriage and was even now on a boat to parts unknown in an effort to escape his obligation. Or that he'd simply decided Pip and Peter weren't important enough for him to take the time to write a letter, letting her know that he was safe and well.

She rested her chin on her fist. In his defense, he could hardly have been in touch with them since he would not have known exactly where they'd be at any given time. Still, she couldn't help the resentment that mounted with every additional week of his absence, even though she'd wished him gone. She didn't exactly understand why she now wished him back, but she did, and more so with each passing day. Silly, she told herself. Utterly stupid, since when he did see fit to return, she would probably take his head off for his negligence.

Heaving an impatient sigh, she waited for the sun to go down and night to fall, bringing not only cooling breezes but the safety of darkness so that she could creep off the boat and go walking without fear of anyone spotting her.

She ate her dinner in solitude as usual, then slipped carefully away, looking over her shoulder to make sure she hadn't been spotted by the ever-vigilant Hassad. As much as she'd come to love him, he felt a strong need to be her shadow, and she'd had to shoo him away on more than one occasion.

Settling herself on a small hummock that overlooked the Nile, she drew her knees up and wrapped her arms around them. Across the river on the west bank stood the two powerful and impressive temples that Ramses II had constructed more than three thousand years before, their giant portals carved out of the foot of a sandstone cliff.

The first temple Ramses had created as a monument to his greatness, with four vast seated statues of himself set against the recessed cliff face at the entrance. The second, smaller temple to the north he'd erected as a tribute to his beloved wife and consort, Nefertari, and at this entrance her statue was enthroned next to his.

Ignoring the sandflies biting at her exposed ankles and hands, she reflected on the eternity of life. No matter how brief one's own presence in the world might be, this monument, among so many others, stood tribute to life itself.

She rested her cheek on her knees, thinking of Ramses' absolute love for Nefertari. Despite the difficulties of his very complicated life, he managed to find one true love, one woman in whom he could trust and find inner strength. The temple he built for her was a testament to that love, and she couldn't help but envy Nefertari for Ramses' devotion to her.

How many women were that fortunate? Pip felt sure that human nature had remained the same over the centuries. Men and women still wanted to be loved without condition, but very few ever found their perfect mates, regardless of their background or breeding. Most settled for poor copies and suffered for the choice. Only the lucky ones ever found counterparts who were their equals—partners who spoke to each other's soul.

She had once hoped that she might be one of those fortunate few, but fate had intervened. She and John Henry had become yet another couple bound together merely by a legal document that entangled them for the rest of their lives. With luck, they would learn to live together with equanimity.

She couldn't help feeling a certain despair. All she'd ever wanted was to be loved the way Will loved her mother. Since she'd never met a man who shared her stepfather's intelligence, compassion, and devotion, she'd settled for independence, and now even that had been taken from her.

So be it, she thought with a heavy sigh. She'd made her bed, and now she must only lie in it—alone—but she also had Peter to think of. His life would turn out differently, she would see to that. He'd have love and security, and, when the time came, he would find a wonderful woman who would make him completely happy.

Maybe that was where her destiny lay, in seeing to Peter's future, making sure that he grew up to be a man of merit. Unlike John Henry, her son would marry for love and not just to further his ambitions.

"What a stunningly beautiful sight," a familiar voice said softly from behind her. "I had no idea."

Pip nearly jumped to her feet, thinking for one idiotic moment that her ruminations had conjured John Henry out of thin air. She turned and stared at him. He was as solid as the rock on which she sat.

"What—what are you doing here?" she demanded, her heart racing with a combination of alarm and something she couldn't define.

"That's a silly question." John Henry dropped down next to her and wrapped his arms around his knees. "As I recall, we're married. Imagine, I actually believed you might welcome my return."

Pip shivered. "I do, of course I do. You just gave me a shock. Where have you *been* all this time? I thought you had been kidnapped by bandits!"

"Nothing so exciting," he said. "I was held up in Cairo, the negotiations proving more difficult than I'd anticipated. I'm sorry, Pip. I've worried about you and Peter the entire time, if that helps at all. I honestly didn't have a way to get word to you."

"No, I understand," she replied, struggling to mean what she said despite her resentment.

"Somehow I wonder if you do." He looked at her, his face lit by moonlight, his strong features cast partly in shadow. "Pip. We must talk."

"Yes, of course we must," she said nervously, not at all sure she wanted to hear what John Henry had to say. "How did you find me?"

"In Abu Simbal, do you mean, or here in this spot? Abu Simbal was easy enough—I merely had to ask about your progress on my way up the river. I knew you would travel as far as you could, but as for this particular place, Hassad told me that you come here every evening."

Pip groaned. "He knows? I thought I was being so careful."

"Not only does he know, but he also follows you every night to make sure you are safe." John Henry smiled. "He's actually not so far away right now.

Mohammed directed me to him. They have an interesting agreement—Mohammed watches out for you on the boat, and Hassad watches out for you whenever you decide to leave it."

Pip felt like a fool. "Oh," she said. "I suppose I should have known."

"Why? They've been careful to protect your privacy as well as your person. I asked them for both, and I also asked them to be discreet about it. They've obviously done a brilliant job if you never realized they were keeping an eye on you."

Sudden anger coursed through Pip's blood. "Do you mean you asked them to *spy* on me?" she demanded. "How could you, John Henry? I don't need looking after. What sort of pathetic woman do you think I am? I managed well enough before you came along, and I've been managing perfectly well since you vanished."

He looked at her long and hard. "The problem with you," he said, bringing his temper under control with an effort, "is that you think you're so damned independent that nothing could ever happen to you. Have you ever considered that *you* might be the victim of bandits, that you actually might have some value to them? They wouldn't give twopence about your safety, comfort, or even your life, you idiot, if they thought they could hold a wealthy British woman for ransom."

Pip paled. "That's—that's just silly," she said, shaken, since she hadn't ever considered anything of the sort. The political unrest hadn't affected her in any way, and she'd believed that she would be under the protection of the British consulate should anything untoward happen.

"Silly? I wonder how silly you would feel being swept away on the back of a horse by a group of Arabs out for blood and held hostage in one of their tents, that being the best of the scenarios. Surely you know as well as I what the political climate in this country is at the moment, never mind that you've been close to the Sudanese border. You are a prime target, my dear, which is exactly why I felt so reluctant to leave you." He looked away. "That is also why I asked Mohammed and Hassad to keep an eye on you. I had no choice but to go, given the prior commitments I'd made, but I wasn't about to take a chance on your safety, or Peter's."

"I hadn't realized," she said tightly, clenching her hands in her lap and looking off to one side, not wanting him to see how much his words had distressed her. "I suppose I should thank you."

"Please don't bother," he replied, his voice bitter. "You owe me nothing. You, after all, pointed out that this marriage is no more than an arrangement. I am only ensuring that the arrangement stays intact. Your abduction would be a huge inconvenience."

"John Henry—" She stopped abruptly, not sure what she wanted to say, not sure what she felt other than confusion. "I don't want you to think me ungrateful," she managed, the words nearly choking her. "Of course I appreciate everything you've done for me and for Peter. I just don't want to be under your thumb for the rest of my days, so I think that we need to straighten out how we're going to manage our lives together. You've said that you expect some facsimile of marriage, but I cannot see how we can do that—not with any sort of honesty."

John Henry didn't respond. Instead his gaze focused in the distance, on the tombs of Ramses II and his beloved wife. "Honesty," he said eventually, "is one thing I do expect from you." He glanced at her, his expression solemn. "I'll abide by whatever you decide; I've told you that, and I won't impose myself on you in any way. You, on the other hand, need to find a way to reconcile yourself to our marriage. We're in this for better or for worse, and I meant my vows, even if they were spoken under unexpected circumstances."

Wanting to crawl under the rock she sat on, Pip could think of no reply, since she hadn't taken the vows seriously. Still, she knew that she too was in the marriage for better or for worse. Hadn't she just come to the same conclusion?

"I'll give you honesty," she said, coming to a decision. "If that's what you really want." She drew herself up straight, steeling herself to hand that truth to him with no reservation.

"I'm grateful to you," she continued. "I don't know what I would have done if you hadn't shown up when you did. Peter owes his life to you, and I owe you for making him legitimate in the eyes of the world." She paused for a moment. "I have told you that I will honor this marriage between us, but I consider it no more than a simple bargain, something we contracted for the sake of the baby. The friendship we shared as children is long in the past. We barely know each other at this point."

He looked down at his clasped hands, his expression neutral. "That can be rectified. However, I cannot rectify it on my own. For the time being, you go back to England with Peter. I've booked passage for you both and for Aafteh, should she wish to go with you." He looked up briefly at her, then back down at his hands. "The ship leaves in a month, which will leave plenty of time to get to Alexandria if we start back straightaway. From there you go the usual route to Calais, then to Dover and on to Alconleigh. I've made all the arrangements. You should be perfectly comfortable."

Pip's mouth dropped open. "You've made all the arrangements?" Her throat was suddenly dry. He had arranged her life without even consulting her? Her eyes glittered in the moonlight as anger surged through her. "Did it ever occur to you that I may not wish to leave just yet? What gives you the right to tell me what to do?"

Then, with a growing sense of horror, she realized the weapon she had handed him. Now that she was his wife, John Henry had complete control over her life.

She swallowed hard. "So you expect me to go trotting back to England like an obedient little wife?"

"I do. Most of the Europeans are leaving now to avoid the coming heat." He folded one hand over the other, his elbows resting on his knees, and regarded her steadily.

"And what about you?" she said. "Aren't you coming with us?"

"I go to Cairo. Unfortunately I was unable to complete my business, but I will follow you as soon as that is done. Oh, and I found a woman who is taking the same ship, a Mrs. Cornelia Hitchens. She has kindly agreed to keep an eye on you."

"Ah, another of your spies," Pip said between clenched teeth, feeling the trap closing around her. Apparently John Henry thought to keep her under lock and key for the rest of her days.

Well, he would have to think again, she decided, her blood boiling. Once she got to Alconleigh, all that would change, since he could hardly command her life there. Alconleigh was *her* home and he had no authority there, whatever he might believe now.

"Fine, John Henry." She smiled at him sweetly. "Whatever you say."

"Why do I not feel at all reassured?" he said dryly. "Oh—that reminds me." Reaching into his jacket pocket, he withdrew a small package and unwrapped it.

Pip caught the glimmer of gold and regarded him curiously. "What is it?"

"Your wedding ring." He took her hand and slipped the plain gold band onto her finger before she had a chance to realize what he was doing.

She stared down at it. Somewhere in the back of her mind she heard the sound of a prison door slamming shut, a great final *thud*.

"Pip? Why do you look as if the world just came to an end? It's only a ring, after all."

She didn't know what to say. The ring, now firmly ensconced on her finger, made the marriage more real than it had seemed before. "I—I just didn't expect it," she stammered.

"Perhaps not, but you needed one. People would wonder if you *didn't* have a ring, don't you agree?"

She nodded, feeling numb. How well she remembered the day Will had married her mother, the moment he had slipped her wedding ring onto her finger, a symbol of his love and commitment, and the look of happiness shining on both their faces. This moment couldn't have been more different. She fought back tears. So this was how an arranged marriage felt—a void where one's heart should be.

John Henry gazed off into the distance as if the ruins were the most fascinating things he'd ever seen. He didn't say a word, and after a few minutes Pip managed to compose herself. She stole a glance at him, wondering what he was thinking. Nothing of his feelings showed on his face. The light breeze picked up strands of his dark hair, blowing them back off his face.

She was reminded anew of what a handsome man he'd grown into, the bones of his bronzed face finely chiseled, his mouth strong, the lower lip fuller than the upper, above a chin that showed great determination.

That determination she'd experienced firsthand, and she didn't know what to do with it. She'd always thought herself more determined than anyone, but John Henry had a way of stymieing her at every turn, using calm logic rather than anger to get his way. How was she to fight that? Really, he was too infuriating.

She looked down at the ring again, twisting it around and around on her finger. He might just as well have put a yoke around her neck.

"Peter's grown considerably," he said. "I looked in on him when I arrived. He's acquired some hair as well. I was surprised by how dark it is. The first crop was much lighter."

"Yes," she said, forgetting her annoyance for a moment. She enjoyed talking about Peter above all other subjects. "He's started to do all sorts of things. He blows bubbles and gurgles."

"Does he? What a handy fellow."

"He's always smiling, too. I imagine once he gets the way of it he'll move on to rolling over." She hesitated. "John Henry?"

"Yes?" he replied comfortably.

"Do you think that Peter might end up being a little, well . . . slow? I know he's too young for anything to show up now, but since he was born so early, I couldn't help wondering if he might be at a disadvantage." There. She'd said it. She'd worried for weeks that her darling Peter might end up with problems other than just being small. She remembered a girl in the village back home who wasn't quite right, and someone had said she'd come too soon.

"Peter is bound to be slightly behind," John Henry said, not looking at all concerned. "I have a brother who also came six weeks early and at first he didn't progress as quickly as the rest of us, but by the time he'd reached two years, he more than made up for his delays. He led us a merry dance ever after."

"Oh, do you mean Thomas? I hadn't realized," she said, feeling immensely reassured. Thomas Lovell had been a handful, forever into mischief. She'd never have guessed that he'd been born too early.

"Yes, and he hasn't stopped since. The last I heard he'd set the barn on fire, lighting candles while cavorting with the milkmaid. Fortunately the fire was extinguished before too much damage was done." John Henry chuckled. "I think Thomas is still making up for lost time."

He put an arm around her and lightly squeezed her shoulder. "Don't worry, Pip—Peter will be fine. He's alert and happy, isn't he? I believe a little delayed development will serve our story well. It might be suspicious if he can walk at what people would assume is eight or nine months."

"I suppose so," she replied, distracted by the feel of his hand resting beside her neck, its heat seeping through the thin layer of cotton. She rose abruptly.

"We should get back," she said. "The hour grows late and we must make an early start tomorrow if we're to head back north."

She didn't wait for his reply, setting off quickly toward the rough path to the river.

A muted laugh came from behind her, and she did her best to ignore it. She didn't find anything amusing in their situation.

The trip to Alexandria was surely going to be hell and she didn't look forward to a single minute of it.

One thing she did know: If John Henry intended to play king, he'd have to play by himself. She had no intention of becoming his subject.

As it turned out, the journey to Alexandria was uneventful, since they avoided each other as much as possible. Pip held her peace for quite a while on the subject of John Henry's presumed kingship, but she finally made her point the night before the ship embarked.

John Henry had taken her late that afternoon to meet Mrs. Cornelia Hitchens, the wife of one of the British Consul's assistants, who was traveling back to England to visit with her two school-age sons. As Pip shook her hand, taking in the plump, dowdy woman somewhere in her early thirties, her heart sank.

She knew a thorn in her side when she saw one, having dealt with women of exactly this type for many years now. John Henry had chosen the perfect person to make sure that Pip's life would be dreadful for the next few weeks. Pip would be expected to dine, converse, and generally fill up Mrs. Hitchens's time, while Mrs. Hitchens made sure that Pip didn't have a breath of freedom and bored her to tears in the process. Oh, yes, John Henry truly had the shackles in place.

They had tea in a restaurant on the harbor a block from their hotel. Mrs. Hitchens carried on about her sons, who sounded remarkably tedious. She went on to condemn the Egyptian heat, its unsanitary conditions and food, following that with an elegy to England and its superiority to all other places.

By the time she and John Henry left Mrs. Hitchens, Pip was seething. John Henry had arranged things nicely for himself—he stayed in Egypt, the home of her heart, and sent her packing with a small baby, an Arab woman, and a dimwitted chaperon.

She rounded on him the minute they were outside. "A word with you in private," she said, taking him by the arm and dragging him off to the waterfront where they wouldn't be overheard.

"Pip, what are you doing?" John Henry said, shaking her hand off. "Are you mad?"

"I am furious," she shouted, giving vent to her rage. "You decide I am to go back to England without you, consigning me to the care of that—that *cow*, and you go merrily on your way?"

He regarded her evenly. "You are my wife. Peter is now my son. I am looking after you both, as is my duty. Check your temper, Pip. It's not as if we didn't agree to this course of action a month ago."

"I didn't agree—you presented me with a fait accompli. Need I remind you that I'm an independent woman, accustomed to making my own decisions?" She clenched her fists, feeling a strange urge to punch him straight in his smug face.

"Need I remind you that I am your husband and am responsible for your welfare?" he said, a muscle in his jaw twitching. "And I'm telling you that, like it or not, you leave tomorrow on that ship."

"And if I don't? What will you do then?" she cried, enraged that he was not only tearing her from her beloved Egypt but was tearing to shreds the fabric of the freedom she'd prized for so many years.

"If need be, I will take you over my shoulder and throw you on board," he said, his eyes flashing with anger. "You are the most spoiled, stubborn woman I've ever had the misfortune to know, so selfish that you cannot see what is right under your nose. Do you not think that I've given careful consideration to what is best for you?"

"What would you know about what is best for me?" she said, close to tears, turning her back to him so that he could not see the pain his words had caused. "You think me spoiled and selfish, but that is only because you resent the life into which I was born. You have always wanted to elevate yourself," she continued, lashing out in blind hurt and frustration. "You took advantage of my desperate circumstances to do just that—you didn't even bother to deny your motives at the time. Now you think that because we are married, you can command me like some kind of slave."

She paused only to draw breath. "I am nothing more than chattel to you, a means by which to better yourself—even as a boy, you talked of how you wanted to be king of your domain. Obviously nothing has changed in that regard, but understand this: Despite the laws that govern marriage, I will never, *never* be ruled by you, even if you do have the law on your side. My will and my heart remain my own, always, and I shall fight you to the end if you try to take that from me."

John Henry didn't reply. He leaned against the rail that separated the sandy stretch of beach from the street, his dark head bowed, one fist pressing hard against his mouth.

The sounds of waves rolling gently to the shore filled Pip's ears along with the the slow wheels of carriages and the muted cries from street vendors selling their wares. The smell of herbs and spices from sidewalk merchants permeated the air, mingling with the tang of the salt sea, and the hot breeze that carried all the scents that were Egypt.

Pip covered her face with her hand, her throat aching as she realized that this life she'd so come to love was coming to an end. She had only hours left in this country and the chances of her ever returning were small. Her future lay ahead in a land where flowers bloomed but never in such violently exuberant profusion, where the sky wasn't a brilliant, cloudless blue but usually a muted gray, occasionally graced by a few hours of sunshine, and those hours unsure.

In England, when the rain fell it usually drizzled down, but here in Egypt when the rain finally came it did so with a passion, not letting up until it had soaked the land so thoroughly that the desert flowered overnight. In England one could never walk out late and catch the scent of jasmine and orange blossom drifting in pockets over the night air, surprising and delighting the senses. In England the winters were cold and dark, and people walked down the streets with heads lowered against the bitter wind. No one sat on brightly fashioned cushions in the streets smoking water pipes, talking about the day's business as camels passed by, laden with goods.

In England . . . She stopped herself abruptly.

She was going home to her family, for stability, for Peter. She knew she had to focus on that thought if she was to get through the next few weeks.

Pip lifted her head toward the sea breeze, wiping away hot tears that leaked from her eyes. She couldn't expect John Henry to understand what she felt.

She turned to him. "I will do as you ask because I must, because I realize this is best for Peter, but beyond that, I will not promise anything."

He placed his hands lightly on her shoulders, turning her to face him. "All I ask right now is that you get on that ship tomorrow, Pip. Whatever you might think of me, I do hold your best interests at heart."

"The truth is that you only have your own interests at heart—otherwise you would be sailing with us, not leaving me to make all the explanations when I arrive home by myself with a baby and no husband by my side. You haven't even bothered to explain why your business is of such almighty importance that you can't see us safely home yourself."

"I see no reason why the details should be of any significance to you. I have to stay for the time being, and that is that."

She shrugged off his hands. "Very well. Be an autocrat. I am sure we will manage very well without you."

"I am sure you will. Go now." He looked away. "I

shall see you in the morning and make sure that you board safely. I think our conversation is done. You've made yourself very clear."

"As have you," she said tightly. She regarded him coldly for a moment. Then, gathering her skirts in one hand, she moved quickly down the street toward the hotel, doing her best to keep her tears and resentment at bay. So be it. She would leave on the morning tide, and when and if she saw John Henry again, it would be on her terms.

She had no idea why she felt as if her heart were breaking.

6

July 10, 1836
Norwich, England

Pip clapped her hands in delight as the great structure of Alconleigh appeared, her heart singing at the sight. She'd never been so happy to see her home, despite her reluctance to leave Egypt. Although the journey back had been boring, irritating, and thoroughly depressing, arriving at Alconleigh gave her a renewed sense of hope. She knew her family would embrace her, care for her. All she'd done for the last year was to care for everyone else, and she had reached the point of exhaustion.

She looked at Aafteh, who gazed at the approaching house with her mouth open in astonishment. Then again, Aafteh's mouth had been open in astonishment ever since they'd left Alexandria.

Pip had no idea what Aafteh would make of

England or England of her, but she continued to serve Peter's best interests, still providing him with milk and love. How well she would adjust to an entirely different culture remained to be seen.

The carriage drew up in front of the enormous house. Pip's heart leaped with joy when she saw her mother dash out to greet them.

Before the carriage even came to a complete stop, Pip threw the door open, jumped down, and enveloped her mother in an enormous hug.

"Mama—oh, Mama, how happy I am to see you," she cried, burying her head in Louisa's neck and drinking in her familiar scent, so long missed.

"And I you, my darling," Louisa said, stepping back and examining Pip's face carefully. "You look exhausted, and little wonder. A rest, I think, and then we'll all have dinner and catch up. Where is your adorable baby?" She looked expectantly toward the carriage, and quickly covered her mouth as Aafteh, draped in her Egyptian garb, emerged with Peter in her arms, smiling hesitantly.

Louisa quickly recovered her composure and walked over to Aafteh. "*Salaam,*" she said, lightly touching her arm. "And this is Peter, of course." She beamed at Pip, who had walked beside her. "Oh, darling, he's absolutely adorable." She lovingly ran a hand over his head, and Peter kicked and gurgled in response, his arms flailing in a mutual greeting.

"How grown-up he is! I suppose I still thought of him as a tiny infant. He's a fine, healthy boy. I'm so happy for you, Pip. Just wait until Will sees his first

grandchild—he's been beside himself with anticipation, as have we all."

Pip felt like the lowest-crawling worm to be deceiv-
ing her family so terribly, despite how much she loved
Peter. She told herself that Peter was as much a part of
the family as she.

She took Peter from Aafteh's arms and passed him
to her mother. "Here, Mama. Why don't you get to
know your grandson a little? He's very easy. I'll make
sure Aafteh gets settled in, since she won't understand
a thing anyone tells her. At least she can make sense of
my Arabic, as inadequate as it is."

"Oh, yes, that's a good idea. I have the nursery all
set up and her rooms are ready." She shot Pip an inquiring look. "Do you really think it wise to bring an
Arab nanny here, darling? She'll be most terribly isolated, not knowing the language or the—the dress."

Pip couldn't help laughing. Her mother was the
most educated and successful of women, a highly regarded novelist, but sometimes Pip wondered if she
wasn't lacking in imagination when it came to the real
world. "Aafteh," she replied, "will adjust over time, but
if she doesn't, she can always return home. I doubt
that will happen since she has very little to return to,
and furthermore she loves Peter. If you're worried
about the servants . . ."

"Oh, no, dear. That wasn't my concern at all,"
Louisa said, cooing lovingly at Peter. "They are accustomed to all sorts of eccentricities, as you know well.
No, I was more concerned about things like her diet,
which must be very different from ours. Then there's

the matter of church—she surely cannot attend with the other staff."

"She has never attended services of any kind," Pip replied. "Women weren't allowed in, or at least not into the inner sanctum, and Aafteh grew up in a village far away from any mosque. Please don't worry, Mama. I'll see to Aafteh."

Pip knew it was going to be difficult bringing Aafteh into the world of rural England. Cornelia Hitchens had treated Aafteh like a leper throughout the voyage, flinching whenever Aafteh came into view and turning away with a handkerchief pressed against her mouth and nose.

Pip had wanted to put this down to the prejudice of one stupid, myopic woman. The remaining trip home, however, had definitely alerted Pip to trouble. Despite being in Pip's respectable company, Aafteh was largely shunned by innkeepers and carriage drivers, who tolerated her only for Pip's sake—and then only because Pip carried the cachet of her stepfather's title.

"Let us go inside, Mama," she said. "I can't wait to catch up. Goodness, it's been a long time since I've slept in my own bed—what a luxury that will be."

"I can imagine," her mother replied. "We'll get you settled, and then you must begin to tell me absolutely everything. Will and I have so many questions, and I in particular want to know how you happened to come across John Henry and decide to marry him in such a precipitous fashion."

Pip steeled herself for the onslaught, hoping against hope that her fabricated story would convince them.

She'd sacrificed too much for everything to go wrong now.

July 25, 1836
Cairo, Egypt

John Henry sank into a chair at Shepheard's Hotel, ordered a large whiskey, then settled back with a British newspaper, weeks old, and caught up with events back home. He wondered if Pip and Peter had arrived safely at Alconleigh. According to his calculations they ought to be there by now, if they had not been delayed. He also wondered how well Aafteh was managing in a completely foreign world. He'd had his reservations about sending her along, but in the end he'd been persuaded by her devotion to Peter.

Odd, how such a small child had changed their lives, which now revolved entirely around Peter's needs.

He felt a tap on his shoulder and looked up in surprise. Egyptian waiters did not have the habit of tapping shoulders. But instead of the waiter, he gazed with astonishment at the face of an old friend from India.

"Good heavens, Simon Forrest, of all people!" He jumped up and shook Simon's hand. "What brings you to these parts? The last time I saw you, you were taking Bombay society by storm."

Simon, who with his ebony hair and brilliant green eyes had earned a wide reputation as a rake during his time in India, merely shrugged. "Bombay lost its charm. Rather like yourself, I'd had enough of India and decided to return home, but also like you I was given a small mission here in Cairo. Nothing of a diplomatic sort, mind you." He cocked an eyebrow. "Still, I do hear things. I gather that Mehemet Ali is not cooperating as fully as you had hoped?"

"He is making a bloody nuisance of himself as far as we're concerned, but I do understand his reticence. After all, he's already ceded limited rights to Indian routes via the Isthmus of Suez and the valley of the Euphrates. The problem is that he's not fully honoring the convention of Kutaya, and it's been, what—three years since we reached that agreement?" John Henry pressed his fingers against his temples; his head had begun to ache.

He hadn't given away anything that wasn't public knowledge, but he was so exhausted that he knew he'd have to watch his words very carefully for fear of saying something he shouldn't.

"Oh, dear," Simon said in sympathy. "I do believe you've either had too much sun or too much diplomacy today. You look done in, my friend, whichever your complaint."

"To be perfectly honest, if I never have to deal with a pasha or his emissaries again I shall be eternally grateful, but unfortunately that is not the case. Mehemet Ali's attentions are at present turned to conquering Syria, and since Sultan Mahmud is bent on revenge, you can probably imagine that my petitions are not foremost in Mehemet's mind."

"These Arabs are unfathomable," Simon said, waving a finger to beckon the waiter. "I have only just arrived and am doing my best to arrange for some pieces to be exported for a third party, but I have run into one obstacle after another. Really, I cannot understand how you manage, although you did work wonders with the damned Indians, getting your way at nearly every turn. Little wonder the British government showed you their gratitude."

John Henry chose not to respond, since he had the utmost respect for the Indian people, unlike the vast majority of the British who lived in that country. Indeed, he had good reason to be enormously grateful to the Indian people, and to one man in particular. If Simon thought for a moment that John Henry had manipulated the Indians for his own ends or the ends of the British government, he could think again.

Uncomfortable, he abruptly changed the subject. "Tell me, what is the latest news? I've heard very little since my departure."

"Nothing much," Simon said, picking up the whiskey the waiter had delivered. "Oh—Colonel Jenkins's wife ran off with Captain Trevallyn, but that's not exactly news. We all saw it coming—well, all but Colonel Jenkins, that is." He grinned. "And you? Anything to report?"

John Henry took a long sip of his whiskey. "I married and had a son since I last saw you."

Simon stared at him. "I don't believe it. You, married? You must be joking—we all placed a bet that you'd end up in a monastery. Oh—sorry; I suppose you didn't know that." He fiddled with his glass. "We just assumed, given your penchant for keeping to yourself. You were never much for the women," he added, looking embarrassed.

John Henry didn't mind the assumption, since Simon was correct. He'd never had any interest in the colonial culture, even less in the brothels or the married Englishwomen who were happy to spread their favors around. "Nevertheless, I am married now," he said. He wasn't about to explain his lifelong love for Pip to Simon or anyone else.

"Good heavens, man, then this is an occasion for celebration. Where is this mysterious wife of yours, and how did you meet?" Simon gestured for another round.

"She is back in England, and we met—or met again, I should say—here in Egypt when I first arrived." At least that was true enough. "I thought that she and my son would be safer with her family while I finished sorting out matters here."

Simon nodded. "I can easily imagine why. But who is she? You say you knew each other previously." He regarded John Henry with keen interest.

"We were childhood friends—neighbors, actually," John Henry said. As much as he liked Simon, the man had a habit of nosing around. "We quickly realized that what we felt toward each other as adults was a little different. I don't think I need to spell out the rest."

"Indeed not," Simon said, looking delighted. "How

marvelous, a true romance. So who is this woman who ensnared my monkish friend?"

John Henry raised his eyebrows. "What makes you assume I behaved like a monk? You know virtually nothing of my personal business, since I went to great lengths to keep it to myself."

"My good man, you're not saying that you had some sort of relationship with a . . . well, with a *native* woman, are you? I don't mean to imply that we didn't all have a dip here and there, but in and out is the policy, you know."

John Henry had to resist a desire to laugh. Simon was no different from most others born and raised in England. Natives, as he put it, no matter the country they sprang from, were to be suspected and usually despised as inferior and possibly insurrectionist.

John Henry knew he had to be very careful, but he'd had one hell of a day and the double whiskey wasn't helping. Simon, given the provocation, would eagerly spread gossip even if it bore no resemblance to the truth.

"No," John Henry managed to say evenly. "I did not become involved with anyone while I was there, native or otherwise. I simply meant that I am employed as a diplomat. I cannot feel that the government would be happy should I reveal anything of my dealings, personal or otherwise." He raised his glass and looked Simon squarely in the eye, challenging him to say anything else.

"No, naturally not. Discretion is everything in your

business. So who is this mysterious woman? You have yet to tell me."

"Her name is—or was—Portia Merriem."

Simon choked on his drink. "Portia *Merriem*, did you say?" He put down his glass abruptly, his eyes watering. "Forgive me," he said, coughing into his hand. "Went down the wrong way. Portia Merriem," he repeated when he'd recovered. "Isn't she the stepdaughter of the Marquess of Alconleigh?"

"Indeed. Have you ever met?" John Henry said, wondering why Simon was so astonished. Did Simon think him too low born for Pip? That was a distinct possibility, and an attitude he would have to become accustomed to.

"No . . . but I did hear that she refused every offer that came her way. Good God—I confess to amazement. The word was that the girl was the toast of the town but would never give any of her suitors the time of day when they came to the point. She had earls, dukes, whatever, begging for her hand, and she turned them all down. How on earth did you manage?"

John Henry rubbed a finger over his mouth. "As I said, we've known each other for many years. Do you find the match astonishing because our stations are so disparate or because she married at all?"

"Don't be absurd. She was bound to marry eventually, and you've been given a knighthood, so that puts you in her circle in a roundabout way." He grinned. "I suppose I'm just surprised to hear that you, who once had no time for women, married the unattainable Miss Merriem. There is a certain irony, don't you think?"

If you only knew the irony, John Henry thought. But he merely shrugged. "I suppose. I can tell you only that we are happy and the gift of a son has only increased our happiness."

"My congratulations to you both," Simon said, finishing his drink in one gulp. "I wish you both every joy and long life to your son."

"Thank you. He's a fine, strong boy." John Henry wanted nothing more than a quick meal down the street and then bed. He certainly didn't want to answer any more questions. "How long do you stay?"

"Heaven only knows. I must complete this transaction, and then I might travel around."

John Henry nodded. "A worthwhile idea. There's much of interest to be seen. As for myself, I leave tomorrow for England, to rejoin my wife and son."

Simon shook John Henry's hand. "A safe journey, then. Marvelous running into you like this."

"Absolutely. Enjoy your stay. I will undoubtedly see you back in England and you can tell me all about it."

He threw some coins on the table, collected his hat, and strode out of the lounge.

7

October 18, 1836
Norwich, England

"Pip!"

Twelve-year-old James bounded into the nursery where Pip sat with Peter, who was busily playing with his wooden blocks, flinging them about with cries of delight.

"What is it, James?" she asked as her brother came to a halt in front of her, something held behind his back.

"A letter for you," he said, his ginger hair, the exact same shade as his twin sister's, practically standing on end. "It just came, and you'll never guess from where."

"I couldn't begin to guess, so you might as well just give it to me."

"It's from Plymouth," he said breathlessly. "It's from John Henry."

"John Henry?" She felt her heart sinking. She knew he would come home eventually, but she'd been so happy the last few months, living a quiet, ordered life at Alconleigh with her family, that she'd managed to put it out of her mind. John Henry was half a world away. Or so she'd thought.

She reached out, took the letter, and opened it.

James was hopping up and down on one foot. "What does he say? Is he coming?"

She looked up, her mouth dry, her heart pounding. "Yes. He's coming. He should be here anytime. He is going to stop briefly to visit his family, since he hasn't seen them for many years, but he doesn't plan to linger."

"Why don't you look happy?" James asked, dropping onto the floor next to her. "Mama is always thrilled when Papa comes home after he's been away."

"I'm just surprised," Pip hedged. Surprise was the least of her emotions. Dazed was more like it. She felt as if her safe, secure world were about to be turned upside down. The thought of having to put on the pretense of a happy, loving marriage in front of her entire family was almost more than she could endure.

She'd painted a picture of wedded bliss, lied through her teeth about how she and John Henry had met again at the ruins of Karnak, and immediately married because they realized they couldn't possibly spend another day without each other.

Her mother and Will had fallen for the story without question and were delighted for her. Why wouldn't they have believed her? She'd never lied to them before. Now she would be exposed for her deceit, as they were bound to see the truth of the situation.

She felt utterly sick. Fortunately, James's attention had turned to Peter and both were engaged in throwing blocks at each other. She rose and walked to the window, where she gazed out at the deep green fields surrounded by great stands of trees, their leaves turning brilliant shades of orange and red against the gray sky.

What on earth was she going to do? She could feign illness, she supposed, but that wouldn't last long, and besides, she was never ill. Her parents would be so alarmed that they'd call in the doctor, and he'd know soon enough that there wasn't a thing wrong with her. Running away with Peter was out of the question, as tempting as the thought was.

Clearly, she would have to face things head-on and do her best to appear madly in love. John Henry would have to work hard to play his part, since she knew he'd never been any kind of actor.

Pip groaned. If her parents did notice any tension between them, she might be able to explain it away by their time apart.

She saw the years stretching ahead, she and John Henry ensconced at Alconleigh, both of them acting a lie.

A flying block hit her foot, jarring her out of her reverie. Peter regarded her with wide blue eyes, one hand clutched in his dark ringlets. She picked up the block and carried it to him. "Try to be a little more careful where you aim your weapons," she said, stroking his silky hair. "You don't want to knock your mama over, do you?"

He chortled merrily, and her heart turned over with love. She scooped him up into her arms and kissed him soundly on his smooth, plump cheek. At least she had him, and she could hardly complain about that.

Aafteh walked silently through the door with Peter's lunch. She smiled shyly at Pip as she placed the plate of buttered bread, mashed vegetables, and custard on the table.

Pip returned her smile. She admired Aafteh enormously, knowing that the woman suffered greatly from the cold—not only the cold of the climate, so different from her own, but the coldness dealt out to her by the other servants. Poor Aafteh had nothing in common with any of them, her customs, dress, and beliefs so different from their own. In that prediction, Pip's mother had been right.

Still, as much as she obviously missed her country, Aafteh dealt with her new life bravely. Her devotion to Peter kept her heart strong.

"Thank you, Aafteh," Pip said, settling Peter into his high chair, his plump legs kicking enthusiastically as he eyed his meal. "He's a hungry boy, as usual."

Aafteh regarded her blankly. Pip was trying to teach Aafteh English to make her fit in more readily, although so far her efforts had met with little success. "I'll be back later," she persisted. "Come along, James, and let's let Peter get on with his meal."

She held out her hand to her brother and left the nursery, to the sound of Peter happily banging his spoon on the tray of his chair.

November 10, 1836
Norwich, England

John Henry, tired, chilled to the bone, and dusty from travel, took in the enormous edifice of Alconleigh as his hired carriage pulled up the long, tree-lined drive. The house, built of gray stone, seemed to stretch on forever. He'd never imagined anything quite so imposing. The parkland that surrounded it was equally magnificent, clothed in autumnal colors.

He waited impatiently for the carriage to stop, then merely nodded at the footman as he alighted, heading straight for the massive steps to the front door. He desperately longed to see Pip again, although he had no idea how she would receive him, given her angry farewell in Alexandria. He wanted just as much to see little Peter, whom he'd missed enormously.

He wondered if Peter would remember him after all the months that had gone by. Thankfully, that could be remedied in a matter of hours. Pip was another question entirely. She'd been constantly on his mind, although he doubted he'd been much on hers.

He wasn't entirely sure how to behave toward her. Loving husband? Near stranger? Despised fortune seeker who'd forced himself on her for his own nefarious motives?

"Good heavens! John Henry Lovell, if I'm not mistaken. I hate to say it, but how you've grown."

John Henry turned abruptly to see Will rounding the corner, his face wreathed in a broad and welcoming smile.

"Lord Alconleigh," he said, removing his hat, relieved that at least one person looked pleased to see him.

"It's Will, and we have much to say to each other. Pip told us two days ago that you would be arriving sometime soon, and we've all been on tenterhooks waiting for the moment." He clapped John Henry on the back. "Come, let us go inside. It's chilly out here, and you must be exhausted from the journey and in need of refreshment and a warm fire."

"Thank you. I made the best time from Dorset that I could." He rubbed his gloved hands briskly together.

"I can imagine. Unfortunately, Louisa and Pip have gone off to make morning calls, but they should be back soon. However, that does give us time to catch up," he said, leading John Henry into the great hall and giving orders to another footman.

John Henry looked around him as yet another footman divested him of his coat, his heart sinking as he took in the vastness of the place, the great expanse of marble and pillars and fine furniture, ancestral portraits lining every inch of wall.

How could he possibly compete with this kind of grandeur? He had little to offer her in comparison, despite the efforts he'd made in Dorset to buy her a comfortable home. Manleigh Park would look like a shanty next to this, even though he'd thought it rather magnificent at the time. He planned to order a total refurbishment, new rooms added, everything brought up-to-date. The reconstruction was going to be enormous in both price and scope, but he hadn't cared, wanting to offer both Pip and Peter a fine life in their fine new home.

Given what she was accustomed to, Manleigh would be a paltry estate, its house laughable with only fifteen bedrooms and five reception rooms and a mere six hundred acres.

He winced, now realizing that he could never give her anything approaching the luxury she'd known. Long gone was the little girl who had been happy milking a cow with him or swinging off a tree limb or chasing down the sheep. Maybe that was the problem—he'd stayed essentially the same in his values, despite his recent change of circumstance. He'd always be a farmer's son at heart, whereas Pip had been briefly forced into farm life by a bad financial turn, her real nature molded by her birth into the upper class.

"Let's go sit where there's some real warmth," Will said, comfortably stretching his arm across John Henry's shoulders and guiding him into a library that was clearly Will's private enclave. Fronted by a desk and chair and lined with overflowing bookshelves on three sides, the room also contained two comfortable wing-backed leather chairs and a sofa that sat in front of a crackling fire.

Sinking gratefully into one of the chairs, John Henry took his bearings yet again. Every overblown image of Alconleigh that had confronted him since his arrival only minutes ago was now directly contradicted by the simplicity of this particular space. Thin, autumnal sunlight streamed in through long windows, slanting across oriental carpets, their rich colors further warming the room. The one wall that wasn't shelved held prints of steeplechasing.

He rubbed a hand over his brow, trying to reconcile himself to this new atmosphere. He supposed he shouldn't be surprised; he'd known Will for many years, dating from the days when Will had acted as a farmhand at Broadhurst. None of them had known anything about his real identity then. He'd been simply Will Cutter, man-of-all-work, living in a single room above the stables, well liked by everyone. That he lived at Alconleigh now was due only to his elder brother's untimely death.

"I'd forgotten you'd never been up here," Will said, settling in the opposite chair. "Alconleigh is a far cry from Broadhurst, but I imagine it's also a far cry from a maharaja's palace."

John Henry grinned. "You could use a bit more gold trimming, and some peacocks might spruce the place up."

"Frankly, I couldn't bear the noise. Goodness, what adventures you've had since I last saw you. You were thoughtful to keep me apprised of your activities."

"After what you did for me, I would have been remiss if I hadn't written. I never would have gotten to India if not for your help."

"Perhaps not," Will said with a smile. "However, I

only gave you a start. You did the rest, and you made a fine job of it. Tell me, do you plan to carry on in diplomacy?"

John Henry shook his head. "My use is at an end. I'll keep my business interests in India, but I'd really like to turn my hand to estate management."

"Any estate in particular?" Will asked, gesturing at a footman, who put down a tray of coffee and swiftly departed. He poured two cups and handed one to John Henry.

"As a matter of fact, I've just purchased a property in Dorset, near the coast. Manleigh Park is the name. The farming is good, plenty of pastureland and fields."

"Really?" Will said. "I'm delighted to hear it, although Pip mentioned nothing about it."

"That's because Pip doesn't know. I only made the acquisition a few days ago. I wanted to surprise her." He scratched his cheek. "Manleigh's rather run down, but I thought we might enjoy putting it to rights together."

"I daresay Pip will be thrilled. She's never been one to lead an idle life. I'm curious about something, if you don't mind my asking." He took a sip of coffee. "Pip has said nothing about your knighthood. She calls herself Mrs. Lovell. Any particular reason for that?"

John Henry put down his cup and clenched his hands together, feeling acutely uncomfortable. "I've told Pip very little about my time in India."

Will shot him an incisive look. "I see. I cannot help but wonder if your reticence doesn't have something to do with the way Pip behaved toward you ten years ago. She did herself no credit, but she was very young and had just come straight from a Parisian finishing school where her head had been filled with a lot of nonsense. I told you that at the time, but I think you were feeling too devastated to take my words in." He stood, walked to the windows, and looked out. "Perhaps it was pride that prevented you from telling her how far you've risen in the world, for fear that she wouldn't marry you just for yourself?"

John Henry looked at the fire, his cheeks burning just as warmly. Will had, as usual, gone straight to the heart of the matter, although he had no way of knowing that Pip wouldn't have married him no matter what his rank was, had necessity not intervened. He struggled to find something to say but came up blank.

Will turned around. "Why do I have the feeling that something is amiss here? Come, John Henry—whatever you choose to tell me will stay between us."

John Henry considered his answer. He hated lying to Will, who had been so good to him, but he was also loath to betray Pip's confidence. On the other hand, he desperately needed to talk to someone, and he valued Will's advice. His conscience gave him no guidance at all; whatever he did, he would be in the wrong.

"Hmm," Will said, breaking into the heavy silence. "I thought as much. Pip hasn't looked like a woman pining away for her husband, as much as she dotes on little Peter, and you don't have the look of a man who is counting the minutes until his reunion with his wife. The only conclusion I can draw is that the two of you became carried away and Peter is the result. Well, never mind. I'm disappointed, but marriages have been made on that basis from time immemorial."

"Not this one," John Henry said in alarm, not wanting Will to think that Pip had behaved dishonorably in any way. "I swear to you, that's not why we married. I would never behave in such a manner, and I have far too much respect for Pip ever to compromise her."

Will frowned. "But do you love her?"

John Henry nodded, as miserable as he'd ever been in his life. "I've always loved her. I tried to put her out of my mind but was never entirely successful. When I saw her again, I realized that she is and always has been the only woman for me." That, at least, was the truth—a truth that had been eating at him all this time, for he was clearly not the man for Pip. She'd forced that point home on several occasions.

Will tapped a finger against his mouth. "I confess, I am baffled. Here the two of you are, married with a child, and that marriage and child happened swiftly indeed. You say you have always been in love with Pip and that she discovered her love for you in Egypt. Therefore, I have to ask myself why you both look so thoroughly unhappy."

"Pip and I . . . argued," John Henry said. That also was true—he hadn't forgotten for a minute the unholy row they'd had the night before she sailed. "She was angry that I was sending her and Peter back to England alone while I stayed behind. I couldn't tell her why my business was so important, given its delicate nature, so she thought I was being unreasonable."

"Is that all?" Will chuckled. "I wouldn't worry. Pip's

always been headstrong—you of all people should know that. I'm sure that the minute she sees you she'll forget all about your quarrel, as will you." He walked over and rested a hand on John Henry's shoulder. "Married people quarrel all the time, especially in the early days as they become accustomed to each other. Louisa and I have had some blazing arguments, and Pip is just as stubborn and passionate as her mother when she has a point to make. I've survived very happily, I might add, and so shall you."

John Henry sighed heavily. "I hope you're right. There's a little more to it than that, though, and I was hoping I might ask your opinion on the best way to proceed."

"Naturally," Will replied sincerely. "Ask away and I'll do my best to give you some decent advice, although no man will ever understand what really goes on in a woman's mind." He sat down and gave John Henry his full attention.

Choosing his words carefully, John Henry said, "This concerns what I've omitted to tell Pip about the last ten years of my life. She has no idea that I have money of my own, or at least not that I have anything substantial, any more than she knows about my title or my . . . reputation." He colored, embarrassed to mention that subject. "You were right in your assumption. I want Pip to care for me as the person I've always been, but she still has some misgivings about my station, and I fear she regrets the marriage." Lord, how he wished he could just come out with the whole story instead of talking around it with half-truths.

"What sort of misgivings?" Will asked, his brow lowering. "Are you saying that she has demeaned you in some way? I find that hard to believe, given that she chose to marry you as you represented yourself. Heaven knows, she had enough chances to marry for position and wealth."

"I believe . . ." John Henry stopped for a moment, feeling his way through very tricky straits. "I believe that Pip questions my reasons for marrying her. Her doubt was at the heart of our argument, you see. She thinks that I used her to improve my position, and I wasn't about to tell her the truth at that point. Pride or no, I will not be accused of such low behavior, especially when there's not a grain of truth in it."

Will drummed his fingers on his knees. "What do you plan to do?"

"I'm not sure," he said helplessly. "I've been thinking about the problem for months now. I could of course tell her everything, but I don't believe that would convince her of my love. I have a plan that might work, though, but perhaps it wouldn't be fair to Pip."

"Why don't you tell me about this plan of yours?" Will said, leaning back in his chair and folding his hands together. "You didn't earn your reputation as a diplomatic genius for nothing." His eyes gleamed with interest and not a little mischief.

"Since Pip and I will have to live elsewhere while Manleigh is being restored, I thought that instead of renting a nearby house, we might just live in the gatehouse. That way I can more easily oversee the entire project. The trick would be to have Pip think we were living there as the hired help, my being the steward rather than the owner. Only until we have the marriage worked out and I'm sure she loves me for myself, as she did as a child."

Will threw his head back and laughed heartily. "Oh, I do see," he said, wiping tears from his eyes. "You give Pip exactly what she's expecting from you, is that it? Brilliant—absolutely brilliant! Although how you'll keep the truth under wraps for long is beyond me."

"That part's not so difficult. The sale has yet to be finalized and I can easily have my solicitor transfer the title into another name, fictitious, of course. When I looked at the property, I said nothing about my personally being the interested party, so I can pretend to have been acting as agent for . . . well, for whomever."

"Aloysius Alfonso Blimp," Will said with glee. "Mr. Blimp can be a man of mystery."

John Henry looked at him in puzzlement. "Who the devil is Aloysius Alfonso Blimp?"

"No one at all. I made up the name when I was a child. I gave it to a pheasant of particularly fine plumage. He liked to parade about in the woods when he thought no one was looking, but the moment he sensed anyone around, he squawked in alarm and fled. I thought him a most curious creature, all show and no substance."

John Henry laughed. Will had always had a perverse sense of humor. "I see, the showy yet invisible Mr. Blimp. That will do nicely. But seriously, what about Pip?"

"What about her? I love her dearly, but more to the point, so do you. If you told her everything right now she might be mollified, but she wouldn't learn a blessed thing about the nature of real love." Will's face sobered. "Pip needs to learn that you want nothing from her but what she can give you from her heart. In her defense, do keep in mind that Pip's father married not for love but for money and broke her mother's heart in the process. She has her reasons for being cautious, if not suspicious."

"I am aware of Pip's history, which is one reason I've kept my silence. But until she trusts me, we will never be happy," John Henry said. "What about your wife? Will she go along with this plan?"

"I understand your position, and I believe Louisa will as well," Will said. "You see, when I fell in love with Louisa my position was much the same: I pretended to be a farmhand with no prospects. You are not so far away from that pretense, but the difference is that you really did start out on a farm, whereas I started out here, with every advantage save that of love."

"At least I had that growing up," John Henry said. "Which is why I intend to settle for nothing less in my marriage."

"Yes, and that Louisa will understand. I'll have a word with her as soon as you solidify your plans." He paused. "Pip explained about the unusual circumstances under which you were married overseas. I thought you might want to consider writing for a special license so that you can be remarried here in

England, should you so choose. Just to be sure the marriage is never questioned, you understand."

John Henry suppressed a groan. One wedding to an unwilling Pip had been enough. He could hardly imagine her agreeing to another. "I'll speak to her when the time is right," he said. "The minister did assure us that the marriage was legal and binding, but I see your point. I must write to my parents as well, do my best to explain all of this to them."

Will rose as a soft knock sounded at the door. "I believe we begin the charade, since this will be Louisa and Pip. Start as you mean to finish, and remember, John Henry, that you have the advantage of knowing exactly who you are and what you want. Keep the courage of your convictions as you always have, and Pip will find in the end that she's made a very good bargain indeed."

John Henry nodded at Will, then stood, his heart pounding in his throat. Pip waited on the other side of that door, and Will had the right of it—this *was* the beginning of their new lives.

8

"I really cannot understand what Mrs. Birdsley meant by saying she thought Reverend Smythe's Sunday sermon unfit for any decent woman's ears," Pip said, pulling off her gloves. "Do you think she referred to his mention of nakedness in the Garden of Eden? I thought he was speaking metaphorically, or at least that was the way I took his reference."

"Divining anything about Mrs. Birdsley is beyond me, my darling," Louisa said. "She takes offense at everything and everyone. The only reason I bother to call on her at all is because her children are friends of James and Kate, and I hesitate to sever the connection." She tapped again on the door of the library. "Will must have decided to spend his morning away from his ledgers," she said, turning away. Just as she spoke, the door opened, and Will appeared, his large form filling its frame.

"Hello, my dears. Did you have a happy morning?" he asked casually.

"I'd answer that with a guarded agreement," Louisa replied, throwing a smile over her shoulder at Pip. "What about you? You took ages to answer my knock. Do you have a fancy skirt hiding under your desk?"

"Don't I always?" Will retorted. "Actually, I have a much better surprise." He stood to one side. "Look who has arrived at last."

Pip stifled a gasp as John Henry stepped into her line of vision. Her heart seemed to stop in her chest as she took him in. His face still bore the healthy tan he'd had when she'd last seen him, but he looked strained. Little wonder. His face reflected what she felt.

"Hello, Pip," he said, stepping forward and taking her hands between his. "You look well." He bent down and kissed her cheek.

This and the light peck on the mouth he'd given after their wedding vows were the only kisses she'd received from him. Despite her resolve not to let him affect her in any way, she couldn't help the shiver that ran down her spine at his touch, as innocuous as that touch was. Her hand crept involuntarily to her face, where the imprint of his lips still burned.

"H-hello," she stammered. "Welcome home. How was your journey?" She tried to assume the role she meant to play, especially with her parents looking on.

"Tedious," he said. "I am grateful to be back with you. I've missed you and Peter both, but you most particularly."

"And I you," she said, forcing a smile. "Peter will be thrilled to see you," she added, diverting the conversation. "He's grown enormously."

"I imagine he has." He took a step back and bowed to Louisa. "Forgive me, Lady Alconleigh. In the excitement of the moment I have been rude. How do you do?"

"I do better for seeing you safely home," Louisa said, "and you might as well leave the formality behind, John Henry. You are my son-in-law now, and although it might be unconventional, I insist that you address me as Louisa."

He remembered how much he'd always enjoyed Louisa's easy warmth. "As you wish, Louisa. If you won't think me ruder yet, I would most appreciate some time alone with my wife. We have been apart for these many weeks, and we have much to catch up on."

Pip summoned a look of delight that completely belied her dismay. "Do you mind, Mama?"

"Don't be absurd. Off you go. Perhaps we'll be fortunate enough to see you at dinner, but feel no obligation to attend. Trays can always be sent to your room if you wish."

Pip turned beet-red at her mother's implication. "I am sure we can manage to make ourselves present at dinner," she said hesitantly. "As John Henry said, we just need some time to catch up."

"Naturally," Louisa said. "I suggest you begin immediately."

"Thank you for understanding," John Henry said, rescuing Pip by taking her hand and drawing her away.

He led her up the first flight of stairs, then stopped on the landing. "I have no idea where we're going," he said, scraping his hand through his hair.

"Then you had better follow me," she replied, taking the lead. Now what? Her bedroom was the only choice. Just the thought of being alone with John Henry in her room filled her with panic—silly, she knew, since she'd been alone with John Henry in a myriad of situations, but somehow this was different.

She drew up abruptly in front of the door, looking anywhere but at him. "This is my room. Our room, I suppose," she said, her cheeks hot. "My parents would never understand any other arrangement."

John Henry looked at her, then at the door, then back at her. "Where is the nursery? I imagine that's where Peter is?"

Pip released a huge breath of relief. Of course—why hadn't she thought of that herself? Naturally John Henry would want to see Peter, and that would take up quite some time. Then she could show him around the house, and that would take up even more time, given its size. Hopefully the dinner hour would come around shortly after, and since the children, with the exception of Peter, dined with them, they'd have lots of distractions.

After that . . . Well, she'd just have to think of something, since she couldn't possibly share her bed with John Henry. "Pip?" he said, examining her face far too intently for her liking. "Do you not want me to see Peter for some reason?"

"No—oh, no," she replied quickly. "I was just trying to work out the time, but he's not due for his afternoon nap for another hour. I am sure he'll be delighted to see you."

"If he has any recollection of me," John Henry said quietly. "I'm not expecting much."

"That is no fault of mine. You were the one who sent us away, as I recall."

He dropped his gaze. "Pip . . . I am sorry for my absence. I have not forgotten your resentment that I did not come with you, but I truly could not. Let us put all of that behind us now and start anew."

Pip heard the real regret in his tone and realized that he was apologizing. She could choose to accept his overture, or she could choose to turn away from him yet again. Suddenly she was tired of being angry, tired of the constant frustration she'd been feeling.

"Very well," she finally agreed. "We will put our argument behind us, but don't think that anything else has changed. Despite the fact that my parents think this marriage is based on love, we have an agreement, and I expect you to abide by it."

John Henry just looked at her.

"Furthermore," she plowed on, her cheeks tingling with embarrassment, "although we are married in name only, the face we present to the world must be that of a happy couple."

"Of course. But please, let us talk about this later. I have a burning desire to see Peter. Tell me, is he sitting up on his own yet?"

"Yes," she said, relieved to change the subject. "He

sits up and he plays with his toys and babbles away in his own language, although he hasn't yet started to crawl. You were right about his being perfectly normal, if a little behind."

"That is good news indeed." John Henry's face lit up with pleasure. "Not a day has gone by that I haven't thought about him and wondered how he was coming along."

Pip couldn't help softening at his expression of eager anticipation, nor could she help feeling a twinge of annoyance that he hadn't mentioned whether he'd thought about her. She pushed the thought away. "Come, the nursery is this way," she said, looking forward to John Henry's reaction when he saw how Peter had thrived in his absence.

John Henry drew in a deep breath as he spotted his son for the first time in many long months. Peter sat on a blanket on the floor, one hand holding a stuffed rabbit covered in slobber. John Henry drank in the sight of him like a man parched with thirst, his throat tight with amazement and love.

Peter had changed so much that he might not have recognized him. He was no longer a helpless infant but very much a little boy, with a head of dark curls and bright blue eyes, a small, round cherub with pink cheeks and a smile that made the world light up.

Peter shouted with delight when he saw Pip and held his arms out toward her, his eyes sparkling, but his face crinkled in uncertainty when he spotted John

Henry behind her. He shoved a fat fist into his mouth and looked quickly back at Pip as if to check whether he should burst into tears at this intrusion of a stranger into his personal territory.

"It's all right," she said gently. "This is your father, sweetheart. You're perfectly safe. He's come a long way to see you."

Peter removed his fist, now covered with drool, and gave them a lopsided smile, showing several newly cut teeth.

"Hello, little man," John Henry said, slowly approaching, his voice thick with emotion. "You have grown up, haven't you?" He knelt down in front of him, careful to keep some distance between them. "You are a fine young man, aren't you?" he said, feeling overwhelmed with love.

Peter looked away, then back at John Henry, and then he suddenly burst into laughter and held out his very wet rabbit.

"Thank you," John Henry said, solemnly taking the toy as if it were the most precious object in the world. To Peter it probably was, and John Henry had no doubt of the trust Peter had just displayed. He couldn't help wondering if the boy did retain some vestige of memory of him, although he couldn't imagine how—Peter was only three months old when John Henry had last laid eyes on him.

He glanced up at Pip. "He looks very well indeed. He's obviously a happy child."

"That he certainly is. Peter has a gift of making everyone around him happy."

"And Aafteh? How is she faring?"

Pip nodded toward the corner, where Aafteh sat quietly watching, her expression serene.

"Good heavens," John Henry said, startled. She'd always had a way of making herself invisible when she chose, an Arab trait he'd long admired. He quickly stood and bowed his head in a gesture of respect. *"Salaam,"* he said.

Aafteh blushed at his acknowledgment of her presence and bowed her head in reply.

John Henry turned back to Pip. "Has she found the adjustment difficult?"

"Let us say she's managing. I think her devotion to Peter makes her happy. He is her entire world and she mostly ignores everyone else."

John Henry easily imagined that she might. He was pleased to see that she hadn't traded in her customary robes for the tight-laced English fashions. "I suppose everyone ignores her as well. Poor Aafteh. I can't think she finds this new life easy."

"She's trying her best," Pip said, bending over and picking Peter up in her arms. He gurgled and dug his face into her neck, then looked over at John Henry shyly, one finger in his mouth. "She doesn't speak of Egypt or her life there, and I respect her privacy."

"That's probably wise." He laughed as Peter flung his arms out and leaned toward him. "Do you mind?" he asked, hungry to hold his son.

Pip hesitated, and for a bad moment John Henry thought she might not comply with his request.

But then she held Peter out toward him. "Of

course," she said, and handed over Peter's wriggling body.

John Henry took him easily into his arms, breathing in his scent. He smelled like powder and milk and fresh air. John Henry looked down at him, returning his toothy grin, and quickly dodged a flailing fist, which he caught in his hand, dropping a kiss onto it. "Well, my young fellow, you are not lacking in energy," he said, rubbing the rabbit against Peter's round tummy.

Peter reached down with a shout of glee and took possession of his stuffed animal, shoving it straight into his mouth with a vigor that made John Henry think that Peter's attentions had nothing to do with him and everything to do with reclaiming his prize.

Not wanting to press his luck, he gently placed Peter back on his blanket and touched the top of his head, then smoothed his fingers through Peter's silky curls. "Devour away, little man, and God help the rabbit. I believe you've had enough of me for now, but we'll visit again soon."

He straightened reluctantly and turned to Pip, whose face bore an entirely neutral expression. He couldn't be sure whether she was annoyed that he and Peter had gotten along so well or was actually happy about it.

He spoke on impulse. "I could use a long walk, and the woods are beautiful this time of year. Will you come with me?"

Pip slowly nodded, although she looked as if he'd suggested pulling her teeth out one by one. "A walk would be nice. I'd enjoy some fresh air."

———

Pip glanced at him as he threw back his head and drank in a deep breath of air. "I know," she said softly, as if reading his mind. "I didn't find coming home easy either. The walls have a way of closing in on one in the beginning. I've become accustomed to the ways of England again, but still, I don't think I'll ever forget how free I felt living on the river, with nothing to hold me in. I loved taking my meals outdoors and sleeping with the cabin windows opened wide, the breeze carrying the scent of water and blossom and elusive spice."

John Henry squeezed his eyes closed for a moment at the enticing image of Pip lying on her bed clothed only in a thin shift. He forced himself to concentrate on what she was saying.

"Yes . . . I do find returning difficult," he admitted. "I suppose the best way of describing it is that I feel . . . stifled." He looked away, not wanting her to know how flustered he was and how well she had divined his feelings.

He looked into her sapphire eyes and for a moment it seemed that she truly did understand everything he felt. But of course she didn't have the first idea of what he felt in his heart right now.

The hell of the whole thing was that he couldn't tell her. He still had a shred of pride, and through painful experience he'd learned to guard his feelings where Pip was concerned.

"Which way would you like to go?" he said against the knot in his throat.

"There's a nice path to the west," she replied, slanting a smile at him, which didn't help his composure. "It winds through the woods and back around over a field."

"That sounds perfect. Lead the way. We can talk as we go."

In the end, though, they hardly spoke at all. John Henry couldn't bring himself to discuss the burning issues at hand, too tired for another confrontation, content to absorb the beauty of the countryside. Doves cooed from the trees and a flock of redwings swept overhead. He breathed in the heady scent of fallen leaves and damp earth, happy just to have Pip at his side.

He began to feel as if they'd been transported back in time, the two of them walking comfortably side by side as they had as children, with no need to talk. But of course they were no longer children, and by a strange quirk of fate they were now married.

Start as you mean to finish, Will had said. Good advice, although John Henry was damned if he knew what it meant in this situation. Maybe if he behaved as if they were strangers just getting to know each other Pip might relax a little. Maybe . . . His step slowed. Maybe the answer stared him right in the face. What Pip needed was a courtship of sorts, a subtle sort of thing. John Henry hadn't been employed in a diplomatic capacity for nothing. Subtlety was the key in that game, subtlety and the gentle art of persuasion.

His original strategy had been more along the lines of *The Taming of the Shrew,* but he doubted that Pip would respond well to being bullied into submission. No, the velvet glove would work far better.

He smiled to himself. He'd never run away from a challenge. He would just approach Pip like a diplomatic problem to be solved. Engaging the enemy, a little thrust and parry, advance and retreat—that should do the trick. Manleigh Park seemed just the place to wage the battle. Unfamiliar territory would provide an advantage to him, keeping her off balance. Mr. Aloysius Blimp was looking more convenient by the moment.

"What are you looking so smug about?" Pip asked.

"Was I looking smug? I beg your pardon. Actually, I was about to tell you about a job I've accepted."

"A job?" Alarm was written all over her sweet face.

"Yes," he answered, already beginning to enjoy himself. Phase one: the engagement—laying the cards on the table. "Do you know Sidmouth, a town in Dorset? It's east of Exeter."

"Vaguely. I've never been there." She stopped and turned to face him. "What sort of job?" she asked suspiciously. "Are you planning to desert us again?" She looked torn between liking the idea and hating it.

"Not in the least. You, Peter, and Aafteh will come along. There's an estate near Sidmouth called Manleigh Park, which is in sore need of repair, and the owner thinks I'm just the man for the job."

Pip stared at him, stupefied. "You've taken on a job as a *stonemason*?"

He lifted one eyebrow. "Really, Pip, must you always go to the lowest common denominator? I've taken on the job of steward. The house is in a tumble-down way after years of neglect, and the land is in no better condition."

She blinked. "And—and you want to take us away from the comfort of Alconleigh and ensconce us in a rundown house with leaking roofs and drafts and plaster falling down about our ears?"

Pip's expression of horror made John Henry want to laugh, but he managed to keep a straight face. "Actually, I thought we'd live in one of the outbuildings. There's a nice little gatehouse—well, it's not in much better repair, but I had a look at it and it will do for the moment."

"No," she said, folding her arms across her chest. "Absolutely not. It's out of the question."

"Now, Pip," he said in a reasonable tone, "I thought we'd resolved this issue back in Egypt. We are married now, and I have no intention of living apart from you and Peter. Don't you think that would look a little odd, especially given the lecture you just made about presenting a united front?"

"If you want a job, why don't you ask Will for one? We could—we could live nearby. There's the dower house right here at Alconleigh. Think how much more comfortable we would be."

"You are mistaken if you think I would take advantage of Will and Louisa's generosity. It is my duty to provide for my family and that is exactly what I intend to do. I'm sorry if you don't like the idea, but that is the way it's going to be."

Pip dropped her arms to her sides. "I see," she said in a small, miserable voice. "I have no voice in this?"

"No. Believe me, Pip," he continued more gently, "I do not wish to make you unhappy, but I believe this will be for the best—for us and for Peter. You don't want him growing up thinking his father was content to live off others, do you?"

"No," she admitted, which John Henry considered a large concession on her part. "I wouldn't want Peter to think that. I know how I felt about my own father's lack of regard for my welfare. I just—I just want Peter to have the advantages that a life here at Alconleigh would offer him."

"A life of advantage doesn't necessarily build character," John Henry pointed out. "Indeed, sometimes it does exactly the opposite. You must have seen that, given the society you've mixed with. Even if I could offer Peter the world, I would be loath to do so, because I strongly believe that real happiness comes from the satisfaction of making one's own way."

"You say that because that's the only way you know," Pip replied, tilting her chin up. "Look at Will— he was born to a life of privilege and it didn't ruin his character, did it?"

"Will is an exception to the rule, and in any case, he had his own struggles to contend with—life was not always easy for him. I'm not saying that everyone born to privilege is condemned to weakness and profligacy, or even that struggling with adversity is the only way to form character. I'm only saying that given our own circumstances, I would rather give Peter a life that teaches him the satisfaction of earning what he wants, rather than having everything handed to him on a silver platter." He ran his fingers through his hair, trying to think how to get his point across without making Pip believe that he disapproved of the life she'd led.

"Take yourself," he said finally. "You were born into wealth and privilege, and then, because of your father's ill-advised actions, you found yourself living at Broadhurst Farm, your mother struggling to make ends meet. Granted, Will came along and took you away to Alconleigh, and your family fortune was restored at the same time, but during those years at the farm, you were not unhappy, were you? You helped out with the chores, you and I had plenty of time for our adventures, and you went to bed every night knowing that you had lived a full and productive day."

Pip glared at him. "So you think that by taking me back to that sort of life and giving Peter the same experience, you will mold us into better people, is that it? You've already told me that you think me spoiled and selfish, so I can only believe that from your point of view I became that way after I left Broadhurst and came here to Alconleigh, where life was not a constant struggle. Ergo, I was ruined by Will's good intentions."

"Don't be absurd," he said. "Both Will and your mother have done their very best by you, and money has nothing to do with it. Look at your mother, Pip. She doesn't sit around eating chocolates all day—she is a successful author and works hard at her job, even if the rest of the world has no idea that she is the person behind M. J. Peter."

"I don't see what my mother's novels have to do with anything," Pip said hotly. "She enjoys her work, and she doesn't need or desire acclaim, which is why she's never acknowledged authorship."

John Henry was utterly frustrated, but the art of diplomacy did not involve indulging in irrational outbursts. He tried again. "The point is that she's doing something meaningful with her life, unlike most women of her station," he said, striving to keep a calm and reasonable tone.

"Oh, and you think I haven't?" Pip countered, her eyes flashing dangerously. "I suppose you think I've been twiddling my thumbs all these years, cramming chocolates into my mouth while lounging on a sofa and fanning myself."

"I said nothing of the sort!" he shouted, the art of diplomacy abandoning him, along with his resolve. What was it about Pip that inevitably caused him to lose his temper? He *never* lost his temper. Indeed, he prided himself on keeping a level head in the worst of circumstances.

"I said," he continued through clenched teeth, "that I admire your mother for working as hard as she does when she doesn't need to. That statement was not a reflection on you, and whether you choose to eat bonbons until the cows come home is no concern of mine." He couldn't help himself. "If you are in the habit of eating bonbons day and night, however, you might as well resign yourself to giving up the practice.

Once we get to Manleigh you'll have other things to occupy your dainty little fingers."

"You really are a beast," Pip cried. "I knew you had an ulterior motive! Maybe I was wrong about you— maybe you didn't want to elevate yourself through me; you wanted nothing more than to humiliate me—to bring me down to your level." She shoved her hands onto her hips, her eyes filled with rage. "I've never heard of anything so low. If I didn't know better, I'd think you'd been plotting this for years just to get back at me for rebuffing your attentions."

John Henry couldn't take another word. "Think what you wish," he said coldly. "You always do think the worst of my motives, no matter what I say or do. I'm going back to the house. I am badly in need of a bath and a change of clothes. I do like to be clean, even though I was born in a sty."

Pip turned her back on him, her slim body shaking.

"Oh, and Pip—I suggest you pull yourself together before dinner tonight. You wouldn't want your family thinking that there was anything between us but the greatest affection. I know I can count on you for that, knowing how well practiced you are in deceit."

He didn't wait for a reply, turning abruptly and storming back down the path, barely able to see where he was going for the fury clouding his eyes.

9

Pip splashed her face with cold water, then reached for a towel. She raised her head and examined herself in the mirror, hoping that the hot and angry tears she'd shed in the woods hadn't resulted in the telltale signs of puffy eyes and a red nose.

As far as she could see, her face looked normal. She didn't *feel* normal—anything but. John Henry had once again managed to turn her world on end.

He ought to consider himself lucky that he wasn't in the room right now, for she would cheerfully have taken his head off. She still couldn't believe his colossal nerve, saying such horrible, hurtful things to her. Not to mention his idiotic plan to take her and Peter away to some awful ruin of a place and make her work her fingers to the bone.

He might not realize it, but she had a scholastic tome in progress, an account of her experiences in Egypt that she'd been hard at work on for months, complete with sketches and watercolors. She wasn't about to tell him about it, either, given his disgraceful attitude. Bonbons, indeed. How dare he insult her in such a fashion? What would he know of scholarly work, anyway?

All he thought of was tilling land and milking cows. She'd chosen to pursue a more high-minded profession, and she wasn't about to let him interfere with her goal.

Bonbons indeed! she thought, working herself into another rage.

She furiously brushed her hair out, then quickly arranged it into a twist on top of her head, without waiting for her maid. She didn't need a maid. She didn't need anyone. Hadn't she proved herself in Egypt? She, Portia Merriem—well, Portia Merriem Lovell, she amended with a scowl—was an independent woman who could manage anything, including an impossible husband who wasn't even a husband.

John Henry was a blight on her existence, and he would soon see that she wasn't someone to be manipulated. Her family would back her up. They wouldn't stand for him taking her to a nasty, dilapidated estate and forcing her to work at hard labor. They would never allow any such thing.

She took an evening dress from the wardrobe and hastily pulled it on over her petticoat. She fumbled with the tiny buttons on the back, then gave up, realizing that she needed her maid after all.

"May I help you?"

She spun around at the sound of John Henry's voice. "I'll wait for my maid, thank you," she snapped. "What are you doing in here?"

"As you might recall, this is my room, too," he said. "I didn't mean to disturb you. I was actually next door in the dressing room, fetching my evening coat. I left it earlier to hang, not having a valet to iron the wrinkles out." He'd dressed in trousers and a stiff-collared shirt covered by a white brocaded waistcoat, his neckcloth neatly tied, the formal coat slung over his arm.

"Then put it on and go," she said curtly, resisting the tug of tears.

"At least let me help you with your dress, since I'm standing here."

He moved toward her, and Pip in her misery did not object. She turned, then jumped as his fingers brushed the bare expanse of skin at her waist. Something about John Henry's touch against her flesh made her go hot and weak. Her breath caught in her throat as his warm hands journeyed slowly up her spine. For once she wished she hadn't been so adamant in her refusal to wear corsets, since at least that would have provided some protection between her flesh and his fingers.

Telling herself she was being ridiculous, she stood still as he finished doing up the final button, which was just between her tingling shoulder blades. "Th-thank you," she said, trying to collect herself as she turned back to face him. "You are very kind."

"I'm pleased that you can find some kindness in me," he said, his dark brown eyes gazing steadily into hers. "If I upset you earlier, forgive me. My words were ill-chosen, and I should have been more thoughtful of your feelings. Will you accept my apology?"

Pip's cheeks flushed with heat. He seemed sincere, but so many matters lay unresolved between them.

"I accept your apology for speaking precipitously," she said, choosing her words very carefully. "I cannot accept your decision, however."

"How unfortunate," he said with a sigh. "That, you see, is the one thing that I will not negotiate." He shrugged his coat on over his broad shoulders and chest, pulling it into place over his narrow waist and hips.

Pip couldn't help staring at him. She'd never seen John Henry in dinner clothes before, and the dark coat completed the image of a gentleman. He looked as accustomed to the attire as if he'd always worn it.

"Shall we go down to dinner?" he asked, giving her a quizzical look as he offered her his arm.

Embarrassed to have been caught staring, she dropped her gaze. She stepped forward and reluctantly rested her hand in the crook of his elbow, acutely aware of the warmth of his body and his scent of soap and outdoors and—a touch of sandalwood? She blushed, unable to believe she was thinking about the way John Henry smelled. What was wrong with her?

He was just John Henry, after all. And anyway, she re-minded herself firmly, she was still furious with him.

He led her through the cavernous house and into the drawing room, where the family had assembled before dinner.

"Ah, there you are," Will said, walking toward them with two glasses. "Sherry?"

"Thank you," John Henry said easily, as if he ac-cepted glasses of sherry from marquesses all the time.

Louisa introduced the twins, who stared at John Henry with avid interest. Throughout dinner they plied him with questions, one starting a sentence and the other finishing it. Their steady interrogation had mostly to do with his travels, and whether he'd ever been attacked by Arabs, ridden a camel, or perhaps been buried in a sandstorm.

He didn't seem to mind the barrage, answering with good grace, and Pip laughed lightly. She was par-tially at fault, having fed James and Kate the kind of exaggerated stories that twelve-year-old children most enjoyed.

He shot Pip an amused look over the rim of his sherry glass as he fielded yet another storm of inquiry. "No, I can't say that I ever witnessed an insurrection in India, although I did once go on a leopard shoot and on occasion rode on elephants. Will that do?"

Kate and James sighed in unison, their freckled faces alight, their brown eyes starry. "Oh, yes, sir," James said happily, "that will do nicely. Did you actu-ally kill any leopards?"

"No. Nor was I even imperiled by one. I merely watched from a distance." He smiled down at them. "I'm sorry to be such a disappointment to you, but I tend to be a peaceful sort of man, not much given to guns or violence. Now, my friend Walter Jeffries, he would be much more to your liking. He shot leopards and tigers and boars all the time, and once he even took on a whole band of rebels single-handed and thoroughly trounced them, thereby saving the party of Englishwomen he was escorting to Calcutta."

The twins shouted with delight and begged him for details.

Pip listened in fascination as the story unfolded, wondering at yet another side of her husband. He was kind, gentle, and attentive to the children, and she was learning more about John Henry's time in India from his conversation with them than she'd ever learned directly from him.

She couldn't help feeling curious and slightly hurt. He'd never told her much regarding that period in his life, yet he willingly talked to her brother and sister about it at length. She was his wife, after all. Surely she had a right to know how he'd spent the last ten years.

Then the realization dawned that she'd never really asked. Not properly, not with serious interest. They'd spent most of their time together talking about Peter's welfare and their awkward situation. John Henry had barely mentioned India, let alone what he'd done there. She'd assumed that he had traveled around, working here and there, looking for adventure.

The picture he drew now for the children didn't fit

that scenario. He'd obviously led a rich and interesting life in India, although the details he gave were no more than little vignettes and did not provide a complete picture.

Pip poked at her food, contributing little to the conversation. She couldn't do more—she had nothing to add. On several occasions she noticed her mother glancing at her with a curious expression, as if trying to divine Pip's thoughts.

Each time Pip caught her mother's look, she did her best to smile, even as her food stuck in her throat. She drank her wine, which did nothing to help her churning stomach. She nodded, and every now and then tried to look fondly at John Henry, which didn't help her appetite.

All she could think of was the night to come, when she and John Henry ascended the staircase to her bedroom. One bed, two people. The idea of having John Henry lie next to her throughout the night under the same sheets and blankets made her heart pound with anxiety.

Would he try to touch her? She shivered and took a long drink of wine. If he did, what would she do? Resist him?

She looked down at the plate of bread pudding the footman had slid in front of her and reluctantly picked up her spoon, knowing that her family would notice if she didn't at least sample it, since bread pudding was one of her favorite dishes. Tonight it tasted like sawdust. She lowered her spoon, unable to swallow another bite.

John Henry had promised to leave her in peace, but he'd made that promise months ago and might very well have changed his mind, given his behavior today. For all she knew, he planned to pounce the first moment he had her alone.

Pip sneaked a look at him. Engaged in conversation with Will and Louisa, he didn't appear at all nefarious. Indeed, he looked entirely harmless. But once the lamps were out, who knew what kind of person he would be? She eyed the knife on the cheeseboard and had the wild thought that she should slip it under her wrap and take it with her to bed.

Looking back and forth between her daughter and John Henry, Louisa rose. "I would leave you gentlemen to port and conversation, but I think John Henry and Pip would prefer to retire," she announced, oblivious to Pip's panic. "Don't you agree, Will?"

Will smiled into his napkin. "We are all tired after a long day. James and Kate, off to bed with you. We will all say our good nights here and let everyone find some much-deserved rest."

Pip stood numbly as John Henry came to her side. This was it, then, her condemnation to hell itself, dealt by the hands of her loving parents, who thought they were sending her off into the arms of bliss.

John Henry said a polite good night to the assembled company, then placed an arm firmly around her waist and led her out of the room and straight up the stairs.

He released her when they reached the bedroom door. He stood back to let her enter. "I'll go into the dressing room," he said. "Your maid will want to ready you for bed. I'll join you when you've finished your preparations."

She turned away from him, her heart pounding so hard that she thought she might collapse. John Henry had a way of setting her every nerve on edge.

"Very well," she said, not about to let him see the state she'd worked herself into. Breathing a huge sigh of relief when he vanished into the dressing room next door, she rang for her maid.

Beth appeared only moments later, her round face wreathed in a broad smile. "Would you like me to lay out your best nightgown, the one with the lace and ribbons?" she asked, her eyes sparkling.

"What, you would have me freeze half to death? I think my usual flannel nightdress will do very well, thank you, Beth." Did everyone in this house think she was about to spend the night in connubial joy? She couldn't really fault Beth for her enthusiasm—the girl had come to Alconleigh to be her maid some six years before. A local farmer's daughter, Beth had always been cheerful and kind, thrilled to be up at "the big house," as she called it, and she wished only the best for her mistress.

Pip wanted to speak her own thoughts now, but that was a luxury she couldn't afford. She went through the usual bedtime routine, letting Beth help her out of her clothes and into her night shift, then washed her face and brushed her teeth as Beth stoked the fire, for once not chattering. As soon as Beth left the room Pip slipped under the sheets and pulled the covers right up under her chin. She lay staring up at the canopy, trying to still the trembling of her body.

The problem wasn't so much that she felt a *complete* conviction that John Henry would attack her. Indeed, if she was truly honest with herself, her anxiety stemmed more from the thought of spending an entire night with him lying right there next to her. She'd never shared her bed with anyone save for her pet cats when she was a child, and John Henry was about as far away from a pet cat as she could imagine. If anything, he made her think of an adder lying in the grass, ready to strike at any moment.

A moment later, John Henry tapped lightly on the adjoining door and came through. She heard a muffled snort of laughter and turned her head to see what he thought was so funny.

He stood halfway across the room, his eyes dancing with mirth, one arm resting across his chest as he looked down at her.

Her eyes narrowed. "I cannot see how you can take any amusement from this situation," she snapped, trying to ignore the fact that he wore nothing more than a long linen nightshirt, his calves and feet bare.

"Can't you?" he replied, grinning. "You should see yourself, Pip. I can't help but wonder if you have a carving knife concealed beneath the blankets."

She colored furiously, given that she'd considered the idea only a short time before. "I would hope I have no need to hold a weapon on you," she retorted.

"And I would hope that you feel comfortable

enough with me to know that I pose no danger to you." He walked to the bed and Pip had to force herself not to shrink away as he pulled back the covers and slid under them, the mattress creaking under his weight.

Rolling onto his side, he blew out the lamp, casting the room into darkness. The only illumination was the low light of the fire burning in the grate, which threw tall, flickering shadows onto the wall.

He settled down, his dark head resting on the pillow that lay directly next to her own.

Pip realized that she'd been holding her breath and released it very slowly. She didn't want him to think that he intimidated her in any way, although every muscle in her body had stiffened. She felt the heat of his body next to hers, although no part of him touched her, heard his slow, even breathing, smelled that elusive scent she'd noticed before. She wished him a thousand miles away.

"Do you remember the last time we spent the night together?" he asked into the silence, startling her.

"I've never spent a night with you," she said indignantly. "If you're referring to all those nights on the boat, they don't count since we had separate cabins."

"No, I was actually referring to the night in the Broadhurst hayloft when we were children. Don't you recall? We were caught in the most ferocious storm, wind howling, trees blowing down, rain flooding the fields."

"Oh, yes . . ." Pip said, a reluctant smile on her lips.

That had been high adventure. "I do remember. We were playing out in the woods when the storm hit, and the cow barn was the only shelter within reach."

"Exactly. The wind nearly blew us over as we ran for cover." He laughed softly. "I remember both of us stripping down and diving under the hay for warmth, nothing visible but the tops of our heads."

"And later when we were both starving, you went down and milked one of the cows, and we drank warm, frothy milk from a bucket."

"I was so hungry I nearly raided the cattle feed," he said, turning his head on the pillow and smiling at her. "You wouldn't let me. You said . . . let's see. That's right, you said that stealing food from the animals' mouths would be the lowest form of behavior and you'd never speak to me again. You were all of six, but even then you had your standards."

Oh, she *did* remember. Despite their fear, that had been a wonderful night, John Henry holding her protectively throughout. She'd never given a moment's thought to their nakedness—all she'd cared about was sharing his warmth, feeling safe in his arms. They'd been so young and innocent, the best of friends. "I remember the next morning equally well, when our frantic parents discovered us. I thought we'd be condemned to nothing but bread and water for days, but you explained everything and in the end came out looking like a hero."

"Well, not exactly a hero, since my father roundly pointed out that I should have read the signs of the coming storm, but our parents were all so relieved we hadn't come to harm that they decided to let the incident drop." He turned on his side and propped his head on the palm of his hand, his fingers resting along his cheek. "Odd . . . I haven't thought about that in years. Who would have thought then that we'd be here now?"

Pip, brought suddenly back to the present, realized that John Henry's face loomed only inches from her own, far too close for comfort. The easy innocence they'd once shared had changed into something dangerous and unsettling.

She sat up abruptly, holding the covers tightly against her. "This isn't a hayloft," she said tightly, "and no storm is raging outside." *Only inside,* she thought miserably, her heart once again starting to pound.

"No, we're not in a hayloft, and we're not children, but I do hope one thing hasn't changed."

"What is that?" she asked, turning her head to look down at him, and quickly wishing she hadn't, for John Henry's eyes burned into hers in a way that caused the pit of her stomach to feel hollow. His body was clothed in a nightshirt, but the expression on his face was completely naked.

"I hope we still have trust between us," he said very quietly. "I don't like repeating myself, Pip, so I'll say this one last time. I will never harm you or let you come to harm. You can sleep soundly tonight in the knowledge that you're safe."

She couldn't help the shudder that ran through her, this time not one of fear or anxiety but of something else, something that tugged at her heart and reminded her of days long gone, when she'd known what real trust was. Days when life had been simple and carefree, and John Henry had been woven into the fabric of her life as inexorably as the intertwining threads of a tapestry.

"Thank you," she said, her voice thick with sudden emotion. "I am sorry if I've been behaving in a difficult fashion. I'm just not accustomed to sharing my bed, and I wasn't sure . . . I wasn't sure what your intentions were."

"Oh, and you think I was oblivious to your concern?" He sat up to face her, taking her gently by the shoulders, the warmth of his hands seeping into her skin and causing her to tremble all over again. "Pip. Listen, and listen carefully. We've been apart for a long time and we need to learn to know each other again, but I'm not completely without sensitivity. Do you really think I was unaware of your feelings tonight at dinner, why you hardly spoke and only picked at your food?"

"I wasn't hungry," she mumbled, unwilling to let him come so close. Her defenses were all she had left to keep John Henry a safe distance away, and he had an unsettling way of breaching her walls with very little effort.

"You weren't hungry? You, the woman with the appetite of a horse? I can only imagine your disinterest in your food was caused by an overactive imagination and what you thought might transpire in this room tonight. Given the fact that I could see very little of you save for your nose when I came to bed, I believe my theory to be sound." He dropped his hands. "At least be honest with me."

Feeling dangerously close to throwing herself into his arms and sobbing out her troubles and fears, Pip stiffened her resolve to keep her distance. "I've given you honesty," she said, rounding on him. "I've told you how I feel, what I expect from you. Don't think you can seduce me with words, because you can't—no one has managed to seduce me yet, and I have no intention of falling into your arms just because you invoke our past history. And if you're so sensitive to my feelings, then why do you insist on taking me away from all that I know and love, to install me in a rundown house in the middle of nowhere in a situation you know I will despise?"

"There really is no getting through to you, is there?" John Henry said, his tone cool. "Very well. But understand this: Since you are adverse to sharing so much as a bed with me and are clearly made uncomfortable by my presence in the midst of your family, we shall go to Manleigh tomorrow. You and Peter will be ready by midday. When we arrive, you will have your own bedroom. I assure you that I shall not trouble you again with my attentions." He leaned toward her, his eyes gleaming with anger. "I wouldn't dream of intruding on your desire for celibacy."

Pip stared at him, taken aback. She'd never known John Henry to speak in such a manner.

"I suppose you know all about the pleasures of the bedroom," she said, shoving at his broad chest and knocking him off-balance. "I should have known that you would be exactly the kind of man who would avail himself of such dubious pleasures at any opportunity."

He straightened slowly. "Why should you object? Was I meant to deprive myself when those opportunities were offered freely? I had no obligation to you or anyone else."

Pip couldn't bear to look at him a moment longer. She slid down in the bed without another word and turned her back on him, pulling the covers up around her shoulders and closing her eyes. She'd just go to sleep, that was all there was to it. He didn't deserve another word, let alone her respect. John Henry had proved himself to be like most other men, a philandering hedonist. She wouldn't be surprised if he hadn't spent the majority of his time in India frequenting the brothels.

For all she knew, he had illegitimate children running all over the subcontinent. Well, she wouldn't have his children: That was one thing she knew with absolute certainty. He'd never lay so much as a finger on her. Even if she wanted him to, which she didn't, he'd made himself perfectly clear yet again—John Henry found her thoroughly undesirable, no more interesting than that childhood playmate with whom he'd once sheltered in a storm.

She heard him settle down and felt the mattress move and the tug of sheets and blankets as he covered himself, but most of all she felt his burning anger as if it cloaked them both as thoroughly as the blankets did.

The night passed in agonizing slowness, Pip not sleeping at all, aware of every movement John Henry made, each shift of position, each turn of his head on his pillow. He made every effort to stay as far away from her as he could. She couldn't be sure if he slept, but in case he was secretly awake, she decided to let him think that she at least slept soundly, oblivious to his presence in her bed. The task proved more difficult than she'd imagined, for she had to breathe evenly and stay very still, which was not in the least restful.

She must have finally nodded off, for when she woke, Beth was pulling back the drapes, letting thin sunlight stream into the room. Pip sat up, rubbing her scratchy eyes, and stretched. To her relief, John Henry was nowhere in sight, the only evidence that he'd spent the night beside her being the indentation on the pillow and the rumpled covers.

"Have you seen Mr. Lovell?" she asked, puzzled as to how he'd managed to slip away without her realizing.

"Aye, missus. He rose much earlier and took his breakfast downstairs," she said with a smile, settling a tray on Pip's lap. "He thought you might want to take your own up here in privacy, thinking you might be tired."

"How very thoughtful," Pip said dryly, then belatedly remembered that she was supposed to be in a state of ecstasy, having spent the night in the arms of her loving husband.

"He asked me to pack your belongings, missus. I understand you're going to your new home. My, but we'll miss you and little Master Peter. The house will feel empty, that it will."

"Thank you, Beth." Pip's heart fell as she realized that John Henry's pronouncement the night before had been no idle threat. He really did intend to take them away and install them hundreds of miles away in a cloud of plaster dust. "Where is Mr. Lovell now?"

"I believe he is in the library with his lordship. At least that's where I saw them go after Mr. Lovell had a word with me. I'm sorry I won't be going with you," she said with a sigh. "Mr. Lovell said you'll be making other arrangements."

"I'm sorry too," Pip replied, her annoyance growing. How high-handed could the man be, dismissing her maid without a word to her? She'd have kicked up a fuss, but she knew that Beth wouldn't really be happy taken away from her home and dragged into the plaster dust with them, despite her loyalty to Pip. "Never mind, we'll be back to visit, and often, I hope."

"I hope so, missus," Beth said, pulling Pip's trunk from the dressing room. "The water's hot," she called from next door. "Best wash as soon as you've finished your breakfast or you'll be bathing in ice."

Pip, who had no appetite, took a sip of hot chocolate, which was about as much as her stomach could manage. She then lugged herself from the warm bed and padded across the room to the pitcher and bowl on the stand next to the bureau. Once she'd washed, she felt more awake. Beth came to help her dress, then went back to the packing, chattering away about poor George's toothache.

Pip couldn't help smiling. She knew that Beth held out high hopes for a match with the handsome groom, another reason to leave her at Alconleigh. With any luck they'd soon be married, and Beth would be busy looking after babies instead of Pip, who had never really needed much looking after anyway, much to Beth's dismay.

"The tooth will probably have to come out," Beth said through the rustling of tissue paper. "Can you imagine the agony? He's so brave, though, that he won't murmur a word of complaint."

Pip doubted that. George had been moping about for the last two weeks, his hand clasped to his swollen cheek, looking like a kicked dog, every now and then emitting a pitiful groan.

"The sooner the tooth comes out, the better," she said, helping Beth to fold a voluminous dress. "He's put the matter off long enough, and you don't want infection to set in. Perhaps you can persuade him to see the surgeon today. I don't think the poultices have been doing much good." In a way she felt relieved to talk about the mundane matters of Alconleigh rather than focus on her uncertain future.

If John Henry had an abscessed tooth, she decided with satisfaction, she'd offer to pull it herself, just to watch him kick and squirm. Unfortunately, John Henry possessed a very healthy, white set of teeth that did not look as if they were going to go into decline anytime soon, thereby depriving her of the pleasure of removing them one by one.

Someone tapped at the door, and Pip froze, praying the caller wouldn't be her sound, abscess-free husband.

Instead, her mother appeared. "Good morning, darling. Good, you're dressed." She cast an eye around the room, which was strewn with clothes. "I'd like a word with you. Would you come for a walk in the rose garden with me? The air isn't too terribly chilly this morning and the stroll might do you some good."

Pip searched her mother's face, not reassured by the vaguely troubled expression in her eyes. Pip admired and respected her mother enormously, and they'd always had a close relationship, but she worried that her mother might have divined a little too much about the one thing Pip didn't want her to know—the true state of her relationship with John Henry.

In that, Pip was right. As soon as they reached the wide garden, a few brave shrubs still showing blossoms, her mother tucked Pip's arm into hers.

"Darling, John Henry told us at breakfast that you leave today for your new home in Dorset. Naturally we shall miss having you here, but I cannot help feeling that he is right: You need to establish yourselves in your own house, and from what I gathered he's found a lovely spot."

Pip nodded and smiled cheerfully, but her heart ached because she couldn't pour out her troubles to her mother. "So he has said. I imagine I will take great pleasure in returning to Dorset. I have missed living near the sea, and I—I think . . ."

Her face fell and she covered it with her free hand, her shoulders starting to shake.

"My darling girl, what *is* it? You looked so unlike yourself yesterday when John Henry arrived, and last night at dinner—well." She inclined her head. "Now you have dark circles under your eyes and I cannot believe they are a result of a happy night. I can only put your behavior down to nerves since you'd been so long apart from each other, but I have to wonder. Is there something you haven't told me?"

Pip shook her head, trying desperately not to pour out every last bit of the truth she'd been hiding for so long.

"Ah . . ." Louisa said. "I think I see. Everything has changed, hasn't it? You and John Henry had a whirlwind courtship in a most romantic location, married and conceived a child almost immediately, and then had to go through a long separation. Perhaps you expected everything to be exactly the same when he returned, but England is not the same as Egypt, and the fairy tale you created there doesn't match the reality of home."

She gathered Pip into her arms without another word, letting Pip weep onto her shoulder until she had no more tears left.

Then she held her daughter at arm's length and regarded her with a firm eye. "Now that all of that is said, I want you to listen to me. All you need is time to become reacquainted with each other, and the best way of doing that is to go to Manleigh Park and remember what brought you together in the first place. You need to make a *real* life together and one that I am sure will bring you great happiness. One . . . well, one difficult night does not presage the rest of your life."

Pip couldn't bring herself to look at her mother.

Louisa obviously thought that their experience in bed had been unsatisfactory. If she only knew the truth . . . but Pip couldn't tell her mother that either.

"I understand," she said, sniffing, wiping her eyes and nose with the handkerchief that she'd fortuitously remembered to bring along. "Thank you for your wise words, Mama. I am sure John Henry and I will work everything out. You're right, of course. We have been too long apart and need to learn to know each other again in a different environment."

Her mother said nothing for a long moment as she regarded Pip closely. "Perhaps. And perhaps you need to give your husband the benefit of the doubt, for something tells me that you have not learned to separate the boy from the man. That, my dear girl, could be a serious error of judgment." She gently cupped Pip's chin in her hand. "You've made your choice. Do your best to make the most of it."

Easy enough for you to say, Pip thought, feeling like ten kinds of fool. She had made her choice, and as a result she was on her way to Manleigh Park with a man she barely knew and who clearly despised her, a man who was bent on making her life a misery and dragging Peter straight into the middle of it.

10

$\mathcal{S}$truggling to keep her composure, Pip stood outside the carriage that Will had graciously loaned them for their journey, hugging her brother and sister and sharing a few words with each of them, then moving to Will and holding him close.

"Goodbye," she said. "Thank you for looking after me so well for all these years. I love you."

"And I you, my dearest," he said, squeezing her tightly. "All will be well. We love you always, never forget that."

"I shan't," she said. She turned to her mother, tears blinding her eyes. "Mama . . ." She was unable to go on.

"Goodbye, my darling," Louisa said, taking Pip into her arms, her eyes just as misty as Pip's. "Remember what I said."

Pip nodded against her mother's cheek. "I'll try," she promised, feeling a painful lump in her throat. She moved away from her mother's embrace, feeling as if with that one step she was creating a chasm between her old, happy life and the new, bleak one she now faced.

Taking one last look up at Alconleigh, the huge gray stone structure representing everything safe in her life, she said a silent goodbye and turned her face toward the future.

Aafteh stood to one side, holding Peter bundled up against the cold, her eyes lowered.

"It's time to leave," Pip said to her in Arabic. "Take Peter into the carriage, where you'll both be warm."

Aafteh stepped without a backward look, her head bent over Peter as she crooned a gentle Arabic song in his ear, soothing his unsettled cries.

As Pip slipped in opposite her, she imagined that Aafteh was soothing herself in equal measure, uprooted once again in this foreign land and not really understanding where she was going now.

John Henry, after speaking quietly to Will, entered the carriage and took his place next to Pip, who made a point of creating as much distance as possible between them on the seat. They'd barely spoken a word to each other that morning.

The carriage pulled away and Pip averted her face, not wanting to see the home she loved so much disappear in the distance. She looked down at her hands, not knowing where else to fix her clouded gaze.

She listened to the creaking of the carriage, the

clopping of the horses' hooves, and Aafteh's soft singing. Peter had blessedly fallen asleep, his wails quieted by the rocking of the carriage and Aafteh's efforts. Aafteh fell asleep as well, her head resting on the top of his silken curls, bobbing up and down as the carriage rocked over the uneven terrain.

Pip looked up to see that John Henry had turned his head to the window and was steadfastly gazing out at the passing countryside clothed in the last of its autumn splendor.

His profile was sharp against the wintry light, and Pip couldn't help examining it. She could see only the long, straight line of his nose, one high cheekbone, the arch of a dark eyebrow, and one side of his sensual mouth set in a grim line.

His dark hair curled softly against the collar of his coat, his hand resting against his nape, fingers lightly curled. Her gaze traveled lower, to where his coat had fallen open, exposing one thigh, the shape of his hard muscles clearly outlined against the material of his trousers.

Heat filled her cheeks as the image of his bare calves, well shaped and covered in fine, dark hair, played through her mind. She pushed the memory away. Thinking of John Henry in his nightshirt did her composure no good at all, any more than did remembering the heavy weight of his body in bed as he lay next to her, his dark eyes regarding her through the flickering firelight.

Thank heaven she didn't have to endure the experience again, she thought, blindly looking out her own window. He'd promised her that she would have her own bedroom at Manleigh, and she could only be grateful. That was about all she could find to be grateful for at this moment.

Exhausted, she lay her head back against the velvet squabs, the swaying of the carriage sending her into much-needed sleep.

"Pip?" John Henry gently touched her shoulder as the carriage neared the posting inn where they were to spend the night. He was relieved that she'd slept the last few hours, knowing that she'd been awake most of the preceding night, as had he. How could he not know?

Each soft breath, each shift and turn of her slim body, had set his blood on fire. He'd needed every ounce of control not to take her into his arms and soothe away her fears. He'd finally turned over, facing away from her, and hugged the far side of the bed for fear that he might inadvertently move against her in the night. The last thing in the world he needed was for her to realize how much she aroused him. Lord knew he'd suffered enough from her slings and arrows in the past, but he'd suffered equally from lying in such close proximity to the woman he physically longed for in a way he'd never experienced with another woman.

He squeezed his eyes shut for a brief moment, then opened them, slowly shaking his head.

Odd, he considered, his hand lingering on her

slight shoulder, his fingers lightly stroking her fine wool coat. Odd how the fiery young girl he'd known and loved had become a stranger in so many ways and yet now had the ability to undo him with the slightest look, the merest touch. Odd that she could send his heart reeling in one moment with her beauty, her smile, her quick intelligence, and in the next make his blood boil in fury when she used her sharp tongue with him.

He really didn't know how he was ever going to convince Pip of his sincerity, given that she took every last thing he said and did and turned it into an attack against his integrity. He would just have to keep trying, he supposed, and not let her goad him into anger. Sometimes he wondered if she didn't intentionally provoke him, just to keep him at arm's length.

He looked down tenderly at her sleeping face, so vulnerable, so soft and sweet. The thought of kissing those perfect, full, rosy lips, of running his hands over her smooth cheeks, her long creamy neck, down over her round breasts . . .

He jerked his hand away and ran it over his face. *God, deliver me from this torment,* he prayed. *Give me patience, give me the strength to forbear until I can make her understand. Give me the understanding to read what is in her heart, what makes her so reluctant and fearful of me. I am only a man, dear Lord. Help me to be the best man I can be, I beg you. I really don't know how much longer I can restrain myself.*

At that moment his beloved tormentor woke up and stretched, yawning, one hand pressed against her rose-petal mouth. He quickly looked away, anywhere but at Pip, whose cheeks were flushed with sleep, her sapphire eyes hazy as she slowly came to full awareness.

She blinked and looked around, then suddenly sat up straight, as if she remembered she was sitting in a carriage with her worst enemy. That hurt him as much as any harsh words she'd ever thrown at him, and, God knew, she had dealt him a lifetime's measure already.

"Where are we?" she asked, rubbing her eyes.

"Just coming to our first stop. This is where we spend the night," John Henry answered, forcing his attention to the tasks at hand. "We'll change horses and be off again first thing in the morning."

"Oh." She looked out at the courtyard in which the carriage had halted. "I trust the rooms are clean? I wouldn't want Peter to catch lice or bedbugs—or some awful disease."

John Henry responded evenly, although he had to make a serious effort to do so. "The rooms are clean. I stayed here on my way up to Norfolk. Furthermore, Will recommended the place. He often stops here himself."

Pip nodded. "In that case, I cannot be worried. At least Will knows whereof he speaks."

Suppressing a strong desire to wrap his hands around Pip's throat, John Henry looked over at Aafteh, who'd slept soundly throughout the journey. Peter rested easily in her arms, one hand curled on his cheek.

The noise of the ostlers shouting around the carriage woke him, and his eyes flew open in alarm, as did Aafteh's, as she looked out the window.

"Tell her that she will shortly be safely tucked away in a room," John Henry said to Pip before he swung down from the carriage and strode into the inn.

After securing three bedrooms and a private parlor for dinner, John Henry returned to the carriage to see Pip, Aafteh, and Peter safely inside. He tried to ignore the curious stares as Aafteh entered, while doing his best to shelter her from the jeers that came from the taproom as men pushed and jostled to get a better look at the foreigner.

He hurried Aafteh up the stairs to the bedroom she would share with Peter.

"What a pathetic display of ignorance," he said in disgust, turning to Pip. "Is that what you met with all along the way to Alconleigh?"

Pip nodded, angry tears in her eyes. "I cannot believe what Aafteh has endured since leaving Egypt. I don't think she had any idea when she agreed to come to England that she would be treated so cruelly. She has been nothing but good and kind and loyal, but can you imagine being shunned and mocked in such a fashion, John Henry?"

"I have experienced being on the outside of other cultures, but I have almost always been treated with kindness and respect, no matter how simple the people—no matter how elevated either, when it comes to that."

He looked over at Aafteh, who huddled on the

floor in a corner of the room, her veil pulled around her face, her arms clutching Peter as if he were a lifeline. "Go to her, Pip. Please. Comfort her—let her know not all Englishmen are unfeeling savages." His face twisted with disdain for his countrymen.

Pip lightly touched his arm. "I will do my best. As I said, this is not the first time she's experienced such treatment. Leave us for a time and I will speak to her."

He nodded. "I'll go to my room—it's just next door, should you need me. I've booked dinner downstairs in an hour's time and also requested a tray sent up to Aafteh and Peter. Don't worry," he added before she could protest. "I saw the suckling pig grilling outside and made certain that she would be served lamb."

Pip smiled in relief. "Of course. Forgive me." She lowered her head. "I honestly forgot for a moment that you know all about Egypt. I've become accustomed to having no one understand what that life is like."

He picked up her cold hands and held them fast between his own. "If you remember nothing else, Pip, at least remember that. Now go and look after Aafteh. I'm going to change my clothes and then go downstairs and make things right with those idiots. A well-placed story or two should do the trick." He released her hands. "You might be amazed at what a good yarn can do to change the tide of opinion."

"I heard you weave your tales last night," she said with a weary smile. "If you can impress them as well as you impressed the twins, you will have done well."

"That crowd of dolts downstairs is going to be a lot

easier to bamboozle than Kate and James, I assure you. By the time I'm finished with them they'll want to stand me drinks all night, which naturally I'll have to refuse, given that I have my wife and son to look after. Aafteh will by that time have reached heroic proportions, her sacrifice in leaving her own people to care for our son already on the way of becoming a legend in this village." He grinned. "Give me an hour or so—can you wait that long for your supper?"

"As long as you swear to give me chapter and verse of everything that happens," Pip replied, flashing a brilliant smile.

Taking one last look at Pip, who had turned to kneel on the floor opposite Aafteh, John Henry left the room, softly closing the door behind him.

"What happened after the terrible sandstorm that we barely survived?" Pip asked, her eyes dancing with laughter, her fork poised in midair. John Henry's account of his hour in the taproom was too good to be true.

"Well, then," he said, taking a sip of his wine, "aside from the sandstorm, I also remembered the twins' burning desire for an Arab raid, so I fabricated one of those, too. I said that we were camped out in the desert later that week, when we heard the blood-curdling war cry *Ghazou, ghazou* go up all around us. The marauders poured into the camp on horseback, lances aimed directly at us."

"Good heavens," Pip said. "What did we do?"

"Naturally I sprang out of the tent, waving my pistol about in one hand and a saber in another, shouting commands to the guards. We parried the savage attack, fighting hand to hand. Here's where Aafteh's great heroism comes in: As soon as she heard the war cry, she took you—you were with child, you see—and she hid you under a pile of rugs to keep you safe, placing herself in front of them. She was prepared to give her life for you."

"How terribly brave of her," Pip said, spearing another piece of roast pork.

"Indeed. We owe her a great debt, for I feel sure that had the attack been successful, you and our unborn child would have been discovered."

"But you repelled the raiders."

John Henry shot her a look of mock disdain. "Of course we repelled the raiders, straight back into the night. What sort of man do you think I am?"

Pip burst into laughter. "I beg your pardon. I suppose I owe you my life as well."

He shrugged. "You wept copious tears of joy and relief, threw yourself into my arms, and told me that you would never forget my heroism. Then we had our dinner, since I was very hungry from all that exertion."

"Oh, really," Pip said dryly. "What did we have for dinner?"

"Dinner? Didn't I say? That was a desert partridge caught by my hawk that afternoon. Aafteh cooked it in broth and we drank fresh camel milk with our meal, from one of the camels who had managed to survive the sandstorm."

Pip choked on the wine she'd just swallowed. "Honestly, John Henry—where on earth did you learn to tell such tall tales?"

"I have always told tall tales. Did I ever tell you that when I was in India I saved a maharaja's eldest son from drowning in a raging river? Despite the threat to my own life, I threw myself into the torrent and dragged the boy to safety just before he was swept away to his death."

"I suppose the maharaja rewarded you with jewels and vast amounts of gold?" she said, highly entertained.

"How ever did you know?" he replied, keeping a perfectly straight face, but his eyes were alight with laughter. "As it happens, he was one of the wealthiest and most powerful maharajas in all of India. He wanted to give me one of his palaces, but I said, 'Thank you, honored sir, but I have no need of a palace.' So he threw some more money my way instead. I could hardly offend him by refusing that as well."

Pip threw her napkin at him. He caught it with a laugh, then rose to stir the fire back to life.

She watched his tall form as he pushed the glowing logs about with a poker. The fire caught and leaped, casting a halo of light around his dark head. Not that John Henry deserved a halo of any sort, she reminded herself.

Then with a start she realized that at this moment

she felt no animosity toward him. Tonight he'd been nothing but good company. Indeed, she hadn't laughed so hard since . . . well, she couldn't remember when.

He was such an enigma to her, one minute cold and curt, another an entertaining companion. Sometimes he was even kind and gentle, as in the way he'd come to Aafteh's defense, turning the tide of opinion about her in the taproom.

Pip shook her head. She needed to remember that at heart he was an ambitious blackguard, or she'd find herself deluded by his easy charm, and then where would she be? He'd probably used this technique on scores of women before, telling silly stories, charming them straight into his bed.

She picked up the decanter, filled her glass to the top, and drank half of it in two swallows.

Funny—she'd never thought of John Henry as charming before tonight. Annoying, yes. Arrogant, definitely. To be fair, he had shown remarkable presence of mind and courage when Peter had been born, but that was an isolated incident. After that, his behavior had been overbearing and impossible. He'd practically forced her into marriage with no forewarning whatsoever, had shoved her onto a ship without consulting her, had taken a job designed to humiliate her—and, to add insult to injury, he didn't even find her the least bit appealing.

Not that she wanted him to, she quickly reminded herself. She just wished that he might look at her with at least a semblance of desire, so that she didn't feel so *uninteresting* around him. Lots of other men found her attractive. She'd spent years fending off suitors, hadn't she? She bit her lip, wondering if maybe her age had something to do with it. Or maybe John Henry still viewed her as a little sister.

Her eyes widened in horror at the thought. Maybe *that* was the problem.

She filled her glass again and downed the contents. That must be the reason for his lack of interest, she decided, although she no longer regarded him as a brother in any sense. Last night when they'd lain in bed together John Henry had felt like anything but a brother. Her entire body tingled as the memory rushed back, and she shoved the thought to the back of her mind, feeling thoroughly depressed. There she'd been, foolishly worried that he might make advances on her, when that had been the farthest thing from his mind.

He turned around as if he'd divined her thoughts. "I was thinking that we might . . . What is it, Pip?" he asked, the smile on his face quickly fading.

"Nothing," she said, fiddling with her empty glass, praying her face hadn't given her away. "What were you going to say?"

"Only that I thought we might take a brief stroll before retiring, but you suddenly look strained. Forgive me—you must be exhausted. I should have seen you up to bed earlier."

"I am tired," she said in all honesty, but she was equally relieved at the prospect of being alone, an entire bedroom away from his. She didn't know what had come over her. The wine, she decided. Wine and lack of sleep were a bad combination. No wonder her thoughts had wandered in such a peculiar direction. She must be a little in her cups. She was sure of it, since her head felt unusually thick.

He held out his hand to her. "Come. We have an early start, and you should get a full night's sleep."

Wrapping his fingers around hers, he helped her to her feet. Pip could have done without the physical contact just then, for it only made her feel more light-headed. She really must watch her wine consumption, she told herself firmly. John Henry placed his other hand around her waist and steered her out of the parlor and up the stairs.

"Steady as you go," he said with a short laugh as she stumbled on a step.

"I'm fine. I'm just a little stiff from the long journey today," she lied.

"You?" he said with incredulity. "The woman who rode camels across the desert, survived a sandstorm and an Arab raid? I can hardly believe that a trip across England in a well-sprung carriage would do anything more than bore you to tears."

Pip looked up at him, a mistake because his eyes laughed down at her, sending another rush of tingling through her body. "That was your story, not mine," she replied unsteadily, looking away.

"Perhaps so, but the Pip I know can gallop a horse across twenty miles of terrain leaping everything in the path and never miss a breath." He stopped on the landing and turned her to face him, his hands resting on her shoulders. "Are you sure that you're not suffering from an entirely different malady?"

"If you mean that I've had a little too much to drink, yes, I probably have," she shot back with annoyance. "I am not accustomed to sharing an entire bottle of claret."

"Oh? I'll have to keep that in mind, although I've never noticed your being affected by wine before."

"That was in Egypt," she explained, stepping away from his touch. "The wine there was not so heady."

He regarded her steadily. "I didn't notice. I never noticed your cheeks flushing, either, but perhaps that was due to the warmth of the fire."

"Yes," she agreed, grateful for the excuse he'd just handed her. "I found the room suddenly warm. I'd like to go to bed now, if you don't mind." She turned and went blindly down the hall, desperate to escape. She found her door and rattled the handle with annoyance, unable to understand why it refused to turn.

"Pip? The key might be useful," he said from behind her, his voice oddly thick.

She spun around. He was dangling the key between his fingers. "Oh. The key," she said, feeling like an idiot. She held out her hand, but he moved in front of her and slid the key into the lock. She heard a soft click as it turned. He pushed the door open.

Her heart nearly stopped. Did he expect to come in? A treacherous part of her, the part of her brain that the wine had affected, almost wanted him to. She couldn't help staring up at his mouth, that enticing lower lip slightly fuller than the upper, imagining how it might feel on hers.

She shut her eyes, overcome by the most terrible trembling. She felt hot—too hot—and had the horrible thought that she might faint. She swore never to drink another glass of wine.

"Thank you," she managed to say, passing a hand over her fevered brow.

"That's it." John Henry scooped her up into his arms and carried her into the room, nudging the door closed with his foot.

Pip gasped, shaken by being held against him so closely.

He gently deposited her on the bed, then straightened and looked down at her. "Do you want me to wake Aafteh and have her help you out of your dress, or should I just do it myself?"

Pip swallowed hard. "I—I can do it myself," she said.

"That I doubt. Here, turn your back. Aafteh needs her sleep and I'm here and wide awake."

She did as she was told. He deftly undid her buttons, his breath close and warm against the thin cloth of her chemise where he bent over her, intent on his task. Her neck arched involuntarily as she half-expected him to drop a kiss on it. That would be nice, she thought hazily, relaxing into the feel of his fingers against her skin. So warm, so gentle, so very nice . . .

"There. You should be able to manage the rest," he said, stepping away.

"Oh," she said, her head swimming. "I suppose I

can. I loathe these stupid clothes. I cannot think why I have to wear petticoats—I draw the line at corsets, you know."

"I noticed. Very sensible, as I'd draw the line at them too. I've always valued the ability to breathe freely."

She nodded adamantly. "When I was in Egypt, I didn't bother with anything fashionable. I loved living in loose clothing, and if I'd had my way, I'd have worn the Egyptian robes, which make far more sense, but Isabel was scandalized that I even voiced the idea." Pip leaned back on her hands, ignoring the fact that the back of her dress flapped open. "I scandalized Isabel all the time. She adored Egypt but felt we must keep our English sensibilities. I think she was worried about me, since I loved riding on camels and donkeys and 'communing with the natives,' as she put it." Pip frowned. "Do you remember when we were small how we used to talk about how exciting it would be to live in foreign lands? How we wanted to be adventurers?"

He sat down next to her on the side of the bed. "I remember very well," he said. "We accomplished that dream, though, didn't we?"

"Yes, we did, each in our own way. You spent all those years in India, and I spent only those few months in Egypt, so you have the better of me in that. John Henry?"

"Yes?"

"I don't want to live my life forever in England, not when I have so many adventures left to experience. I want to go back to Egypt." She sat up straight, the repressed desire she'd restrained for the last six months pouring forth. "I want to go to Syria and Lebanon—I want to live in a tent in the desert. Not forever, you understand, just for a little while."

"I imagine that could be arranged," he said equably.

"No, I really mean this. Please don't appease me. I honestly don't want to live in plaster dust for the rest of my life while you tear walls down and build them back up. I have . . ." She hiccuped and covered her mouth. "Pardon me, for I truly have had too much to drink, but regardless, I have ambitions of a different nature, and I want to fulfill them."

"I can imagine that you do. However, my sweet Pip, I think the one ambition you need to focus on right now is a good night's sleep."

"Are you putting me off?" she demanded, squinting at him. "I have the funds to support myself, you know. I can manage perfectly well on my own." She nodded sleepily in self-agreement.

He chuckled. "You are the most self-sufficient woman I've ever known." So saying, he slipped her dress down off her shoulders and proficiently lifted her to slide it over her hips, leaving her in nothing but her chemise.

He deposited her under the covers. "Sleep well," he said, dropping a kiss onto her brow as her eyes closed. "Tomorrow will bring its own set of challenges."

Pip turned onto her side and tucked her hand under her cheek, falling straight into a deep slumber.

John Henry covered her up, a smile hovering on his lips. So. Pip was not as invulnerable as she claimed to be. Granted, she'd had a bit more to drink than was good for her, but at least she'd spoken a little of what was in her heart. Not only that, but she'd most definitely shown him that she wasn't entirely indifferent to his attentions. She might have been three sheets to the wind when she gave him that indication, but he still had a modicum of hope that he might eventually be able to bring her around, and that was far better than no hope at all.

Patience, he reminded himself as he slipped out of her room and into his own.

His last thought before he closed his eyes was that love was absolute hell.

11

$\mathcal{P}$ip wished she were dead. Her head pounded and her stomach churned. Every jolt of the carriage only reminded her that she'd had far too much to drink the night before. But far worse than that was her excruciating embarrassment over her wanton behavior. She couldn't imagine what had gotten into her, letting John Henry undress her like that.

If she'd had her wits about her, she would have insisted that he wake Aafteh—but no. She'd let him strip her practically naked without so much as an objection. Worst of all, she'd hadn't minded, or at least not then. Now she minded very much. He'd probably had no interest in her body, although she couldn't really remember much.

Thankfully, John Henry had been buried in a book all day and had paid her no attention, for she didn't think she could have managed so much as a simple conversation. She hadn't even been able to look him in the eye. Sneaking a peek at him, she couldn't help wondering what he must think of her.

He glanced up then, caught her eye and smiled, and went back to his book without a word.

Pip squirmed on her seat in humiliation. A part of her wished he would speak his mind and get the lecture over with.

Thinking about it, he'd said nothing about her folly, save to insist that she force down some breakfast. Beyond that, he'd left her to her own devices, amusing himself with Peter from time to time when not immersed in reading.

She looked up to see that the sun had topped the trees, sending a soft, golden glow over the landscape. Night would fall soon, and she was grateful, wanting nothing more than sleep.

Eventually John Henry closed his book. "We're nearly there," he said. "We've made exceptionally good time."

"Nearly where?" Pip asked, coming out of a doze.

"At Manleigh," he said, stretching his legs in front of him. "How do you feel? You have some color back in your cheeks, a good sign."

"Oh," Pip replied, realizing that she did feel better. At least her head had stopped aching. "John Henry," she said in a rush, determined to clear the air between them, "I apologize for my behavior last night. I assure you, I really am not in the habit of overindulging. I hope I did not make too great a fool of myself."

He stroked the corner of his mouth where a little smile played. "Not at all. You were overtired to begin with. I am at fault for not watching you more carefully, but you seemed to have polished off the decanter while my back was turned."

Pip groaned. "Please don't remind me. I've never felt so ill. Are you really not angry with me?"

His smile broadened. "I think in future I shall do the pouring for both of us, but no, I'm not angry. Why should I be? You didn't dance on a table or get into any brawls."

She bristled. "I would never behave in such a fashion. How could you suggest that I might?"

"Calm down, Pip," he said, holding his hands up in front of him as if to fend her off. "I was joking. Why did you think I'd be angry?"

"You've said hardly two words to me all day." She hesitated, wondering if she should mention her unladylike behavior in the bedroom, and decided against it. She'd apologized, and that ought to cover all of her transgressions.

"I've kept silent because I know from bitter experience that the last thing one wants the morning after overindulging is a lot of chatter. I assumed you'd prefer peace and quiet."

She dropped her gaze. "Thank you," she said, embarrassed all over again.

"Thank Aafteh. She took one look at you and knew

you were feeling unwell. She's done her best to keep Peter quiet—not an easy task."

Pip looked at Aafteh, who gazed silently out the window, Peter snuggled in the crook of her arm. His dark head lay against her chest, his rabbit dangling loosely from one hand as he sucked the thumb of the other, his eyes half-closed.

"She's wonderful with him," Pip said with a soft smile. "I don't know if I thanked you properly for what you did last night. I did notice a new respect given to her this morning, even through my fog."

"Mmm. Let's just say that contempt turned to curiosity. Aafteh is so composed that I sometimes find her hard to read, but I think she noticed the change of attitude. She actually smiled at the innkeeper's wife when the woman bade her farewell. I thought the woman might faint."

"That silly old cow. I was so angry last night when she behaved as if Aafteh was going to soil her precious establishment. Really, the bigotry in this country infuriates me. One would think that—"

John Henry cut her off with a light touch of his hand on hers. "Look, Pip," he said, his voice oddly husky. "Here is the approach to Manleigh."

The carriage slowed from its fast clip and made a turn down a smaller country road. Directly ahead lay a long drive, lined on both sides by giant oaks. In the distance was a large house built of sand-colored stone. She could make out three wings, one jutting out in front, facing the south. Tall chimneys rose from the shingled roofs, although no smoke curled from them.

Fallow fields stretched out on either side, and behind the house a thick, brilliantly colored wood formed a backdrop.

She drew in a deep breath, absorbing the place that would be her new home, even if that home belonged to someone else.

Still, there was something about the estate, an air of tranquility, as if it existed outside the mundane world, a sanctuary of sorts. She couldn't put her finger on what gave her that impression, only that she felt a sense of peace, the last thing she'd expected.

The carriage passed through a pair of open gates, flanked by stone walls marking the perimeter of the property, and drew to a halt just outside a gatehouse built off the back of the right wall. This was a much smaller structure, built in the same sandy stone and covered with brilliant red ivy over its front.

"What do you think?" John Henry asked. "This is where we shall be living for the moment."

Pip had lived in worse places, and she'd certainly lived in better, but she couldn't deny the charm of the little house, even though she could see that some work would be required to make it truly comfortable. The roof needed repair, since much of the slate had fallen off, and the drains were filled with leaves.

"Pip?" John Henry prompted, regarding her uncertainly. "Is it that bad?"

"No—no, not so bad at all," she replied. "I won't really know until I've looked around inside, but the façade is pleasant enough."

"Good. That's good. Let me take you inside." The

footman let down the steps, and John Henry offered Pip his hand.

At the arched stone entrance, he removed a key from his pocket and fitted it into the iron lock. The lock clicked and the large oak door creaked as John Henry pushed it open.

Pip shut her eyes for a moment and took a deep breath, knowing this was the beginning of her new life. The thought was daunting.

John Henry guided her through the door, his hand cupping her elbow.

As her eyes adjusted to the darkness within, horror filled her heart at the sight of the bare walls and the crumbling plaster.

A battered staircase rose to the left. To the right, an open door led into a front parlor, and the little she could see of the furniture looked frayed and worn.

She swallowed and continued her perusal. Directly ahead lay a hallway, two more doors leading off to the right, with another door straight in front of her, behind which she assumed was a kitchen. She prayed that John Henry didn't expect her to cook, or they'd all starve. They'd have to hire a maid or two as well. She didn't know the first thing about cleaning, and she doubted he'd considered any of those practicalities.

"There are five bedrooms upstairs," John Henry said, interrupting her thoughts. "I asked to have the house thoroughly cleaned and fresh linen put on the beds."

Pip nodded, tears starting to her eyes. "It's—it's very cozy," she said thickly, feeling as if she were in a nightmare. If she'd had the strength, she would have given him a tongue-lashing, but she was too tired to do anything but stare at the shambles into which he'd brought her.

"It's a roof over our heads for the moment," he said. Gently resting an arm around her shoulder, he gave her a squeeze. "I know you're accustomed to much grander surroundings, but we can make it into a home."

Pip shrugged off his hand and moved away. "I'll fetch Aafteh and Peter. You had better light some fires, for they'll surely catch their death of cold. Have you thought about what we're to have for supper?"

"The pantry should be stocked with provisions," he said, his tone suddenly cold. "I also picked up a hamper at the last posting inn when we stopped to change horses. We will dine on cold meat, bread, cheese, and fruit, if that suits your ladyship."

"Do not toy with me," she cried, at the end of her patience. "You talk so much of making a home, but have you given any consideration to our needs?"

He fixed her with a steely look. "I have given every consideration to your needs. You have a clean bed to sleep in, food to eat, and you'll shortly have a fire to keep you warm. I find your attitude perverse, Pip— last night you spoke of wanting to live in a desert tent, where comfort is in short supply, and tonight you're not satisfied with the basic necessities that many families live without."

"Oh, and I suppose you are now going to accuse me again of being spoiled and selfish when all I ask for is a reasonably comfortable home for our son and his nurse, never mind myself?"

He wearily ran a hand over his forehead. "I forget. I was brought up in a pigsty and so know nothing about how to provide for such as you. Will you not be happy until you have Rembrandts and Botticellis lining the wall?"

Pip glared at him. "I have no need for Rembrandts or Botticellis, although what you'd know about such paintings is beyond me. I only expected a warm, relatively well-appointed house to bring my child to."

"If you'll give me a few minutes, you'll be warm enough," he retorted sharply. "I hadn't planned on leaving Alconleigh so quickly—that was your doing, since you exhibited such a horror of sharing a bed with me. I'd actually asked for fires to be lit next week in anticipation of our arrival, but I didn't have time to send word ahead. Thank God I did insist that the house be cleaned and the linens changed immediately, or I'd have even bigger hell to pay."

Pip planted her hands on her waist. "Then maybe you should have thought again about precipitously dragging us away from Alconleigh without a word of warning. That was *your* choice yet again, John Henry, as everything has been from the miserable moment I first set eyes on you in Egypt. If you'd bothered to consult me—a concept that would never occur to you—you would have discovered that I preferred to wait until this house was in order."

"Is that so?" he said. "Then you're saying that you would have also preferred the agony of lying next to me night after night at Alconleigh, tossing and turning, trying to avoid any inadvertent contact, and all for the sake of your precious masquerade?"

Pip curled her fists by her sides, her blood boiling, mostly because he'd read her far too well. "I *never* tossed and turned—indeed, I didn't notice you at all. You may think yourself irresistible, but I find you very boring."

John Henry crossed his arms across his strong chest. "Do you know, I think I prefer you in your cups. At least you're honest then."

Taken aback, Pip flushed bright red. "How—how dare you throw that in my face?" she cried. "I apologized for my behavior last night, and you made light of it."

"This has nothing to do with your behavior last night and everything to do with your attitude now, which I find childish in the extreme."

She turned her back on him and stormed toward the door, wiping away hot tears.

He reached the door before she did and stretched one arm across the frame, his face a black cloud. "Let us get one thing straight right now," he said, his eyes boring into hers. "You might find me undesirable for any number of reasons, and quite honestly at this moment I couldn't care less. However, we are sharing this house, and I have no intention of living in an atmosphere of constant conflict. You will keep a civil tongue in your head, Pip, if not for my sake, then for Peter's. He doesn't deserve to have two parents forever at each other's throats."

Utterly miserable, Pip turned her face away, unwilling to meet his stony gaze for one more moment. "Then keep your distance," she replied tightly. "If this is how we are to live, so be it. I cannot change our circumstances, but at least I can try to avoid you."

He looked at the ceiling, his fingers tightening on the lintel of the door. "This house is not large enough to avoid each other. I suggest we learn to live in peace, or every last one of us will be deeply unhappy. You spoke of choices, Pip. You have one directly in front of you—make up your mind here and now."

Pip considered. As angry as she was with him, John Henry did have a point. They couldn't go on like this, battling constantly, for that would do Peter an injustice. She forced down her pride. "Very well," she muttered. "For Peter's sake I will try. Do not ask anything more of me, though. Civility is as far as I'm prepared to go."

He dropped his hand, rubbing it against the back of his neck as he stared at the floor. "Civility is a beginning," he said, his voice flat. "Why don't you bring Aafteh and Peter in? I'm going to speak to the footmen, see if they won't help me lay some fires before they return to Alconleigh. I'll do my best to get some hot water going once that is done."

Pip pushed past him and walked out to the carriage, her head held high but her heart aching with something she couldn't define even to herself.

12

November gave way to December and frost hung cold and sharp in the air, just as it did between John Henry and Pip, with no sign of a thaw. Pip felt as if she were living in limbo. The world of Alconleigh seemed a million miles away, but her new life at Manleigh didn't seem any more real. She went through her chores as a matter of rote, taking little pleasure from them, as she helped with the cleaning, gave orders, and wrote copious letters to her family and acquaintances.

She particularly enjoyed corresponding with Lady Samantha Merriem, her step-grandmother, who was the most colorful person she'd ever known. Pip eagerly looked forward to her entertaining letters, full of news about what the rest of England was doing, how, and to whom. Since Lady Samantha knew most of English society, her letters usually had Pip in stitches.

For some reason, John Henry had his letters delivered to the main house. She supposed that made sense, since they must have to do with his business. He never mentioned friends, but then he never mentioned anything personal.

Indeed, John Henry paid her next to no attention, and she made an effort to ignore him in kind.

The days marched by, one drifting into another, all the same without any sign of a respite from the tedium. At least Peter kept her entertained, but he could offer nothing in the way of conversation, the thing she most longed for.

She did take pleasure from working on her paper about her time in Egypt, pouring herself into the words, describing the country she'd come to love so well, its antiquities, its people and their customs. She also worked on her pen-and-ink sketches and her watercolors, refining them until she felt that she'd gotten them just right.

Her other pleasure came from walking outside. There at least she felt truly alive, the wind stinging her cheeks, the bare branches of trees starkly outlined against the gray sky. Manleigh Park possessed a unique beauty particular to the Dorset countryside, but it possessed something else besides, a special magic that she was slowly learning to recognize as she explored the woods and meadows.

She couldn't exactly put her finger on what that

magic was, only that her spirit felt soothed and comforted when she walked across the land. One of her favorite places to visit was the lake in front of the main house.

Still and quiet, the expanse of dark water gave her serenity. A stone bridge spanned the narrow portion of the lake, slightly arched, its balustrade a perfect place to rest her arms as she gazed over the glassy surface. She always found a stillness of mind as she stood there, her thoughts drifting away into nothing, like wind-blown clouds crossing the sky. Peace. Heavenly peace that she longed for, a balm to her bruised soul.

And then she'd shake herself loose from the tranquility, realizing that she had to go back to her chores.

Christmas morning came and they celebrated quietly. Pip gave John Henry a muffler she'd knitted and he gave her a pretty little cameo. Aafteh, who was baffled by the holiday, received a necklace of lapis lazuli from John Henry and a shawl from Pip, both presents pleasing her greatly. Peter crowed with delight at his new stuffed bear and a picture book, but he took just as much pleasure in the wrapping paper, which he tore to shreds and threw about. His big present to all of them was learning to crawl, a skill he put to good use and that kept them running after him all day.

Despite the festivities, the strain between John Henry and Pip continued, a bitter note in an otherwise happy day.

Pip stood next to him at Christmas services in the

village church, singing along to the carol, her soprano contrasting with his deep tenor, but she took no joy in the blending of their voices. She took no joy in John Henry's presence at all. He treated her politely at all times, but she couldn't help wanting more than cordiality.

Loneliness ate away at her, her only company Aafteh and Peter, the cook, and the housemaid who doubled as lady's maid. Not that Pip had any need for help. She and John Henry didn't socialize, but then with whom would they socialize? They had no standing in the community.

John Henry was gone for most of each day and often into the evening, returning from the main house tired and dusty. Dinner conversation consisted of a running report on how the renovations progressed and the mundane details of her daily routine. Mostly they talked about Peter.

At least they had him to bridge the gulf between them, she thought, as the sermon began.

She looked down at her gloved hands, twining her fingers together. Christmas was supposed to be a happy occasion, a time for charity and sharing, but she'd never been more miserable. She released a heavy sigh, ignoring the droning of the minister. In her heart of hearts she knew she had asked for exactly this. She'd demanded distance: John Henry had given that to her. She'd insisted on civility but nothing more: John Henry had given her that too. She'd made a point of having separate bedrooms: not only had John Henry seen to that, but he never put so much as a toe inside her room. In short, he'd complied with her every wish, so she had no reason to complain.

She glanced at him. He appeared to be paying rapt attention to the vicar's words.

Pip couldn't imagine what John Henry found so fascinating. The man was usually a terrible bore.

"This holy day is a day for forgiveness," the minister was saying. "Christ came into this world to teach us that we must love each other despite our transgressions. Has not each one of us his faults? Is there one person in this congregation today who can call himself perfect? If so, please step forward so that I might first congratulate you and then give you a lecture on the nature of self-delusion."

Pip couldn't help smiling. She hadn't realized that Reverend Weatherby had even a slight sense of humor, but apparently he wasn't quite as dull as she'd thought.

"Therefore, remember the words of Our Lord: 'He that is without sin among you, let him first cast a stone.' He went on to say: 'Neither do I condemn thee: go, and sin no more.' We all have within us the capacity to forgive as Christ taught us." Reverend Weatherby tugged at his ample earlobe. "Throughout the year, I hear the complaints of my parishioners, the petty grudges they hold, the slights that have been dealt them. And every year I wait for this day of mystery and wonder to remind each and every one of you what the Christ child came to tell us—His message of good tidings and great joy, heralded by the angels on the occasion of His birth."

He paused for effect before continuing. "The kingdom of God is within you. It does not reside here in this humble church where you come every Sunday to renew your faith. You must take His message with you and live it every day of the week, every year of your lives, or you shall be the seed that fell by the wayside. If you cannot forgive, do not expect to be forgiven. If you cannot love, do not expect to be loved. But if you can love each other in whole heart and without judgment, you shall live in the kingdom of God here on earth. I ask you today to make a new beginning, to pledge yourselves to live according to Our Lord's teachings. Take hope, have courage, trust in God's divine mercy. Let us pray."

Pip knelt on the padded stool and bowed her head, touched to the core by the vicar's simple words. The prayer flowed over her, soothing and healing. She blinked tears away, feeling ashamed of herself. She'd been so wrapped up in her unhappiness that she'd given no thought to what John Henry might be feeling, that he must be as lonely and miserable as she, her pride preventing her from letting him anywhere near her.

But what was the point in holding on to her pride? The vicar's words came back to her: *If you cannot forgive, do not expect to be forgiven. If you cannot love, do not expect to be loved. . . .*

She pressed a hand hard against her mouth. Was *that* what she wanted? For John Henry to love her? The thought had never really occurred to her, not since the day that she'd exchanged vows with him. At the time she'd been angry at being forced into a loveless relationship when all she'd ever wanted was to marry someone she adored, who adored her equally. Even then, the idea of being loved by a man had been amorphous, not attached to any one person. She might as well have dreamed of being married to Apollo if she expected that kind of perfection.

She supposed she'd been attached to the ideal, and ideals were fine as philosophical principles, but they didn't work very well in real life, or so she'd discovered. So much for her fine education—it hadn't done her a bit of good when it came to managing her marriage.

John Henry was no more than flesh and blood, a man with his own set of flaws, just like anyone else. He might be stubborn and impossible, but then, so was she. He also might have his ambitions, but did she not as well? Her ambitions might be focused in more scholarly directions, but that didn't make his any less important, she supposed, conceding what she thought to be a very large point.

He did work hard to achieve his goals, she considered. They never went hungry or cold, and even if she didn't have a fine carriage to take her about on social calls, was that really what she wanted? She'd never taken much enjoyment from social calls in any case, finding them all more or less the same combination of polite but empty chatter and tepid tea.

John Henry, on the other hand, had always been amusing company, good company, never without something to say, or at least not until she'd slammed the door in his face.

And since she was responsible for slamming that door, she would have to find a way to open it up again, or she'd live the rest of her life in polite but awkward silence.

She looked up from her folded hands and risked a glance at his bowed head. He wasn't really the enemy—she'd just made him into one, her thwarted ambitions fuelling the flame of her anger.

It was Christmas Day, she reminded herself, quickly looking back down. Surely she could bring herself to call a truce, to make an effort to be nice to him. How hard could that be?

Pip grimaced. She had only one problem left, but it was a rather large one. Since John Henry looked at her as no more than an annoying little sister, the fly that wouldn't go away, he probably would not be very receptive to her being a loving wife and companion.

Not that she wanted him in her bed, she reminded herself quickly, her cheeks suddenly hot despite the chilly air. That would be taking the point too far, especially since he had no inclination to present himself there anyway.

Maybe she should just let him know that she'd forgiven him his trespasses, hope that he would forgive hers, and they could go from there, maybe sharing evenings in front of the drawing-room fire. They might even go on walks together, she decided, rising to sing another carol. That would be nice, a little company.

She shook her head. That plan sounded utterly

sanctimonious. If she were John Henry, she wouldn't put up with it for a minute.

The last strains of "I Know a Rose Tree Springing" died down, and she sat again, turning over ideas of how to create marital harmony while some man she'd never seen before read the Gospel of St. Luke and poorly at that, stumbling over the beautiful words. Too bad, she thought, for this was one of her favorite passages.

"And it came to p-pass in those days, that there went out a, a, er, a degree from . . . from Caesar Augustus, that all the world should be taxed. . . ."

She tried not to listen to the mangling of the words. Then it was time for another pass of the collection basket, and Pip sank to her knees again, still in turmoil, no solution in sight.

She decided to say her own prayer, fervently asking for guidance. *Please, dear Lord, grant me a miracle on this blessed day. I need to find a way back to my own heart, and I need to find a way to show John Henry that I can be a good wife, that I'm not the spoiled, dreadful person he thinks me to be. I need to forgive my own trespasses, for I've made many of them, against Isabel, whom I failed to protect, against my family, whom I've lied to, but most particularly against John Henry. I've not behaved the way a wife should toward her husband, and I ask for your help in showing me how to make amends.*

She raised her head and stared hard at the cross above the altar, tears in her eyes, every ounce of her being poured into her entreaty.

Nothing happened. No insight came to her, no

sense of peace. She felt disappointed, but she should have expected nothing else. She hadn't behaved in a way that deserved any benediction from the Lord, let alone His angels. She'd probably infuriated the entire Heavenly Host, given everything she'd done in the last year.

Wiping her eyes, remorse weighing heavily on her heart, she stood for the final carol, a resounding rendition of "O, Come All Ye Faithful." She couldn't help thinking that she'd been excluded from the flock.

They filed out with the rest of the congregation, shook the vicar's hand, spoke briefly to a few of the village people, and then John Henry led her to the carriage he'd left at the side of the churchyard. He helped her in, took his side, and urged the horses into a fast trot, not looking at her, not saying a word.

Pip twisted her hands together, trying to find a way to create an opening between them. "Mrs. Biggs has probably made a wonderful Christmas meal," she finally said, her throat tight.

He glanced at her with a neutral expression. "Mrs. Biggs has proved herself to be a fine cook. I'm sure she will do herself proud with the roast goose."

"Yes. She said she planned to make Yorkshire pudding and roast potatoes and parsnips as well."

John Henry didn't respond, his gaze fixed on the road.

Pip nervously cleared her throat. "She also told me that she was going to make treacle tart with cream. I remember that you used to love treacle tart," she added, about to sink under the seat in humiliation.

"You used to come over specially when Cook made it at the farm."

He barely nodded. "Cook is—or was—a master."

Pip stared at him, one hand flying to her mouth. "What do you mean 'was'?" Tears started to well in her eyes. "Did something happen to her? She's not—she didn't die or anything dreadful like that?"

He did look at her then, the expression in his eyes hard and unyielding. "I wouldn't expect you to know or even care, but Cook—Mary Lipshot was her name—died five years ago. Her heart failed one afternoon. I heard the news from my parents in a letter they wrote me when I was in India. Apparently her only son was killed in an accident at the mill where he worked. The shock was too much for her." He trained his gaze back on the road.

Pip covered her face with her hands. Dear Cook? Dead? She couldn't comprehend it. Cook had been so much a part of her young life, telling her off roundly whenever she'd transgressed, which was often, and slipping her little treats of freshly baked biscuits or sweets when she was in favor.

Cook was one of those people whom Pip had thought would live forever. Now she was gone, and Pip had never had the chance to tell her how much she'd meant to her, how important her tart words of advice had been. She'd never be able to tell Cook how much she'd shaped the young, confused girl into the woman that Pip had become.

Pip had often felt as if she were a raw biscuit Cook had slipped into the oven and patiently let bake, watching all the while to be sure the child came out according to Cook's plans. But then life suddenly changed and Pip had left Broadhurst Farm for Alconleigh. She'd seen Cook only on rare occasions after that. Although the bond remained, the immediate intimacy had dissipated.

She covered her face with her hands, and her shoulders shook as she cried silent tears of regret. If only she'd taken the time to visit over the years, to stop by and share a cup of tea and some memories.

"Pip?" John Henry's voice penetrated her despair.

She shook her head, unable to bear anything more. One more harsh word and she would shatter.

Instead, she felt his arm gently reach around her shoulder and pull her close against his coat. "I—I can't." She gulped. "Do not ask me to speak now." Her cheek brushed the soft wool and she burrowed her face into it, moving her head back and forth, her body racked with grief. She breathed in John Henry's scent as if it were a lifeline, something that would anchor her, give her a sense of stability.

He shifted and pulled her closer yet. "I'm sorry I distressed you," he said, resting his cheek on the top of her head. "I didn't realize Cook meant so much to you."

"She meant the world to me," Pip sobbed, trying desperately to control herself. "I've been an idiot—I never imagined that just because I left that world it would close itself to me. I just . . . didn't think. I assumed everyone would always be there, exactly as I saw them last, and I could come back and find everything in place."

"Ah," he said, his fingers tightening around her shoulder. "I think I begin to see. Do you know, I might actually understand better than you realize?" He removed his arm and dug in his pocket for a handkerchief and handed it to her.

She wiped at her eyes, then raised her tear-stained face. "How? How could you possibly understand? You didn't abandon anyone. You might have gone off to India, but still you *knew* Cook had died. I was off living my own life with nary a thought for anyone else— or at least not the people I'd left behind at Broadhurst."

John Henry didn't respond, his attention focused on the road ahead. "Listen to me, Pip," he said eventually, not looking at her. "Listen carefully now. We shared an early path in our lives, had many people in common. What you must understand is that you took a different course, and it was only natural that you should put certain parts of your past behind and take up what your future offered you. How could you have done anything else?"

She wiped her eyes again. "You're being very kind, but I don't think I can excuse myself for ignoring the people who meant so much to me in those early years."

He abruptly pulled the horses to the side of the road and halted. Then he turned to her, took her by the shoulders, and looked at her intently, and there was heat in his eyes. "I don't want you taking blame on yourself for something that is no fault of your own. Yes, you could have kept in closer touch, but as you already pointed out you were young and assumed that everyone was going to live forever. The finality of death hadn't marked you yet." He dropped his gaze. "I don't think you realized what death truly meant until Isabel's passing."

She nodded, knowing that he was right. Her father's death had meant very little to her, since he hadn't been a part of her life. Other than that, she'd never lost anyone, or at least anyone important. Not until Isabel.

"Pip," he said, very gently. "You are a good, caring woman who has made tremendous sacrifices for the people you love in the present. Please, at least give yourself credit for that."

She raised anguished eyes to his, her heart aching with so many regrets. "I feel so unworthy," she said, her voice choked. "I listened to the vicar's sermon today and felt like the lowest-crawling creature—worse, I suppose, because there's nothing wrong with a low-crawling creature."

John Henry tried to suppress a chuckle, but it was no use. He turned his head away and howled with laughter. "Sorry," he said, when he'd regained his composure. "You were saying?"

Pip glared at him. "How could you make fun of me at a time like this? Here I am pouring my heart out to you and all you can do is laugh at me." She was tempted to sock him straight in his belly.

John Henry grinned. "Pip, my sweet, forgive me. The last thing in the world I meant to do was to laugh at you. I—I just can't help but be amused by the unique way you have of stating your position. I've never known another soul who has such an imaginative way with words."

Folding her arms across her chest, Pip started to formulate a heated response, but the words just wouldn't come out. She lowered her arms again, sinking back against the seat.

"John Henry," she finally said, determined to make her apology and clear the air between them. "I've been thinking. . . ."

"Have you?" he said, looking over at her. "What about?"

"Well, in church the vicar talked about this being the season of forgiveness, especially on this day, and I decided that I've been perhaps a bit *hasty*."

"Hasty?" he said, his mouth trembling at the corners, which didn't help Pip's composure. "In what way have you been hasty?"

"I—I believe that I have judged you unfairly." The words felt like sawdust in her mouth. "No—no, please don't say anything or I might never get this out," she said quickly as he opened his mouth to reply. "I've been holding a grudge against you because nothing in my life has worked out as I planned, and I blamed you for that instead of accepting that all you wanted to do was to help me out of an impossible situation. I realize that you've made sacrifices too." She swallowed hard, forcing herself to go on. "So I thought that I should tell you that I'm sorry if I've been cold and difficult and—and not very nice to you."

"Not very nice to me?" he said dryly. "I suppose

that's one way of putting it. I would have said that you've been downright impossible."

"Please, don't start being nasty now, when I'm trying to apologize. I'd like to put the last few weeks behind us and start over again." She pulled her coat closer around her, warding off the chilly breeze.

He slowly nodded. "How do you propose to do that?"

"I thought that we might go back to being friends—you know, the way we were when we were young." She cringed. That hadn't come out at all the way she'd intended. "Well, not exactly as we were when we were young, obviously, since I cannot quite imagine climbing trees with you, but we might at least be pleasant to each other, share some real conversation, maybe have a game of chess or two." She frowned. "You do play chess?"

"Mmm," he said. "I've even been known to win on rare occasions."

"Oh. Well, that's good. You see, there's so much I don't know about you and never will unless you tell me."

He nodded again, not looking at her. "All you need to do is ask, Pip. I find some difficulty pouring out my heart to someone who treats every word I utter as either drivel or a deliberate insult."

She colored. "I told you I'm sorry. I know I haven't been very receptive, but I was angry with you."

"No," he said with mock disbelief. "I never would have guessed." His smile took the sting out of the words, and she was grateful to see that he wasn't really annoyed.

"So we can start over?" she said brightly, her heart much lighter for having made her confession.

He did look at her then, his smile fading, and Pip's heart sank straight back into the pit of her stomach, where it had taken up residence many months before. "I don't know about starting over," he said, his expression serious. "I think that what we must do is move forward. I haven't been happy living in this stalemate any more than you have." He took off his beaver hat and brushed his fingers through his hair. "Pip, thank you for your apology. I know that can't have been easy for you, given everything we've been through, so let me tender one of my own. I've been busy and distracted and haven't given you the attention you deserve, and for that I truly am sorry."

"You have nothing to be sorry for," she said, deeply touched for his easy forgiveness and forgiving him every one of his trespasses in return. "I started the battle, so I should be the one to make reparation. Isn't that the way a truce works?"

He burst into laughter. "Ah. The aggressor pays the forfeit, is that it?"

"Something like that," she said with a smile. "Do not push me on the matter, however, or I shall have to reengage hostilities."

"God help me," he said. "I ask for nothing more than amiable neutrality, for I really don't think I could take much more of your turned back. It's a very nice back, mind you, but I much prefer looking at your face, especially when it's smiling."

"Do you know what I'd really like?" she asked in a small voice.

"What is that? Ask and I shall do what I can to accommodate you, as long as you don't ask me to take you off to a desert tent just now."

"No, nothing like that. I was hoping you'd take me around Manleigh House. I've been burning with curiosity to see what Mr. Blimp's future residence looks like."

He scratched the corner of his mouth. "It's a bit of a mess at the moment, but I cannot see why you shouldn't have a look. I didn't realize you had any interest."

"Oh, yes," she said eagerly, forgetting she'd ever borne him a grudge. "I didn't want to let you know, but I've walked all around the house, trying to imagine what the inside is like. I love houses, you see. Each one has its own personality, and there's something special about this one that captured my imagination. I know this sounds foolish, but I can't help feeling that Manleigh is the sort of house that should be occupied by a family, filled with laughter and fun and children dashing about making mischief."

"With luck that will come to pass in a few months," he said quietly.

"Really? Is Mr. Blimp married, then? Does he have children? Is he a young man?" The questions came rushing out, an unleashed torrent of curiosity she'd stemmed ever since arriving.

"Mr. Blimp is indeed married. To date he has only one child, a son, but he hopes to increase his family, which is why he bought the estate. As for his being a young man, he is my age. Whether you consider that young, I do not know, but he is not yet old and withered."

"Oh—how wonderful! For some reason I imagined him to be more advanced in years. Will I like him, do you think?"

"That remains to be seen, but I hope so." John Henry turned the carriage through the gates. "You must first learn to know him and then you can decide for yourself."

"Yes. That is fair. We are going to stay on, aren't we?" For some reason she desperately wanted reassurance that they were. Manleigh had worked its way into her heart, and the idea of leaving it was not one she wanted to contemplate, despite her initial reservations. Much to her surprise, she realized that even the little gatehouse had become dear to her, a house of her very own, as much as she'd ranted and railed against living there. For the first time the smoke curling up from the two chimneys looked warm and inviting, and as they pulled up in front, lovely smells wafted out from the kitchen, portending a delicious Christmas dinner. "John Henry?" she asked again, as he hadn't answered. "We will be staying on?"

"As I told you, Manleigh is our home now. We shall stay as long as you are happy here, and I must tell you that my heart is gladdened to hear that you have not found it the hell you originally thought."

She lowered her head. "I didn't know it then," she said softly. "I don't think I even knew how strongly I felt until today. You're right. Manleigh *is* home, and I shall do my best to make it a happy one for us both. I don't even mind living here in the gatehouse, really I don't. And—and I love the lake and the woods and the reach to the coast, and looking down over the sea, listening to the crashing of the waves against the cliff face and the cries of the seagulls."

John Henry reached out a hand to her and lifted her gloved fingers to his mouth, dropping a kiss onto them. "Thank you for telling me all that. You've given me the best Christmas present I could ever have asked for. I love it here too, Pip," he said, his voice thick. "Maybe now that you've declared a truce we can share some of those things together."

She looked into his eyes, feeling warmth flood through her body at the thought of having a companion again. "I'd like that."

"I must put the horses away," he said, releasing her hand. "Perhaps after dinner we'll take a walk together before the light fails. There's something I'd like to show you." He jumped down and walked around the carriage to help her down, his hand strong and firm on hers. "I shan't be long."

"You had better not be, or Mrs. Biggs will have your head. She's been basting that goose for hours. Two o'clock she said, and not a moment later."

"God forbid we should cross Mrs. Biggs. She's likely to walk out the door in a snit should we offend in any way," he said with a chuckle. "Give me twenty minutes, and I'll be at the table with clean hands, a well-scrubbed face, and a hearty appetite."

"That should please her," Pip said, giving him one last smile before going inside.

All in all, Christmas Day was looking a good deal brighter than it had in the morning, and for that she thanked God and His angels, for they must have heard her prayer after all.

13

John Henry sluiced his face with water, then groped for a towel. He'd always believed in the small miracles of life, but he'd never expected Pip to come around so suddenly or sweetly.

Indeed, he'd been prepared to wait many more months for her to get over her grievances against him, but that she had chosen to do so on Christmas Day made him believe in miracles all the more.

Living with Pip the last six weeks had been hell on earth, and there had been times when he'd questioned his folly in buying Manleigh, let alone installing her in the gatehouse. To learn that she had actually developed a fondness for the place, if not for him, was a balm to his soul, and he could only thank God for His mercy. He wasn't entirely sure just how far God's mercy stretched in this instance, and he didn't want to push the boundaries by expecting more than a little civility.

Still, he wouldn't have been human if he hadn't hoped for just a touch more. His loins ached with longing for her, as they had every day and night for months now. Nights were the worst.

This was a beginning, though, and he intended to do everything possible to gain her trust. This was no time to let passion overcome his common sense, he told himself, brushing his hair and straightening his coat. He'd tamed green horses many times before, and Pip was no different, as skittish as any colt he'd encountered, jumping away from the slightest touch, wary of any encounter other than the most benign. On the other hand, she had made the first overture, which was a good sign.

Slow and steady, he decided, taking one last look at himself in the looking glass above the bureau and deciding that he appeared presentable. A calm demeanor and an even temperament would go a long way toward reassuring her that he had no intention of taking advantage of her—no matter what his true inclination was.

Pip was waiting for him in the front parlor and turned as soon as she heard his footsteps coming across the floor, a tentative but welcoming smile on her lips. "Here you are," she said, moving toward him, but stopping a few paces away. "Dinner is ready. Shall we go in?"

"I'm famished." He offered his arm and took her hand into the crook of his elbow, relishing the feel of her fingers resting against his coat. He prayed that she had no idea what her touch did to him.

Dinner proved to be more of an agony than he'd expected. Pip talked away merrily as if the dark clouds that had marked the last few weeks had blown away to be replaced by a blaze of sunshine. John Henry had to exert all his control to listen and respond to her vibrant conversation, pretending for all he was worth that he didn't notice the swell of her breasts beneath her bodice, the glow of her skin, the slope of her creamy shoulders. The way she had of leaning forward to make a point only emphasized the shape of her breasts pressing against the fine wool cloth that confined them. He wanted nothing more than to strip that cloth away, stroke his hands over that lovely flesh, make her cry out in pleasure at his touch.

Physical longing obliterated his thoughts. He knew he wasn't holding up his end of the conversation in an appropriate fashion, but he couldn't seem to focus properly. He could only be grateful that the table and the napkin in his lap hid his desire.

Thinking about it, Pip had been far easier to deal with when she'd treated him with disdain. That had acted as a good dose of cold water and diverted him from thinking of her feminine attributes, of which there were a multitude.

"John Henry? You look as if you've just swallowed ground glass. Is Mrs. Biggs's goose not to your liking?" Pip asked, her brow furrowing. "Perhaps the orange sauce doesn't suit you?"

"No, everything is splendid, simply splendid," he

lied. What else could he say? That his appetite had nothing to do with roast goose and everything to do with Pip?

He abruptly changed the subject. "Pip . . . have you noticed anything different about Aafteh recently?"

Pip lowered her knife and fork. "Different?" she said. "What do you mean?"

"Only that she seems happier. She has a certain sparkle in her eyes that I've never seen before."

Pip stared at him. "You're not saying that she— No, never mind. Of course you're not."

"What do you think I'm not saying?" he asked, highly amused.

"Well, I thought maybe you were implying that she has developed an interest in the gardener who comes by with the vegetables. I know she always makes him a cup of tea, but I can't think that she is doing anything beyond being polite."

"Oh?" he said, reapplying himself to his meal. "Why shouldn't she have developed an interest in the gardener? By the way, his name is Tobias Jackson, and he's been asking a great many questions recently about Egypt, not the usual sort of questions that one would expect from an English gardener. My guess is that the interest is mutual."

"But even though Aafteh's English is improving daily, she still doesn't have very much in the way of proper conversation," Pip said, looking at him as if he'd lost his mind.

"Who said that he's interested in her conversation?" John Henry retorted. "Aafteh is young and very pretty, and she's certainly exotic. Indeed, I for one am thrilled that Tobias doesn't hold her foreign birth against her as so many others have done."

Pip shook her head. "I think you're wrong, John Henry. Although she hasn't said as much, I'm sure she will want to return to her own people once Peter grows a little older."

"Has it ever occurred to you that maybe Aafteh will not be welcomed back by her people? You know how rigid the rules of Arab society are, especially where women are concerned. She might very well be treated as an outcast, now that she's lived in another country, doing heaven knows what as far as her family is concerned."

Pip's face fell. "I hadn't even thought of that," she said, looking stricken. "I've been terribly selfish, haven't I? When I took her away I thought only of Peter's welfare. Oh, poor Aafteh." Pip's hand slipped to her mouth. "What have I done?"

"I shouldn't worry too much about Aafteh. You have to remember that as young as she is, she's already lost a husband and a child. Perhaps she'd like to start another family. Furthermore, you took her away from a life of poverty. Here, she never has to worry about going hungry, and although the winter weather leaves something to be desired, neither is the summer heat a misery. All in all, she has not made such a bad bargain."

"No, I suppose not when you put it like that. John Henry, do you think that she and Tobias might actually make a match?" Pip appeared to be warming to the idea.

"I think there's a good chance."

"Perhaps I should speak to her." Pip appeared to warm to that idea as well.

"No," John Henry said quickly. "The last thing we should do is to meddle. If Aafteh has any concerns, let her bring them to you."

"Yes, I suppose you're right. I've done enough meddling in other people's affairs."

"I believe you have." He smiled. "You have a family of your own to worry about."

Pip returned his smile, which caused him to forget what he'd been about to say.

Fortunately at that moment Mrs. Biggs, a middle-aged woman with steel-gray hair and an equally steely expression, appeared from the kitchen with the treacle tart. She set it down on the table along with a saucer of whipped cream, took one disapproving look at John Henry's unfinished plate as she removed it, and disappeared back into the kitchen without a word.

Pip burst into laughter. "Oh, dear," she said, carving the tart and handing John Henry a plate along with the saucer of cream. "I fear that you're going to be in disgrace at least until Easter. You'd better eat your ham then or she won't speak to you until next Christmas."

"I can only pray that the Christmas gratuity I'm about to bestow on her will make up for my transgression," he said, digging into his dessert.

"You're very generous," she replied. "Are you giving one to Violet as well?"

"Naturally. She's had to put up with you, hasn't she?" he said with a straight face.

"I have been nothing but kind to Violet," Pip said.

"I suppose you think you should give yourself a bonus as well, seeing as you've had to put up with me?"

"Hmm. I hadn't thought of that, but it's not a bad idea." He looked across at Pip, who sported a tiny dollop of whipped cream on her nose. He resisted the urge to move over to her and kiss it away, tempting as the thought was.

He cleaned his plate, since to do anything else at that point would be a sin of the highest order in Mrs. Biggs's eyes, then folded his napkin and placed it on the table. "Would you like to go for a walk? I have a surprise for you, one that I hope you'll like."

"Really?" Pip's eyes lit up with pleasure. "I adore surprises. I'll check on Peter and then meet you in the hall."

"Excellent. I'll give Mrs. Biggs and Violet their gratuities, do some lavish praising, and perhaps redeem myself."

"I think you've done enough redeeming for one day," she said softly.

Wrapped up warmly, Pip took John Henry's arm as he led her out into the thin sunshine. She didn't know if Christmas Day was working its magic or if she and John Henry had truly broken through their impasse, but she felt a sense of harmony with him, a peace and contentment that had been missing. Other than Isabel and the young John Henry, she'd never had close companions, finding her comfort instead in the bosom of her family.

As a boy, John Henry had always been the very best of company. As a man, he remained the same, at least when they weren't at odds with each other. The only real difference, she told herself as they strolled down the drive, was that he was—well, he *was* a man, who came with all the attendant physical attributes. Still, the fact that he had an appealing physique didn't make him any less of a friend.

He could no more help the way he'd developed than she could help the way she'd matured.

Then why did she have an absurd desire to slip her hand inside his coat and run her palm over his hard chest? Her step slowed slightly as she realized that her thoughts were running in very much the wrong direction. One didn't think of good friends in that context.

"Where are we going?" she asked, trying very hard to ignore his close proximity, the feel of his arm under hers.

"You'll have to wait and see," he said, turning his head and smiling down at her.

Pip's knees went weak. "Is it far?" she asked, just to make conversation, anything to divert her from John Henry's physical presence.

"Are you cold? Do you want to go back?" he said with concern.

"No—I'm warm as can be. I'm just curious."

"Well, you know the old saw about curiosity. You're going to have to wait." He looked up at the trees that lined the drive, their branches dark and bare against the sky. "Just think, Pip. In a few short months all of this will be clouds of green. Daffodils and tulips will appear, or at least I imagine they will. If not, we'll have to plant some. I do know that lilies will bloom on the lake. According to Tobias, they cover the edges and float out into the middle."

"That sounds lovely." She sighed, imagining the picture he painted for her.

"Do you know about water lilies?" he asked. "There are many different types, but Tobias tells me that these bloom at night, staying open only until midday. It's a rare genus of *Nymphaea*, which is Egyptian as it happens, although how they came to be here I don't know. I do know it's not an ancient species, since those flowers were blue, and these are apparently white. And that's all I know."

"As usual, you seem to know a good deal."

He chuckled. "That's generous, but I don't know as much as I'd like about a great many things." He shot her an odd look. "For example, Pip, I'd like to know what's made you such an enigmatic creature. I don't know from one minute to the next what to expect from you."

"You think *I'm* enigmatic?" she said. "I find you just as much of a mystery."

"That begs the question," he said, turning toward the stables. "Not that I consider myself the least mysterious. Really, I'm a very simple man."

"There's nothing simple about you, John Henry Lovell, and one of these days I intend to get to the bottom of who you really are."

"Ah." He looked a little startled. "Well, you have all the time in the world, although you're bound to be deeply disappointed when you discover that I'm the same person I've always been, just a little larger in size."

Pip didn't reply. If John Henry truly believed that piece of nonsense, then he was delusional, she decided.

He opened the stable door and led her inside. Pip adjusted her eyes to the dim light, breathing in the heavenly smell of horse and leather and hay. "What are we doing here?" she asked, wondering if he planned to take her for a carriage ride.

"Come over here," he said, leading her toward the stalls. The last time Pip had been in the stables, there were only the two horses used for pulling the carriage and one gelding that John Henry used for riding about the estate.

But now a new horse occupied one of the stalls, a beautiful white mare with large, doe-like eyes and a delicate head that spoke of Arab blood.

"Oh . . ." she breathed in wonder as the mare moved to the door and pushed her head over the top, nickering gently, her finely shaped ears pricking back and forth. "Who is she? Where did she come from? Did Mr. Blimp send her down for his use?"

"Not exactly. Her name is Mascha. She's of Seglawi extraction, and she is yours."

Pip whipped around to stare at him. "Mine . . . but—but John Henry, *how*? I don't understand. . . ."

"She was given to me in return for a favor I did for a Bedouin sheik and only arrived the other day. She is your Christmas present, Pip."

Tears sprang to her eyes. She could hardly take in the enormity of John Henry's gift. "I can't—I don't know what to say," she gasped.

"You needn't say anything. I know how much you've missed having a mount, and Mascha seemed the perfect solution. I've ridden her, and she is sweet-tempered, willing, and intelligent."

Without thinking, Pip flung herself into John Henry's arms and held him tightly, tears streaming down her face. "Thank you," she whispered against his chest. "I've done nothing to deserve her, but I still thank you from the bottom of my heart."

His arms came gently around her. "My thanks will be seeing you enjoy her," he said quietly, but he sounded uncomfortable.

Pip suddenly realized what she'd done and pulled away. "Forgive me. I didn't mean to embarrass you," she said, turning bright red. "That is, the excitement of the moment . . ." She felt horribly awkward. The worst part was that she'd enjoyed being held by him, could have stood there in his embrace for a good while longer, breathing in his warm scent, feeling his body molded against hers.

"You didn't embarrass me in the least." He moved a few paces away, his back turned to her as he stroked the mare's nose. "It's nice to know that you don't find me completely abhorrent to touch."

"Find you abhorrent?" she repeated in shock. "Is that what you think?"

He turned to her, looking as disconcerted as she felt. "What else am I to think, Pip? You avoid me as if I have some sort of contagious disease, and you've certainly told me enough times that I am to stay entirely away from you."

"But I . . . I . . ." She looked away in confusion. "That was at the beginning when I suspected your motives in marrying me."

"Are you telling me something has changed about that?" he demanded. "I hadn't noticed, other than an apology today for treating me like a leper."

"Which I meant," she said, wishing he wouldn't keep turning things around to suit himself. "I no longer think you married me solely for selfish motives, but you've been treating *me* like a leper in equal part."

He shoved his hands onto his hips. "What am I to do, may I ask? Insinuate myself where I'm not wanted?"

"No—no, of course not, but that's not the point," she stammered, wishing she could think more clearly. Logic had always been her strong point, but somehow John Henry always took her straight down an illogical path.

"Then what is the point?" he asked coldly. "Enlighten me, Pip, for I find myself entirely at a loss."

"The point, you idiot, is that you still regard me as a little sister in braids and a pinafore. You don't seem to have noticed that I've grown up, that I'm no longer a child, and that I have a mind and a will and feelings that—that have nothing to do with climbing trees!"

He gazed at her in fascination as if he'd never seen her before. "What are you telling me?" he asked eventually. "Are you saying you want something else?"

Pip bit down hard on her lip. She hadn't really

meant to say any of that, but now that she had, she couldn't take it back, especially because it was true, she realized. She did want something more from him, a great deal more, and it had nothing to do with politeness or kindness or the gift of a fine horse. She wanted John Henry, pure and simple, and she was appalled at the thought that she could be so foolish, knowing how he felt about her. What would he think if she told him what she really desired? He'd probably laugh himself silly.

He took a step toward her, then another, looking thoroughly dangerous, and she backed away until her spine pressed against the door of an empty stall.

"Is it possible, Pip, that you might want this?" Before she knew what he intended, he pulled her forcefully into his arms and lowered his head, his mouth descending hard onto hers, taking it in a deep, thorough kiss. His hands roamed restlessly over her back as his tongue plundered the delicate recesses of her mouth, causing her to gasp with surprise and unexpected pleasure. Just as abruptly he released her, his eyes blazing. "Was that it?" he said, his voice hoarse, his breath coming quickly.

Pip could hardly breathe, let alone respond. Her legs gave out and she sank to the ground, her eyes huge with wonder. *That* was what a kiss was supposed to be? Something that sucked the air from her lungs and set her body aflame? She'd had no idea, she thought vaguely, as she stared up at him, wanting things she'd never dreamed of before, wanting every part of him, just . . . wanting.

He dropped to his knees and took her hands between his. "I'm sorry," he said, still trying to catch his breath. "I shouldn't have done that, but I'm at the end of my rope, Pip. I want you so much I've hardly been able to bear being around you. If that's a truth you don't want to hear, so be it, but it is the truth."

Pip didn't answer, throwing her arms around his neck and pulling him to her, her mouth claiming his this time, demanding more. She could think only of his feel, his touch, his taste, and how he made her senses reel.

He groaned low in his throat as he returned her kiss in full measure, lowering her to the ground, his body stretching beside hers as he pulled her hard and close to him, his mouth plundering hers.

Pip strained up against him, wanting something unfathomable, something so much deeper. She'd never felt such desire for anything, and she knew that John Henry could meet that desire, fill it in her, turn the heat that consumed her into an inferno.

To her enormous disappointment, he pulled away and sat up, pushing his hands through his hair.

"Pip," he said on a choked laugh, "had I known that giving you a little Arabian mare would lead to this, I'd have arranged for her shipping much sooner. But I think we had better calm down, just for the moment."

"Did I do something wrong?" she asked, bewildered, wondering why he'd stopped kissing her so abruptly and feeling deeply disappointed that he had.

"No—oh, you did everything exactly right," he replied. "Very, very right. I just think we would be more comfortable back in the house, where we needn't worry about being interrupted by the groom returning from his Christmas dinner. I also think, as much as I'm reluctant to say so, that we might be best served by giving ourselves a little time to talk. I don't want to take advantage of you, which I'm in every mind to do, and I don't want you to have any regrets." He stood and helped her to her feet. "Do you understand?"

Pip nodded, brushing herself off, but she wasn't sure she understood anything. The world had just upended itself again, and as usual at John Henry's hand, but this time she didn't mind at all. Not that she felt like talking. Conversation was the very last thing on her mind.

Trying to collect herself, she walked to the mare's stall and put out her hand. Mascha pushed her nose into it, sniffing, and Pip took the opportunity to run her fingers up over her muzzle and along the side of her neck. "I'll see you tomorrow," she whispered into Mascha's ear. "We'll go for a ride."

John Henry came to stand beside her. "Her bridle and saddle are next door. Come, Pip. Let's make the best of the last of the light. I thought we'd walk up to the lake."

She curled her fingers into his, surprised by how comfortable she felt. John Henry led her out of the stable, closing the door behind them and latching it with one hand, never letting go of hers.

They walked in silence back to the main drive and up between the line of oaks, turning as they approached the big house to skirt the side wing. The lake reflected the colors of the setting sun, shining gold and red on the rippling surface.

John Henry led her onto the arch of the stone bridge that spanned the narrowest part of the lake. He paused there, slipping one hand around her waist, his other resting on the balustrade as he gazed over the expanse of water.

A sense of peace flooded through Pip as she stood at his side, listening to the soft sound of the wind through the leafless trees, barely audible over the gentle cry of doves roosting in the dovecote in the woods. In the distance she heard the shrill, high call of seagulls as they swept over the cliffs. John Henry's arm rested lightly around her, his body pressing close to hers. He felt easy and natural, and yet she sensed the undercurrent of physical tension, impossible now to ignore.

"There are things I need to tell you before we go any further," he said, his voice very quiet. "The first is this. I want you, Pip, very much. I have for a long time now, but I've waited because I was under the impression that you didn't feel the same attraction toward me."

"I didn't know what I felt," she said in complete honesty. "I didn't even know until we were in the stables just now that I was capable of feeling anything of that nature for anyone. I've never experienced that sort of desire." For some peculiar reason, she felt no shame at the admission.

"Thank you for being so candid. I'd suspected as much, but I didn't want to address the point too directly. You already gave me a strong hint some time ago, when you spoke of your previous suitors with little enthusiasm."

Pip grinned up at him. "If you'd had to deal with even one of them, you'd have run away in disgust and dismay."

"Understandably so," he said, but his face remained serious. "There's something else I must tell you, and this you might find a little more difficult to accept. I can only pray my words won't drive you away, but we've come to a point where I have to speak the truth to you, or I'll end up betraying both of us."

Pip touched his cheek, seeing the deep pain in his eyes. She couldn't imagine what confession he needed to make. "Save an admission of murder or fraud, and I don't think you capable of either, I don't think your transgression could affect us. We can surely get beyond a minor theft, so tell me. I would rather have no secrets between us. What crime have you committed?"

He released a deep breath, taking her hand from his cheek and lowering it. "Pip, you really can be a horse's ass," he said, turning away.

Pip, who hadn't been called a horse's ass by anyone but the young John Henry, socked him in his arm. "How dare you?" she cried, forgetting her impassioned feelings.

He spun back around, glaring at her. "How dare I? Let us see. When I was nineteen and came to see you with real joy in my heart at finally meeting my great friend again, you made me feel like an insect under your foot. The next time I saw you I happened in on

Isabel's unfortunate birthing, and without so much as a blink you dragged me straight into that nightmare."

He paused only to draw breath. "Then you put me in a position where unless I damn well married you, your reputation might well have been ruined and God only knows what might have happened to Peter. You told me at the same time that I was a greedy bastard who wanted only to line my own pockets and boost my social position, or something of that nature. Furthermore, I wasn't ever to lay a single finger on your sacrosanct self." He pounded one fist on the stone balustrade, then shook it hard. "Damn and blast," he said, wincing.

Pip was astonished. She'd never seen this side of John Henry. He'd always been so controlled, or at least for the most part. "I told you I was sorry for all that," she said. "You didn't break it, did you?"

"My blasted hand, do you mean? Or my heart, which is far more to the point."

"Your hand," she said, thoroughly taken aback. "Your heart seems to be in fine order." She did have to admit that it had pounded rather fiercely when she'd been pressed against his chest, but then, so had hers.

"No thanks to you," he said, hugging his hand to his chest. "You truly are a horse's ass, Pip."

"If you say that one more time I might very well push you over the railing and that will be an end to you."

"Possibly a welcome state, given what I'm dealing with." He grabbed her by the shoulders and gave her a shake. "Pip, are you so much of a fool that you don't understand what I'm trying to tell you?"

"You want to live and therefore will attempt to behave in a civil fashion?" she retorted, although a little unevenly because the look in John Henry's eyes warned her that she might have taken one step too far.

He groaned. "You really can be an idiot. I'm trying to tell you that I'm in love with you and have been for many years. Does that mean anything at all to you?"

The breath left Pip's body. "What did you say?" she whispered, grasping the balustrade, for that was the only thing holding her up at the moment.

"I said I'm in love with you." He looked out across the lake. "That's why I didn't want to take advantage of you in the stables or anytime before that. If we have any chance of a meaningful marriage, we need to have truth between us. That is my truth, Pip. If it's not yours, I would really rather not proceed along the path we are on."

Pip shut her eyes and shook her head back and forth as tears leaked down her cheeks. She realized that her childhood affection had grown into a deep and passionate love. She could no more deny it than she could deny her physical attraction to him.

"I think I see," John Henry said finally, breaking the silence. "I've horrified you with my confession. Never mind, Pip. I took a chance in telling you, and perhaps I should have kept silent, but I didn't want to make love to you without your knowing the truth. We'll forget the last hour ever happened."

"No—oh, no, John Henry, you don't understand at all," she cried, grasping his arm and looking up at him imploringly. "I really *have* been a horse's ass. Don't you see, I'm in love with you too."

He stared at her as if she'd just told him that the moon really was made of green cheese and they'd be having it for supper. "Pip . . . there's no need to spare my feelings," he said tightly.

"Do you think I'd make up something so important just to make you feel better?" She wiped the tears from her cheeks. "I love you, John Henry, and if you can't see that, then you are the idiot. Do you think I could have kissed you as I did in the stable and not mean it?"

He shook his head slowly. "I just never dared to hope," he said. "Are you sure that this is not just gratitude for my Christmas gift of Mascha?"

"Don't be absurd. I know my own mind *and* my heart, now that I've bothered to look, and quite frankly, I cannot see why we're still standing here having this conversation when we could be at home making the point in a far more interesting fashion."

A grin flashed across his face. "If that's an invitation, I would be a fool to refuse. I just want to be sure that you won't take a poker to my head after the fact and accuse me of taking advantage of you."

"I wish you would take advantage of me," she said softly, wrapping her arms around his back and holding him close. "I've never before found the idea the least appealing, but now I find that I cannot wait to discover what ravishment is all about."

He tilted her head back with one hand, dropping a

warm kiss on her parted lips. "I will do my best not to disappoint," he said. "Only promise me that should you change your mind in the process, you will let me know, for I do not want to force you to do anything you don't wish to."

"What I wish is that you'd stop being such a gentleman and pick up precisely where you left off in the stables."

He took her by the arm and led her off the bridge and directly to the house.

14

$\mathcal{P}$ip discovered that she didn't have a shy bone in her body. Now that she'd realized she truly loved John Henry, her impatience to explore the full joy of that love made the walk home nearly unendurable. As soon as they reached the gatehouse, she practically ran up the stairs, pulling John Henry along with her.

He chuckled as she dragged him into her bedroom and locked the door behind them. "Do you know," he said, leaning back against the wood and regarding her with amusement, "I don't think I've ever known anyone so eager to discover the delights of love as you, but somehow I'm not surprised. You always have jumped in with both feet once you've made up your mind about something."

Pip looked at him uncertainly. "Is that a bad thing? I know nothing about the pleasures of lovemaking, other than two kisses in a stable. Should I be more reticent?"

"Reticent? You?" he said, straightening. "I'd think you were sickening of something. However, before you pull me into bed and have your way with me, why don't you let me help you out of your coat. Just so you don't overheat, mind you."

His eyes danced with laughter, and Pip couldn't help grinning. She turned her back and John Henry slipped the coat off her shoulders, his fingers brushing along the exposed length of her neck, his light touch making her shiver.

She turned around again. "Now what?"

"Now I take off my coat." He shrugged it away and deposited it on the back of a chair along with Pip's, then removed his jacket. Pulling off his neckcloth in one easy movement and shedding his waistcoat, he stood before her in only his shirt and trousers. She could see the strong muscles of his chest beneath the fine linen, the bulge in his trousers that spoke of something utterly male and entirely unfamiliar.

Pip swallowed hard. The more clothes John Henry removed, the more she realized what she was about to undertake.

"Pip? Why are you staring at me like that?"

She ran her tongue over her lower lip. "Was I staring? I suppose I was. I'm just not accustomed to seeing you in such a fashion."

"You saw me like this many times in Egypt and never looked as if you were going to jump out of your skin. Are you having second thoughts?"

"Maybe if you just kissed me as you did earlier . . ."

He didn't waste a moment, drawing her into his arms and lowering his mouth to hers, taking her in a heated kiss that left her breathless and weak, reminding her all over again of why he stood in her bedroom half-dressed.

"Better?" he asked, raising his head and looking down at her, his eyes nearly black in the flickering candlelight.

She ran her hands over his hard chest, savoring the shape of his muscles as she slid her palms down to his lean waist.

"I feel light-headed," she said, swaying against him, which gave her the excuse to press herself more closely against his hips.

"Do you? How very interesting. I shouldn't expect your condition to improve, however," he replied, slowly sweeping his mouth down her neck and dropping a kiss in the hollow of her collarbone, his tongue making a languid circle just there.

Pip shuddered with pleasure. "Oh," she said with a long sigh. "That's nice."

"Good," he murmured. He turned her around and deftly unbuttoned the back of her dress. This wasn't the first time she'd felt the touch of his hands on her back, but it was the first time she'd welcomed that warm touch, ached for him to continue.

He slid the material off her shoulders and kissed

the exposed skin, his lips traveling across her nape to kiss her other shoulder.

"You're so lovely," he said, slipping her dress down to her waist and over her hips until it fell in a pool on the floor. Swiftly picking her up in his arms, he carried her over to the bed and laid her down, taking the pins out of her hair and spreading her auburn curls over the pillow.

She reached up for him, and he came down to her, supporting his weight on his forearms as he took her mouth with his, the fevered kiss making her gasp with delight as his tongue tangled with hers in a sensuous dance.

"Do you have any idea how long I've wanted to touch you like this?" he said, his voice husky as his palm slipped down to her breast and cupped it, his thumb brushing over her exquisitely sensitive nipple as his lips caressed her cheek.

Pip closed her eyes, drinking in every blissful sensation, her body twisting up against his as her hands roamed down over his broad back. She'd had no idea how lovely he would feel, all taut muscle and sinew and heated skin that burned like fire through his fine linen shirt.

He shifted his weight and skillfully untied the ribbon that held the bodice of her chemise together, impatiently pushing the edges aside to expose her breasts, and lowered his head to her nipple and running his tongue over it, then drawing it between his lips, pulling gently.

Pip cried out in pleasure as he sucked the hard

nub, causing her to writhe, her breath now fast and shallow. She tangled her fingers in his silky hair, wanting more, so much more.

He gave her just that, his clever hands working magic as they moved down over her waist and hips, brushing over her thighs, then lifting her chemise and running back up over her bare skin, cupping the curve of her buttocks.

Somehow he managed to lift the chemise over her head and discard it, leaving her naked, but she felt no embarrassment, reveling in his hungry gaze that took in every bare inch of her.

"You are beautiful, even more than I imagined," he said with a groan. "You have no idea how much I've imagined, how many sleepless nights I've endured, wondering if I'd ever have the chance to hold you like this, touch you like this." As he spoke, he slid his hands to her breasts, shaping them with his palms until she moaned, tossing her head back and forth on the pillow.

"Please!" she cried. "Please . . ." She didn't know what she was begging for, only that she wanted him to fill the deep, aching need that burned deep and low in her belly, the heat centering between her legs, where her delicate female flesh throbbed. She felt moisture flooding her there, readying her for John Henry's touch.

"Oh, my little love," he whispered. "Wait—wait just one moment." He sat up, stripping off his clothes, then quickly came back down to her, kissing her hard and thoroughly as his hand slipped between the curls at the juncture of her thighs.

He found her cleft, his fingers stroking over her swollen flesh, moving slowly back and forth, finding a place that was so exquisitely sensitive that the breath left her body as he circled one fingertip around it. "So soft, so sweet," he murmured, his skin blazing against hers, his breath coming in ragged gasps.

She pressed her hips up against his touch, her arms holding him close, her face buried against his shoulder as she trembled with unbearable pleasure, a tension building deep inside that threatened to break her apart.

His masculine hardness strained against her belly and she knew with absolute certainty that this was what she needed to complete her, to make her whole. She was just about to ask him to do something useful with it when he slipped a finger inside her aching flesh. She opened her mouth in a wordless cry. She tried to suck air into her lungs as he slid that finger in and out, driving her to a mindless oblivion that left no room for anything but his feel, his touch, the taste of his mouth on hers, his tongue driving to match the rhythm of his plunging finger.

She sobbed against his lips, her hips moving convulsively as her fingers twisted in his damp hair.

In one swift movement he raised himself above her and parted her legs with his knees, the tip of his hard shaft replacing his finger. "I don't want to hurt you, my darling, but I might," he said raggedly. "It's just this once. . . ."

She wrapped her hands around his buttocks impatiently. "*Please*, John Henry. I don't think I can wait another second."

He laughed and groaned at the same time. "You never have had any patience," he said, pushing gently into her. She felt a stretching and a brief, sharp stab of pain, and then he was buried in her, his hard length filling her completely. She shuddered, not with agony but with longing, knowing that this was what she'd been waiting for. John Henry. How could she have been so stupid not to have guessed?

He slowly began to move his hips, gently stretching her even farther, rocking inside her, fanning the fire in her into a brilliant white heat that threatened to extinguish her. She responded with equal passion, drawing him deeper and deeper, sharp cries coming from her throat that she heard only dimly, aware only of his hands stroking her body, his mouth kissing her wet cheeks, her throat, her breasts, as he increased his rhythm, moving faster and harder.

"I can't—I can't breathe," she gasped, her brow knitting as her inner muscles contracted into a desperate knot, a wave that stood on an endless crest, then broke in a furious crash, taking her down and down into a depth of pleasure that had no end. Darkness threatened to consume her, not the darkness of death, but rather the darkness of the deepest pool of life, where all things began.

She heard him cry out, felt him pull back and then plunge deep into that pool with her, his body in a spasm as his hot seed flooded into her. Finally, finally, breath returned to her body and her eyes fluttered open in wonder. John Henry's head lay against her shoulder, his breath deep and slow. He lifted it and dropped a soft kiss on her breast.

"My God, Pip," he murmured. "I've never experienced anything like that in my life."

She propped herself on her elbows and looked down at him, brushing a lock of hair off his forehead, slick with sweat. She couldn't help herself. "Have you . . . have you had a great deal of experience?"

He gave her a wry smile. "Part of me wants to lie and impress you with my insatiable virility, but the truth is that other than the odd encounter here and there, I never had much interest in seducing women— or being seduced, for that matter." He sighed. "It's hard to summon up much passion when one's heart is already engaged, and my heart has never been very far from yours, sweetheart."

Pip bent down and kissed him softly. "Maybe the equation worked both ways. I think that the reason I never married or even properly considered the idea was because somewhere deep inside me I've always loved you. I was just too blind to see it."

He ran his hands down her arms, then lifted her fingers to his lips and kissed them one by one. "And now? Why now?"

"I don't know exactly what happened today, unless God heard my prayers in church and decided to give me a good knock over the head. All these years I felt content with my life, but I always knew something was missing." She ran her fingers through his damp hair. "How could I know that something would be you?"

"You might have looked a little harder before you sent me off like a cur all those years ago."

Pip groaned, wishing that day had never happened. "I was a young girl, full of my own self-importance. I was looking forward to my first Season, about to have my first party. At that point I didn't realize how empty life in the *ton* would be."

She reached inside her for a deeper honesty that John Henry had every right to hear. "There's something else—when I saw you at Broadhurst Hall that day, I was terrified. You weren't the John Henry I'd been so looking forward to seeing. You'd changed, become a grown man, or near enough to leave me shaking with confusion. You'd grown so handsome, and I didn't know what to think or feel, so I did the first thing that came to mind and sent you away, telling both you and myself that you were just a farm boy and meant nothing to me any longer."

His gaze searched her face. "You're saying that you felt differently."

She nodded miserably. "When I saw you coming up the hill, that lovely bunch of wildflowers in your hand, your face lit up with such a welcoming smile, I panicked. No matter how alarmingly attractive I suddenly found you or how happy I was to see you again, I had—I had silly expectations about what I wanted to be, and you didn't fit into any part of my plan."

He just nodded, but his eyes reflected a deep pain. "It would have been easier if you'd just told me that— or easier still if you'd shot me on the spot. I knew, Pip, that I had no real place in your life and wouldn't have asked you for anything beyond a little of your time. But to have you look at me like someone to wipe your delicate feet on, that cut deeply. I never expected that kind of behavior from you."

"I'm so sorry," she whispered, ashamed.

"Never mind. Actually, knowing now what you were really thinking helps heal that wound, truly it does. I should probably have realized that you would never have changed so much, but when you said those things to me in front of your friends, something important died in me."

"Then why did you keep loving me?" she asked, her heart aching. "I thought you despised me from that moment on. That's why I assumed the worst when you appeared in Egypt, why I behaved so horribly to you."

"I never despised you," he said, twining a lock of her hair around his finger. "I was hurt, still disappointed in you, perhaps, but I couldn't help loving you despite all that. You were always my Pip, my best friend. As I grew older, those feelings turned into a different understanding of what we'd always been together. We might have come from different backgrounds, but our values and our interests were the same, and as much as I missed you after you moved away, nothing changed for me. Other than growing up, that is, and then I found myself thinking about whether you'd grown these."

He smiled softly as he touched her breasts with his fingertips. "And this," he continued, reaching down and brushing his hand over the curls at the apex of her legs. "At times I went a little mad, trying to picture you as a woman. No one else ever really took my interest, as crazy as that might seem, but that's how it was."

He rolled over onto his back, wrapping his hands around her waist and pulling her on top of him. "And then the day arrived that I heard you were coming back to Broadhurst, and I worked myself into a frenzy, worrying about whether you would look at me like the same old John Henry or see me as a complete stranger. What happened was definitely not anything I'd ever anticipated."

Pip shook her head, tears dripping down her cheeks and onto his chest. "To think that I hurt you so badly . . ."

"Yes, but as I believe I once told you, had that not happened, I would never have set off for India to nurse my injured feelings and try to forget you. It was in India that I finally became a man, saw and learned things I never would have otherwise, given my limited possibilities here in Dorset. In the end I have much to thank you for, and in the end here we are together, despite impossible odds. How can I feel anything but gratitude?"

"And I," she said, settling down to lie on his chest. "Can you forgive me for my reprehensible behavior that day—and for many days since then?"

"I can forgive you anything as long as you promise to stay here in my arms for as long as we both live."

"I have no intention of going anywhere," she said, nuzzling her face against his warm skin, the soft hair that covered his strong chest tickling her nose. "I can think of nothing more wonderful than living here, having your children if God so wills, and becoming a wrinkled old woman whom you still want to hold in your arms every day and night."

"That's not the primary thought on my mind at the moment, but yes, I will love you until age withers us both. Do you feel strong enough for me to show you again, and just how much?"

Pip pealed with laughter. "You can show me until the cows come home."

"I'll have a word with the cowman to drive them into another county," he said, rolling her over and kissing her thoroughly, leaving her in no doubt of his feelings.

15

$\mathscr{P}$ip sleepily opened her eyes the next morning and found John Henry's arms securely wrapped around her. She smiled in contentment, both body and heart thoroughly sated. She eased herself out of his arms and propped herself on one elbow, gazing down at his face. He slept peacefully, his breathing soft and even. His dark hair lay tousled on the pillow, and long, thick sweeps of lashes fell on the high curves of his cheekbones. Her gaze drifted lower over his muscular body, hidden only partially by the sheets wrapped loosely around his waist.

She shivered as she remembered all the wild, wonderful things he'd done to her in the night, initiating her to the delights of lovemaking, so strong, so gentle, so passionate, all at the same time. Never in a hundred years would she have guessed that anything could be so delightful as to be loved by John Henry. And oh, the things he'd said to her . . . She shivered again, blushing at the memory of his heated words that had driven her into a frenzy.

He stirred, opened one eye, and squinted up at her. A slow smile broke across his face and he reached up, pulling her down against him. "What are you looking at with such fascination?" he murmured, kissing her ear.

"Nothing much." She snuggled closer, breathing in his rich scent. "I was merely contemplating your anatomy."

He chuckled. "That doesn't sound like much of a compliment. I offer my body to you without reservation and you call it nothing much? You could at least prevaricate a little."

"I don't need to. You're magnificent and furthermore you know it."

"*Magnificent* is definitely an improvement over *nothing much,* although I feel my honor is in need of restoration." He shifted, trailing his hand over her rounded breasts. "Now *that* is what I'd call magnificent. And this," he continued, smoothing his fingers over one hip and slipping them into her curls. "And most certainly this," he added, as he found the tender folds of her flesh, already damp and ready for him.

She closed her eyes with a little gasp as he began to stroke her, fanning the embers of the fire he'd lit in her only hours before.

"Mmm, that's nice," he said, lifting her hips and fitting her over him, his shaft sliding easily into her, his hands guiding her into a slow, easy rhythm. "Your turn, madam. Do with your husband what you will, but I beg you, be gentle."

Pip made a sound halfway between a laugh and a moan as she began to move on him in earnest, shifting, finding the position that gave her the most pleasure. She rode him as she would a horse, using her thighs on either side of his hips to anchor her, rising and falling on his engorged shaft until she drew long, deep sighs from him, his brows drawing down as if in pain, his eyes never leaving hers. Pip rejoiced that she could give him so much pleasure. Her blood coursed through her veins, every nerve standing on edge as she fueled their passion with each downward thrust, accepting him deep into the well of her body, withdrawing only to sink down on him again.

She gripped his powerful shoulders as he raised his head and suckled each tender nipple, his mouth imitating the movement of her hips. She threw her head back, her lips parting in a soundless cry as every muscle tensed and then exploded in release as she fell into the blissful abyss where nothing existed but their joined bodies, their mingled cries, a union without beginning or end.

Pip lay against his chest, pulling in deep breaths as her contractions finally subsided. "Oh," she whispered, her tongue softly tracing the line of his collarbone. "Oh, John Henry, I think I finally understand the meaning of eternity."

"Mmm." He kissed her temple. "If you mean boundless love, I think I understand it too. I do love you, so very much. It might kill me, of course, since

I'm the most loyal of steeds and would let you ride me from here to the end of the earth, but I am willing to sacrifice my life for you. I think I just came very close, but then, you are merciless."

Pip, not sure if he meant it, raised her head and saw his eyes dancing with laughter. "Beast," she said, pummeling his shoulder.

"Didn't I just admit it?" He rolled her over, kissed her soundly, then sat up. "I'd like to linger all day, but something tells me that we've overslept. You smell wonderful, like a combination of musk and attar of roses. Lust suits you, my sweetheart. It makes you all soft and malleable and infinitely desirable."

"And lust makes you behave like the cock of the walk."

John Henry grinned. "I absolutely refuse to comment. Look, my love, we should get on with the day. I have work at the house, but I thought we might take the horses out first—only if you're not too tender to sit a saddle, that is."

"I think I might just be able to manage," she said. In truth she was a little sore, although in the most pleasant sort of way.

"Good. Then we can take a tour of the big house. There's something I need to talk to you about in any case, and that seems the best place to hold the conversation."

Mystified, since she thought they'd already said everything possible, Pip just nodded. "I'll wash and dress and meet you downstairs for a quick breakfast. I can't wait to try Mascha out. Thank you again for such a wonderful Christmas present. I wish I'd had something other than a muffler to give you."

"You gave me the gift of yourself, sweetheart, and that was the best Christmas present ever."

He slid out of bed, pulled on his trousers and shirt, and picked up the rest of his clothing from the chair. "I'll see you in twenty minutes or so." He kissed her lightly and slipped out the door, leaving Pip sitting in the middle of the bed, counting her many blessings and so happy that she thought she might burst.

As he sat on his gelding in the stable yard watching Pip mount Mascha and quickly steady her, John Henry felt supreme satisfaction. The look of joy on Pip's face did that alone, as it had all night long. But observing Mascha's immediate adjustment to her new mistress, the manner in which the mare arched her neck and pricked her ears in attention to Pip's whispered Arabic, told him that this was going to be a perfect match. At the time that Mascha was presented to him, he'd had no idea that he and Pip would also turn out to be a perfect match—both in bed and out of it.

He sent up a quick prayer of thanks to God for having delivered him from his agony, for giving him the opportunity to love her as he'd wanted to do for so long, for allowing Pip to accept that love with the generosity and enthusiasm she had. He'd never imagined that she would be so uninhibited and receptive, but she'd exceeded his every wish, surprising him enormously with her admission of love for him, showing him that truth in every way possible.

He felt the luckiest man alive, but he still had one last, large hurdle before him. He could only hope that Pip would accept his confession with grace and understand the necessity of his deception.

Perhaps if she saw the house, saw what he was trying to do to make her life happy and comfortable, she would not hold the duplicity against him. He still didn't know how he would find the words to explain that he was in fact the mysterious Aloysius Blimp, that he owned Manleigh Park, and that he had a title, albeit a minor one, attached to his name.

He knew he would also have to explain about the fortune he'd acquired and why he hadn't kept her in a style commensurate with that wealth. She might not like his reasoning one bit, no matter how much she claimed to have accepted her new life. Nevertheless, his thinking remained sound to him. He prayed that she would see how much they'd both needed to accept each other simply for who they were at heart, with no question between them about the value of station or fortune—or his reason for marrying her.

Pip trotted the mare over to him. "Mascha's perfect, John Henry. She couldn't be sweeter or more compliant. I took her for a turn around the courtyard and she goes as easily as a lamb." A huge smile wreathed her face.

"I saw," he said, trying to control the racing of his heart, which happened every time Pip came near. "Why don't we go a little farther afield and see how she does in the open country?"

"Yes," she said, her eyes sparkling. "Do you think it's too soon to jump her?"

"I can't think why, as long as you choose low obstacles instead of the high hedges you have such a fondness for. She won't have had much experience with jumps, given that she was raised in a desert."

"I wouldn't dream of setting her at something I didn't know she could manage with ease," Pip said, then a sudden shadow crossed her face. "Do you think she's ever taken a jump?"

"I don't know, but if she hasn't, I can't imagine anyone better than you to teach her. I ask only that you be cautious. As I said, when I took her out she was quick and willing, but I set her at nothing more difficult that a gallop across the sands. She was fast as lightning, turned on a ha'penny, but you have to remember that she was bred and trained for desert battle, not for charging across the English countryside."

Pip nodded. "Yes. I see your point, and I will be careful. Oh, John Henry, she really is lovely. Wait until Aafteh sees her! Mascha should make her eyes light up, since you know how valuable these horses are to her people."

John Henry couldn't help but wonder if Aafteh would feel anything but a sense of mourning when she saw the little Arab mare, for Mascha would remind her strongly of all she'd left behind, but he declined to comment. "Why don't we try her out? I thought we might ride toward the coast."

"Oh, yes—that's perfect!"

They rode silently over the dormant fields, Pip's

attention commanded by Mascha's skittish response to such unfamiliar terrain. John Henry admired Pip's skillful handling of the mare, the gentleness of her hands on the reins, the way she corrected and maneuvered with only the slightest touch.

Although he'd been brought up on horses from early childhood, John Henry hadn't really learned the true art of riding until he'd been trained in India under the maharaja's master groom, who had taught him the delicacy of technique necessary to deal with high-bred horses.

He'd always known that Pip had a special gift with animals, willing them quietly to her command, but he'd never appreciated how great that skill had become. She must have learned it from Will, who was a superior horseman. She seemed to adjust her seat and her hands to what suited Mascha best, and the mare responded in kind, altering her gait to whatever Pip asked of her. The two of them appeared equally concentrated on their task, learning a similar language, each eager to accommodate the other.

He couldn't help thinking of Pip in bed last night, just as eager, just as accommodating, so willing to learn and respond. The thought did not prove to be a comfortable one, and he had to readjust his seat as he tried very hard to think of other things. He thanked the good Lord as they approached the coast, the wind blowing up fiercely from the sea, enough to distract anyone.

Pip pulled up as they reached the edge of the cliff, her cheeks blooming like roses. He couldn't hear a thing she called to him, her words taken away by the howling wind, but the shining expression of exhilaration on her face told him everything he needed to know, and his heart sang in response.

He swung quickly off his horse, looped the reins over the gelding's neck, and walked over to her, reaching his arms up to her.

She slid easily down into them and let him lead her to the edge of the cliff, one arm wrapping about his overcoat as they stood looking at the sea pounding beneath, throwing up great sprays of foam against the rocky face below. Seagulls gracefully swooped and dove on the air currents, their cries shrill in the pounding of the waves.

He gathered her close and slipped his hands beneath her coat. "I love you," he murmured against her ear, strands of her hair whipping across his face.

"I love you too," she said, pressing close to his side. "Do you remember the night you came to Abu Simbal, the night you found me sitting by myself overlooking the temples?"

"I remember very well," he replied quietly. "Why do you bring that up now?"

"Because I was thinking then of the love that Ramses and Nefertari held for each other and wishing that I had been lucky enough in my life to experience the same." She sighed. "I thought then that every chance of that had been taken away from me. Now I realize that you stood in front of me at that very moment, offering the very thing I'd pined for but never had the sense to realize."

"I think it's enough that you know it now—enough for me, at least. Those days are behind us, Pip, and we can't take them back—they'll always belong to us as the way we came together, but I have no regrets, not when I can look forward to a long, happy future with you." He hugged her hard. "Why don't we just think of that time in Egypt as a beginning, a gift from God, and it's been up to us to unwrap it and reveal the mystery inside."

She pulled back slightly and looked up at his face, her eyes filled with a soft, tender love that nearly tore him apart. "I treasure those months. I was awful to you, but every moment is permanently etched in my mind, from the instant you appeared at Isabel's bedside to the day you practically shoved me on board the ship to send me back to England. How could I now, knowing what was really in your heart, begrudge you a single one of your actions?"

He rested his head on top of hers, feeling a huge burden lift from his shoulders. "Thank you, Pip. Thank you for understanding. There are still some things I need you to hear and understand, and we are both growing chilled out here, so let me take you back home—or to the main house, if you would like that."

"I would," she said, her face alight with pleasure. "I'd like that above anything except climbing back into bed with you."

He nearly choked. Pip was proving to be insatiable, not that he had a single complaint. He just hadn't yet become accustomed to her candor when it came to matters of lovemaking. The few women he'd known in that way had made an art of dissembling, of pretended blushes and affected demureness.

Pip, on the other hand, approached lovemaking as she would a banquet, with a hearty appetite and a willingness to sample everything.

He thanked God, for he couldn't seem to restrain himself either. "Bed, my beloved, will have to wait until later, since I really do have some work to do. The roofers have been good enough to come in today, and I'd feel shabby indeed if I didn't make a showing and give them some supervision. We don't want the entire west wing to cave in just because I decided to spend the day in bed with my wife."

"I understand completely," she said. "We have years ahead, and it wouldn't do if Mr. Blimp's roof collapsed."

He gazed at her distractedly, cursing the day he'd come up with his scheme to create a fictitious owner. This was it—he would have to come clean, and as soon as possible. He'd already decided that the best place to do that was in the house, once she'd seen the possibilities, just as he had.

"What is it?" she asked, her smile fading. "You suddenly look very uncomfortable. Am I not supposed to mention lovemaking outside of the bedroom?"

He dropped a kiss on her ripe, impossibly desirable lips. "You may mention it anytime at all, as long as no one else is in earshot. You don't want to scandalize half of England with your unmitigated lust for your husband. That would be most unseemly."

Pip pealed with laughter. "Oh, do you think they won't see what's right under their noses?"

"They might see, but that's their concern, not ours. My concern at this moment is to get you out of this cold wind, so let us start back." He kissed her one last time, his mouth releasing hers reluctantly.

They rode back over the fields at a fast canter, John Henry's thoughts on the difficult task ahead as he prayed that he wouldn't make too bad a mess of it.

Taking John Henry's arm, Pip walked up the steps of Manleigh Hall, filled with anticipation. He opened the enormous wood door and stood back, letting her inside. She ignored the sound of hammering from somewhere above and drank in the sight before her.

Her first impression was one of delight as she took in the large main hall and the beautifully carved wooden staircase leading up from the center of the marble floor to the next level, which stretched out from a wide landing.

Light streamed in through the long, lead-paned windows, giving enough illumination so that she could appreciate the fine wood paneling and the oil paintings that hung on the walls.

Her gaze traveled over the huge fireplace, its mantelpiece made of honey-colored stone, past the pair of closed, double-sided doors to the left side, then wandered over to the right side of the hall, where another pair of double-sided doors overlooked a terrace. Dust sheets covered the furniture grouped around the fireplace, lending the hall a ghostly feel, but she could see that once refurbished, the house would have enormous charm. "It's lovely," she said, squeezing his arm. "Even nicer than I'd imagined."

"Come over here," he said, leading her to the doors on the right and pushing them open. "This is the dining room."

She poked her head inside, taking in the spacious area, the wood-paneled walls. "Oh, my. You could seat at least twenty in here," she said, craning her head up at the ornate plastered ceiling, which held two chandeliers. "Where is the kitchen?"

"Fortunately it's just through those doors in back. I'll show you."

He took her through each room, patiently letting her absorb the feel and dimensions of each one as her imagination ran wild, picturing what they might look like when filled with furniture and draperies and all the odds and ends that gave rooms individual personality. He told her what had been done so far and what had yet to be finished before the house was truly inhabitable.

She couldn't help wishing that she might be the one moving in. Each room seemed more charming than the next, and when John Henry took her upstairs and showed her the nursery, she felt a stab of real envy. The room was a little piece of magic all its own, filled with light, overlooking the back garden so that in summer, she felt sure, the scent of flowers would drift up through open windows along with the sound of birdsong.

"What a perfect place for a baby," she said with a

sigh. "Oh, if you and I are lucky enough to have children of our own, this is exactly the sort of room I would imagine for them."

"Would you, Pip? Would you really?" he said, taking her gently by the shoulders and gazing down at her, his expression suddenly intense, almost pained.

"Would I like to have children with you?" she said, suddenly thinking that she'd hurt his feelings, since he wouldn't ever be able to provide their children with quite such a lovely environment. "Oh, yes—of course. But we can raise them perfectly well at the gatehouse, or wherever we happen to end up. It's not the house we live in that matters, only the happiness and love we give them."

"No, that's not what I meant," he said, dropping his hands from her shoulders. "I meant do you like *this* place, *this* room."

"Yes. I told you I think it's all wonderful, but that's not the point."

"But it is the point," he said, turning away. He walked to the window and looked out. "I want to make you happy, Pip, give you everything you want." He turned around to look at her, and his expression struck her as desperate.

Her heart hurt for him, for she knew she'd inadvertently made him feel less than adequate. She went quickly to his side and took his hands in hers. "John Henry, you've already given me everything I need. Honestly, you have. I've never been happier."

"I don't think you understand what I'm trying to

say." He looked as if she'd just stepped hard on his foot and he was trying not to respond to the pain.

"I *do* understand. We've been through this so many times, and I know I've been dreadful to you about your lack of funds, but that doesn't matter. I have money, even though I know you won't touch it—but if we need it, it's there just in case. So really we have nothing to worry about."

He appeared ready to tear his hair out. "Pip, my love, please listen to me. There's no need for you to offer up your funds, for we really don't need them, as generous as you are."

She ran her fingers down his cheek. "As much as I love you, sometimes I think you can be too proud."

He gazed at the ceiling as if praying for some higher help. "Pride has nothing to do with it," he said after a long moment, finally looking back at her. "Well, that's not entirely true. Pride did have something to with it, but not any longer. The fact of the matter is that I—"

Just then he heard a loud, persistent shouting from somewhere below. "Mr. Lovell? Mr. Lovell! Where are you, sir? Part of the roof has just collapsed. We need you right away!"

John Henry looked toward the open door as if he'd like to banish the roof to oblivion. "Just a moment," he called, then turned back to her. "I'm sorry, sweetheart. I'd better see how serious this is. Please, just hold what I said in your mind, and we'll continue this conversation later."

"You'd better hurry," she said, alarmed not only by the thought of the roof falling in but by John Henry's peculiar behavior, which she couldn't make out for the life of her.

"Thank you." He kissed her swiftly on her cheek and bounded out of the room as if all the dogs of hell were at his heels.

Pip decided that it might be best if she stayed out of the way while John Henry dealt with his crisis. She walked quickly downstairs and out into the sunshine, intending to take Mascha back to the stables.

Before she could even untie the reins from the mounting post, a man came riding up the drive at a fast clip. She looked hard, wondering who he might be, for she recognized neither horse nor rider. And then a thought suddenly struck, and her eyes widened. This was *not* the time for a portion of roof to be falling in. John Henry was going to be deeply unhappy at this ill-timed visit from Mr. Blimp.

The gentleman drew up, dismounted, and looked at her in surprise, although she couldn't think why.

"Good heavens," he said, sweeping his hat off his ebony head and making a bow. "The former Miss Portia Merriem, if I'm not mistaken?"

She wondered how Mr. Aloysius Alfonso Blimp would know her. "That was my maiden name, but I'm now Mrs. Lovell. You're Mr. Blimp?"

"I am not," he said with a charming smile. "Simon Forrest at your service. We've never met, but word of your conquest of London spread all over the British Empire some years back. We all wondered why you never married." He regarded her with curiosity. "Who is Mr. Blimp, and why should you look so alarmed that

I might be he? And why are you calling yourself Mrs. Lovell?"

"Because I did marry," she said, thinking that he was short a sheet or two, since the answer was obvious. "But if you don't know Mr. Blimp, then why are you here?" she asked in confusion.

"Actually, I've come to see your husband," he said, tethering his horse. "We were friends in India, and I heard that he'd taken on the estate. I'm on my way to Cornwall, so I thought I'd just stop by and have a look around. I last saw your husband in Cairo, you know, and was curious to discover what he'd gotten up to. What an elegant mare you have. She must be Arabian."

"Yes," Pip said, pleased that he recognized the bloodline. "John Henry gave Mascha to me for Christmas," she continued, stroking the mare's neck. "She's beautiful, isn't she? But then, you'd be acquainted with the breed if you've been in Egypt. Were you there long?"

"Only for a month. And yourself? John Henry told me that you renewed your acquaintance there and married. I also gather you have a son?"

Pip nodded, now even more confused by his earlier questions. "Yes, we have a son. Mr. Forrest, may I ask you why, if you knew all this about our lives, you appeared so surprised when I introduced myself? You behaved as if you had no idea that I was married."

He shot her an odd look. "Naturally I knew you had married, as I just said. I simply didn't understand why you introduced yourself in the fashion you did. I would have expected you to use your title."

"My—my title," Pip said, desperately trying to remain clear-headed. *What title? I don't have a title, so why would this Simon Forrest, who seems to know a great deal about everything else, make that sort of error? John Henry surely doesn't have a title—does he? How could he?*

The questions flew through her head at lightning speed, but she didn't come up with a single answer. "Why should I use a title?" she asked as nonchalantly as she could manage, while trying to control the trembling of her body.

"I have no idea, unless you are like your husband, who obviously remains reticent in using his. I understood his reasons in India, where he wanted to stay strongly on the side of the natives. I suppose he took the same approach when he was in Egypt, and I imagine for the same reasons. Those Arab sheiks are impossible." He grimaced. "Can you imagine—they actually believe their bloodlines to be purer and nobler than ours. A lot of savages, I call them."

"I don't know if I'd call the Arabs savages, Mr. Forrest," Pip said. "They have a very ancient culture of their own, although it might not resemble ours. Still, I highly respect the nobility among their people, and most especially the Bedouin sheiks, whose code of honor far surpasses our own, from what I've been told."

"My dear Lady Lovell, far be it from me to disenchant you about what is obviously your romantic view of a very brutal part of the world, but I understand that your time there was sheltered, as it should have been. Perhaps your husband has not told you much of his experiences either there or in India, and correctly so."

Pip gazed at Simon Forrest with a combination of fascination and horror. Clearly, John Henry had not informed her of very much, including why this man should address her as "Lady Lovell."

She was determined to get to the bottom of the matter, for if Simon Forrest spoke the truth, then John Henry had a lot to answer for.

"My husband has said little of his time in India," she said, maintaining her composure. "Of course, he's been so busy since his return to England that we've hardly had a moment to discuss anything but his most recent job."

"Yes, of course," Simon said. "He has undertaken quite a challenge, but I am sure he will manage brilliantly. This is nothing in comparison to bringing countries to the negotiating table and actually seeing treaties to the end. Little wonder he was knighted, but still I am surprised that he has chosen not to use his title now that he's back home."

Pip could only stare at Simon speechlessly, so taken aback that she could hardly breathe.

Oblivious to her shock, Simon shook his head. "Then again, your husband always has been a bit of a mystery to us all. Tell me, how is he, now that he's out of all the excitement? One would think he'd be bored to tears, stuck away in the country, but perhaps he finds a bit of peace here, away from the constant demands. Word in London is that no one's seen hide nor hair of him since he returned."

"He's doing very well," Pip said cautiously, knowing she had to say something that didn't make her sound as utterly ignorant as she felt. "As I said, he's enormously busy with the restoration work. I would summon him, but there's some sort of problem with the roof. Where do you stay?"

"I'm at the White Cockerel in the village. I leave first thing in the morning, though. Any chance of my seeing him before then?"

"You are welcome to take dinner with us," she said, jumping at the opportunity to gather more information— and better yet if John Henry was present to confirm or deny that information. A furious anger built in her as she began to realize how badly he'd deceived her.

"How kind of you," Simon said, his green eyes lighting with pleasure. "I'm sure your fare will outdo anything the inn might provide, and I would most enjoy the company. I would like to catch up with your husband, and I'd also enjoy the opportunity to further my acquaintanceship with you."

"Thank you," she said, at the same time frantically wondering what she could provide for a proper dinner at the last moment. "We stay down the drive at the gatehouse, if you'd like to present yourself there at seven this evening."

"I would be honored." He bowed again. "I look forward to our conversation this evening."

"As do I," she replied, thinking that he had no idea how much. Her thoughts quickly turned to the question of how far their food supplies would stretch. She hoped that Mrs. Biggs had made soup from the leftover meat and bones of the goose. There was cold ham, which could be served with a mayonnaise sauce, and they had root vegetables aplenty, but a sweet would have to be concocted. Maybe a prune pudding might suffice, followed by . . . followed by John Henry's severed head with an apple stuffed in his perfidious mouth.

"Lady Lovell? You appear to have drifted away."

"I beg your pardon," she said, realizing that he was waiting for some sort of formal farewell. "Good day, Mr. Forrest. We shall see you at seven, then." *Oh, indeed we shall see you at seven, and by nine John Henry will be hanging by his neck from the nearest oak tree, if everything this man has said is true.*

Simon mounted, tipped his hat at her, and kicked his horse into a canter, disappearing back down the drive, unaware that he'd turned what had just become a very happy marriage into a complete disaster.

John Henry had better have an explanation or she'd make him wish he'd never been born. Oh, yes, she'd play him like a pianoforte tonight, sounding out every false note until she had all the discords in place, every last lie, every last piece of dissembling, out in the open.

She couldn't help but wonder what else he hadn't told her.

16

John Henry, exhausted from fixing the small portion of roof that had started to collapse, wearily stabled his horse and walked back to the gatehouse, every muscle aching. The one soothing thought in his head was that Pip would be there to take him into her arms and give him some solace.

He called for her as he entered the house, but received no answer. Assuming she was in the nursery with Peter, he went straight to his room to wash and change for dinner. Looking around the bedroom, he wondered if the time was ripe to suggest to Pip that they share one room or the other, even though the rooms were small.

The situation would only be temporary, since they'd be able to move into the main house fairly soon, but he couldn't bear the thought of sleeping alone again, now that they'd finally found happiness together.

On the other hand, he didn't know how Pip would react to the news of his deception. He was going to tell her over dinner. It was unfortunate: He'd been on the brink of confessing the full truth to her, only to be interrupted by the calamity of the roof.

Putting on his coat, he decided that the only thing to do was to pick up exactly at the point where he'd left off. Pip would understand, he told himself as he went downstairs, looking forward to seeing her and stealing a kiss or two before dinner. Of course she would understand. She might even be delighted by his news, given her enthusiastic reaction to the house.

Opening the door to the parlor, he stopped abruptly at the unexpected sight of Pip speaking to a gentleman whose back was turned to the door.

Pip looked up. "There you are," she said brightly, coming toward him with a smile. "You'll never guess who has paid you a call. You'll remember your friend Mr. Forrest, of course."

John Henry's heart nearly stopped as Simon Forrest turned around and strode toward him, one hand outstretched in greeting. He couldn't believe his bad luck. God only knew what Simon had been telling Pip, but his presence did not bode well.

"Simon," he said, forcing a smile. With a sense of impending doom he shook the man's hand. "What a— surprise. How on earth did you know where to find me?"

"Good heavens, man, you might think you made yourself invisible, but I had little trouble discovering that you'd returned to Dorset. Sir Hector Guild from the Foreign Ministry directed me straight here. He had the address off the letters you've exchanged."

"Yes . . . yes, of course." John Henry wanted to kick himself for his stupidity. He hadn't thought to ask Sir Hector to keep his location a secret for the time being. "I didn't realized that you were acquainted with Sir Hector."

"I wasn't," Simon said cheerfully. "I bumped into him at my club, and when the subject turned to India, naturally your name came up. I merely inquired whether you'd been in touch and he told me you'd re-located here. It's a lovely spot, I must say."

"Yes, it is," John Henry replied, desperately wondering how much Simon might have already spilled to Pip. But since she didn't look the least bit concerned as she handed him a glass of sherry, he breathed a little more easily—only slightly, since at any moment Simon might put his foot in his mouth and reveal far too much. Simon never had been known for his tact. "What are you doing in this part of the country? Surely you didn't come solely to seek me out."

"Not at all. As I told your charming wife, I'm on my way to visit friends, so I thought I'd stop by to see you. I hope I do not catch you at an inconvenient time? Your wife assured me that you had no other plans this evening and kindly invited me to stay for dinner."

John Henry nearly choked on the sip of sherry he'd just taken. "D-dinner? How nice, although I don't know that we can offer you very much in the way of a sumptuous meal. We live very simply." Oh, dear *God*, what was he going to do now? Dinner with Simon could be a disaster.

"Yes, I've seen how simple your life is at the moment, but then, you never did mind living in the most frugal of circumstances, a mystery to those of us who prefer our luxuries," Simon replied.

John Henry merely nodded. "I can imagine. Perhaps we should go in for dinner. I, for one, am famished. Pip?"

He offered her his arm, and she easily slipped her hand onto it, but he couldn't help noticing that the warmth she'd shown him only a few hours before had cooled. Telling himself that he was seeing trouble where none existed—probably the result of a guilty conscience—he smiled at her. She returned his smile, but then quickly looked away.

His heart sank, dread filling him as they all walked into the dining room and sat. Here was trouble indeed, and he had no idea how to deflect it. Despite all the diplomatic skills he'd learned over the years, not a single one came to mind for this situation, other than to do his best to keep the conversation on a neutral course.

"Tell me, Simon, how did your time in Egypt work out in the end?" John Henry asked as Mrs. Biggs put bowls of soup in front of them. "You mentioned that you were concluding a transaction, if I remember correctly, and then going off to tour. Did you enjoy your travels?"

"Oh, very much, although the weather left much to be desired, given the blistering heat. Still, I managed to take in the important sites. I found the pyramids quite interesting."

"Any in particular?" John Henry asked, risking a glance at Pip, whom he thought would be amused by this lumping together of the spectacular and varied assortment of pyramids that stretched along the Nile. She didn't meet his eyes, appearing intent on eating her soup. Since it wasn't really that good, more grease and water than substance, he had to wonder at her lack of interest in one of her most favorite subjects.

"No, just the usual," Simon replied. "The structures at Giza were more than enough for me. After that I'd had enough of the desert sand and those dreadful camels one is forced to ride. Nasty beasts, they are, forever moaning and spitting and trying to bounce one off." He took a large swallow of wine. "I must say, I was rather taken by the Sphinx—a rather peculiar-looking sort of thing, but as an oddity it had a certain quality."

John Henry, who had been awed beyond words by the Sphinx, could find nothing to say to Simon's easy dismissal of one of the world's wonders. Pip, who shared his reaction, still didn't look up, which truly alarmed John Henry. In all the years he'd known her, she had never kept her opinion to herself, especially when she felt strongly about something.

Then she finally spoke, resting her spoon carefully alongside her bowl. "I am so happy you took pleasure in your travels in Egypt, Mr. Forrest. But would you mind terribly if we talked about India, since that is a country I have not yet had the opportunity to visit. How did you enjoy your time there?"

"Ah, well," he said, sitting back as Violet replaced his soup bowl with a dinner plate filled with ham, scalloped potatoes, and vegetables. He picked up his knife and fork and dug in with a healthy appetite. "Now India was an entirely different experience, but then I resided there for a number of years, just as your husband did. I was in the army, the horse cavaliers, you know, so my experience was dictated by where I was sent and what my duties were, unlike your husband, who went where he pleased," he said, chewing his meat heartily. "But then, surely he's told you all about it. My adventures pale in comparison to his."

John Henry wanted to kick Simon if only to shut him up, but that was impossible since Simon was too far across the table. He probably wouldn't have taken the hint anyway. John Henry saw his life blowing up in his face as Simon mindlessly carried on.

"You see, originally your husband dealt in business, which took him all over the country, whereas my job was simply to defend British interests against insurgents. In the end he had much more of an exciting time of it."

"Really?" Pip said, her chin resting on her palm. "Do tell me more."

John Henry quickly interrupted, determined to stop this dangerous line of questioning. "Mr. Forrest, or Lieutenant Forrest as he was known then, was a marvelous horseman. He downplays his role considerably, since he was the best horseman in his regiment, and not only that, but once or twice he actually helped to save the day during attacks by renegades against the British colony he protected."

Pip nodded. "How worthy," she said, although she didn't look the least bit interested. "And you, John Henry? What were all these exciting adventures you were having?"

"Mr. Forrest exaggerates," he said, taking a bite of potato, although his appetite had fled. Nothing soured the appetite as much as complete and total trepidation.

"Is that so?" Pip said. "I wonder why you have always been so reticent to speak to me of your time there. Could that be because you got up to no good?"

She regarded him sweetly, but he knew that look far too well to think she had even an ounce of sweetness in her heart at that moment. Which meant that Simon had already done some serious damage by giving information that John Henry would have preferred to impart himself. In private, and in his own words. He opened his mouth to speak, but he was too late.

"To the contrary," Simon said hastily. "Your husband, madam, is far too modest. He was a hero."

John Henry wanted to put his dinner knife straight through Simon's chest. This was the beginning of the end. Of all the terrible scenarios he might have imagined, being inadvertently given away by Simon Forrest had not been one of them.

"A hero? Really, how thrilling," Pip said, gazing at Simon with complete fascination. "I had no idea. My husband *is* a modest man and doesn't speak easily of his accomplishments. How did he become a hero?"

Simon was so astonished that he dropped his knife and fork onto his plate. "Do you mean you really do not know?"

"Please, Simon," John Henry said, sweat beading on his forehead. "Do you think we might speak of something else?"

"Certainly not," Pip interrupted innocently. "I should like to hear what Mr. Forrest has to say, since you obviously have no intention of telling me yourself." Her eyes flashed at him, not with fire but with ice.

To John Henry's dismay, Simon enthusiastically launched into the tale.

"Well, my dear," he said warmly, "one day about two years after your husband arrived, he happened to be working in the north of the country, mapping out trade routes for the East India Company, or so the story goes."

John Henry abandoned his meal altogether and lowered his head in despair, knowing exactly what was coming.

"John Henry was working during the monsoon season, so of course there was terrible flooding, the rains unceasing, the rivers overflowing their banks, which isn't unusual for that time of year, but very dangerous." Simon stopped his narrative to shove in another mouthful of food. "Apparently the eldest son of the powerful local maharaja made the dire mistake of playing along the riverbank, which then collapsed, sweeping the boy into the raging waters."

Pip glared at John Henry, and he knew she

remembered the story he'd told her that night at the inn when he'd made a tiny sortie at the truth, laying the gentlest of groundwork. Simon had just dug a crater out of his intentions, damn him.

All John Henry could do was to look at her, his heart in his eyes, trying somehow to communicate that he hadn't meant to deceive her, much less toy with her—that he'd only been waiting until the right time to tell her the truth.

Pip averted her gaze, her face turning to stone. "What happened then?" she asked Simon, her hands clenching the side of the table.

"From what I heard, your husband came riding along and saw the boy being carried away by the torrent. He stripped off his boots and coat and dove into the river." Simon took another long drink from his glass. "He swam out into the treacherous current, grabbed the boy around the chest, and somehow managed to get them both safely back to shore. Then he pumped the child's chest to remove all the water he'd swallowed, covered him with his coat, and collapsed alongside the boy. The maharaja's servant came looking for his young charge and discovered them lying on the bank, exhausted, soaked, and shivering with cold, both near to death."

John Henry felt closer to death at this moment than he had ever felt in India. "You make the situation sound much more dramatic than it actually was. I did nothing exceptional, certainly nothing more than anyone else would have done if they'd witnessed the same incident."

"Nonsense," Simon replied, cleaning his plate with a flourish. "If you hadn't risked your life, the maharaja would never have given you his complete trust. Without that trust you never would have been in a position to negotiate the territorial rights for Britain."

"The treaty was sheer good luck," John Henry retorted, wondering how he was ever going to make things right with Pip. With every ill-chosen word, Simon Forrest dug John Henry into an ever-deepening hole. To be fair, it wasn't really Simon's fault. He didn't know how fragile the situation was or how thoroughly John Henry had kept his wife in the dark.

"Good luck indeed, and I don't just mean the monetary reward you were given by the maharaja— after all, the King awarded you with a knighthood as a result. I would say that India treated you extremely well, my friend. Would that all of us had been so lucky."

John Henry was furious. The whole damned India episode was out in the open now and not a word of the truth had come from him. He looked at Pip, who stared down at her plate, her face pale. She didn't say a word, just sat there looking as if the world had come to an end.

He wanted desperately to take her in his arms and explain everything, but he couldn't do that in front of Simon Forrest. If he did, the story of how he'd roundly deceived his wife would be all over England in a matter of days. Simon would see to that and have a fine time spreading the gossip.

All John Henry could do now was to try to control

the damage, starting with curtailing Simon's tongue before he could go any further. "Well, that's all in the past now, and my wife and I have chosen to live quietly here in the country. I've had enough adventures for a lifetime. What are your own plans, now that you've left the army?"

"I haven't made any at this point, although as a second son I need to come up with a career of some sort, since my income doesn't stretch as far as I'd like." He grinned. "Unlike you, I cannot afford to buy an estate and retire to it."

John Henry really did want to kill the man.

Pip's head shot up and she stared at John Henry, who wanted to sink under the table. Two bright spots of color flamed in her cheeks, and she looked as if she might throw her plate at his head at any moment, which he would well have deserved.

"We are very fortunate to live at Manleigh," he said evenly enough, but never taking his eyes off Pip. "It is a pity that you will not have the time to see the estate more thoroughly, but perhaps another day, when the renovation of the house is complete."

"Indeed," Simon said, leaning back as Violet appeared with the prune pudding. "I would enjoy that. I commend you, John Henry, for choosing to live here until your house is completed, when you could easily afford far more comfortable accommodations, but then, you've always been a get-involved sort of fellow. Better to keep an eye on the progress than to let things go awry."

"My thoughts exactly," John Henry said, wondering

how the handsome Simon Forrest would look with prune pudding all over his face.

"Tell me, Lady Lovell," Simon continued, "did you not spend your childhood somewhere in Dorset? I seem to remember a mention of that—perhaps your husband told me."

"I spent the first eight years of my life not far from here. Why do you ask?"

"Oh, sheer curiosity. Dorset is quite a distance from the pleasures of London, but I imagine you will find time to visit. I shall look forward to that. I wouldn't like to be so far away myself, but then I am a city creature. Too much fresh air makes my head ache after a time."

He went on making small talk, oblivious to the tension in the air. Finally, after what seemed to John Henry like hours, he put down his napkin and stood.

"Forgive me, but I must take my leave of you. I so enjoyed the meal and the evening. We must do it again soon."

Over my dead body. John Henry escorted him to the door and practically shoved him out. As soon as he could politely close it again, he turned to Pip, who had come out into the hall.

"Pip—I'm so sorry," he said, feeling miserable that she looked so pale, knowing that he was responsible, and wanting somehow to put everything back the way it had been. "I never in a million years dreamed Simon Forrest would show up on our doorstep and . . . well, spill all of the truth before I had a chance to tell you myself."

She didn't say a word. She gave him one long look that held no expression at all, then turned abruptly and walked up the stairs, her back stiff.

"Pip, please," he called. "At least give me a chance to explain why I didn't say anything before this."

The only response he received was the sound of her bedroom door closing, then the click of the lock turning in the heavy stillness of the house.

"Oh, hell and damnation," he muttered, turning down the lamps. Never mind, he decided. He'd dealt with Pip's temper before, although this time he truly deserved her scorn. What worried him more was her silence. He'd have been much happier if she'd given him a good piece of her mind. At least he knew how to do with that.

He'd simply have to wait out this latest catastrophe and pray that by morning she'd be ready to listen.

But when morning came, Pip had gone, taking Peter and Aafteh with her.

17

$\mathcal{P}$ip stood at the window of Will's London town-house, gazing out over the barren grass and the rain-soaked streets of Hanover Square, not really seeing, her thoughts turned inward.

She'd spent so many happy days in this house, but now, empty of all but a skeletal staff of servants, it seemed bleak and cold, reflecting the exact state of her heart. Even Peter's laughter resounding through the hallways didn't lighten her spirits.

Shivering, she wrapped her arms around her waist, then turned back to the desk where she'd spread out the pages of her Egyptian treatise, which she'd been finalizing for the last week.

But that too gave her no pleasure. She felt as if all

the joy that was inherent in her nature had been stripped away by John Henry's enormous deception.

Sitting down, she blinked away the tears that had become a constant presence and tried to concentrate, anything but think about the man she'd loved so deeply, who had betrayed her so thoroughly. But as hard as she tried, she couldn't focus on the pages, which blurred in front of her eyes.

She had to stop this self-indulgence and get on with her work, she told herself. She had an appointment with the governors of the board of the British Museum in only a week's time, and she had to have everything in order if she ever expected to have her paper published. She owed that much to herself. John Henry might have made a fool of her, but she still had her dreams. She would make a new life for herself, forget all about John Henry. She would live the life of a scholar, as she'd always planned. She would be a good mother to Peter.

Maybe, when Peter was a little older and more self-sufficient, she would even travel again. She would take him with her, naturally, and Aafteh too. They could lease houses wherever they went so that Peter would have a stable, comfortable base. Maybe one day in the distant future her heart would stop feeling as if it were beating only by rote, one painful pulse at time. Maybe one day she'd even forget that John Henry had come back into her life and taught her what real happiness was.

Pip buried her face in her hands, her shoulders

starting to shake with sobs that tore at the core of her being.

John Henry straightened abruptly as he heard a carriage pounding up the drive. Could Pip have finally decided to return to him? He dropped the trowel he'd been using to spread mortar along the front steps of the main house and sprinted down them, training his eyes on the approaching carriage, his heart hammering.

If nothing else, maybe word had finally arrived as to her whereabouts. Pip had left without even a note telling him what her intentions were or where she was heading. He'd written letters to both Will and Lady Samantha, praying she'd gone to one or the other of them, but he had not yet heard back from either.

Every hour of every day passed with excruciating slowness as he wondered what had become of his wife and son. He missed them acutely, longed to hold them, but as ten days had dragged by without a word from Pip, he couldn't help wondering if she hadn't left him for good.

The carriage pulled to a halt, and a footman jumped down from the box and let down the steps.

John Henry held his breath, praying with everything he had in him that Pip would appear from the curtained interior with Peter in her arms.

His heart fell as Lady Samantha Merriem descended, arranging her hat. "There you are, my dear boy," she bellowed, marching over to him and holding out her gloved hand for him to kiss. "My, how you've grown up. I can see why our darling Pip decided to marry you. Now, what is all this about losing your wife like some misplaced valise? She is most certainly not with me—indeed, I haven't heard a word from her, which is unusual since she writes me every three days like clockwork. What on earth did you do to chase her away?"

John Henry took her firmly by the elbow and led her out of earshot of the workmen. "It's a long story," he said, quickly going over the most salient points.

Lady Samantha held her peace until he was finished. Then she simply stared at him. "You are telling me that Will was involved in this absurd scheme? What blockheads you both are—I suppose I shouldn't be surprised, given your sex, not to mention Will's past folly with Louisa. One would have thought that had taught him something, although obviously it did not. But really, John Henry, what could you have been thinking? I was once under the impression that you possessed some common sense."

"When it comes to Pip, my common sense seems to fly out the window. But never mind that. If she's not with you, she must be at Alconleigh."

"I wouldn't be so sure. Pip is proud. She might not want to go running home to her parents, especially if she feels she's been made a fool of by her husband." She looked at him with disdain. "At least Pip doesn't know—or I hope she doesn't know—that Will had any part in this nonsense, or she will be even more hurt than she already is. Men," she snorted.

"Whatever your opinion of men might be," he said curtly, "I still cannot understand why Pip went flying off without a word."

"My dear boy, you seem to forget your wife's history. Her father badly betrayed her mother, and that's not the sort of thing a girl forgets. Valentine Merriem married Louisa for financial gain and financial gain alone, then proceeded to run around with all sorts of fancy women, ignoring his wife and making her life miserable. In the end he abandoned her and their daughter completely, then managed to get himself killed at Waterloo."

"But this situation is entirely different," he protested vehemently. "I *love* Pip. I would never intentionally hurt her."

"But despite your best intentions you did hurt her. You might have misled her for what you thought were good reasons, but I can assure you, no matter your reasons, Pip had every reason to react as she did. You betrayed her trust, and she cannot take that lightly."

John Henry thought hard. Will had mentioned something of the sort a few months back, but John Henry hadn't taken the point as seriously as he should have. He certainly hadn't thought he was betraying Pip, merely finding a way to make their marriage work. "Yes," he said slowly. "I think I begin to see."

"Well, that's a start. At least you're looking properly remorseful, even strained, which is all to the good."

John Henry felt an improbable desire to laugh. He hadn't seen Lady Samantha for at least ten years, and she hadn't changed one iota, her makeup still an amazing mixture of blue eyeshadow and pink rouge, her trademark triple strands of oversized pearls hugging her throat, and her forthright tongue in excellent order. "I *feel* strained," he said. In truth, he was exhausted, hardly having slept at all in the last week. "All I want to do is find my wife and bring her and our son back where they belong."

"That might take some doing, my boy. You've made a proper mess of the whole affair, and Pip is no one to be trifled with. She is a bright, independent woman with not only financial but intellectual resources that have always served her well. I remember very well being her age and having very much the same sense of independence. You did not marry a milksop, John Henry, and you would be well advised to remember it."

"I could hardly forget," he said with a tired smile. "Pip is and always will be a force to be reckoned with. I intend to meet the challenge, if I can find her. I really do love her with all my heart, Lady Samantha, and I don't want to live the rest of my life without her."

"Fine words," she said gruffly, but looked pleased nonetheless. "If I were you, I'd put my back behind them and stop standing around feeling sorry for yourself. Action, my boy. Action is what's called for. When the battle is joined, one must engage."

"I agree, Lady Samantha. The only problem is that it's very difficult engaging in battle when you don't know where the enemy is located."

"True enough," she conceded. "In which case, we must ferret out the camp. Aha!" she cried in triumph. "I believe this is the post arriving right now."

A young boy pulled up on horseback, tipped his hat, and handed John Henry the day's mail. Samantha pulled it straight out of his hand, quickly sorting through the pile like an expert. She produced a letter, waving it in the air. "I believe this might answer some questions," she said, reluctantly handing it to him, clearly itching to open it herself.

John Henry didn't waste a moment, breaking open Will's familiar seal, the frank on the front already confirming his identity.

He read the neat lines swiftly, then released a deep sigh of relief. "Pip is in London," he said, able to breathe properly for the first time in a week. "She went directly there, then sent word to Will that she was attending to some business and would be staying in the family house for an unspecified period of time."

"Give it here, for you're bound to forget the most important details." Lady Samantha impatiently pulled the sheet out of his hand, instantly produced a lorgnette from somewhere inside her bulging reticule and read the letter for herself. "Hmm," she said "Hmm, hmm. Well, that's it, then. Will has gone to London on his own since Louisa is at home with the twins, both of whom have chicken pox. Pity, since she would have made less of a mess of matters."

"I'm sure Will is capable of looking after Pip for the moment," John Henry said dryly, taking back the letter before Lady Samantha could object and tucking i safely away in his coat pocket. "I'll leave immediately. Thank you for coming all this way, Lady Samantha. I'll write as soon as I know anything."

"Don't be a complete idiot," she said. "We will both go to London in my carriage, which happens to be standing at the ready with all my trunks packed—and for your information, you will go nowhere near Hanover Square. Pip is not even to know that you are in London, unless, of course, you would like to chase her back to Egypt or goodness knows where else." She glared at him with an expression that brooked no argument. "You will be staying with me in Upper Brook Street until I can sort out the disaster you've managed to make of your marriage. Then and only then will you be allowed to see your wife."

John Henry glared straight back at her. "Might I remind you, Lady Samantha, that although Pip is your step-granddaughter, she is still my wife, and as such I will see her when and how I choose. I am perfectly capable of sorting out my own disasters."

"And haven't you done a fine job so far." She waved her hand at her carriage, which was immediately pulled up beside her. "Come along, John Henry. Get in and take me to your gatehouse. I will take a cup of tea and some cakes while you pack your bags. You have no more than half an hour, or I leave without you."

John Henry, who knew when to concede defeat, shook his head and offered up a wry smile. "Very well, Lady Samantha. Have it your way. However, I'll walk to the gatehouse, thank you. I need to clear my head."

"Clear whatever you like. I don't want any more

nonsense from you." She climbed imperiously into her carriage, which slowly proceeded down the drive like a royal progression of one.

He looked after it for a moment, then quickly returned to the house to find the foreman and issue instructions that he hoped would suffice in his absence.

Still, even if the whole house fell down while he was away, nothing was more important than making things right with Pip, and he intended to do just that, no matter what the effort cost him.

Pip, writing frantically away on the last stage of her paper, which was more than two hundred pages, started as the door to the study opened.

She looked up to see Will standing in the doorway, a broad smile on his face.

"So, my darling girl. I see that you have big business afoot. Is this what brought you all the way to London?" he asked, gesturing at the piles of paper scattered all over the desk. He kissed the top of her head as she scooped the pages together, wishing she could collect herself as easily.

"Will," she said, standing and hugging him hard. "I didn't think my letter would tear you away from Alconleigh. I didn't mean it to."

"It didn't," he said easily. "I had already made plans to come to town. Parliament opens shortly and I have a speech to prepare. Unfortunately I had to leave your mother at Alconleigh as the twins are covered in revolting red spots, and she felt she ought to oversee them lest the entire staff defect from the result of their ill tempers."

"They're not seriously ill?" Pip asked with alarm.

"Do you think I'd be here if they were? Actually, I'm more concerned about you. You are distinctly pale, Pip, and I don't like the dark circles under your eyes." He rested his hands on her shoulders and looked straight into her eyes. "Is there something you want to tell me? I cannot believe your appearance is a simple matter of overwork on whatever this project is."

"I'm fine," she said, then promptly burst into tears, sobbing against his strong chest, taking comfort in the safe harbor of his arms as she had when she was a small child.

He held her tightly, waiting until the storm had passed, then guided her to the sofa close to the blazing hearth. "Now that's over," he said, handing her a handkerchief, "why don't you tell me the truth? Something's sent you haring up to London, and I don't think it's this manuscript or whatever that huge pile on my desk is."

Pip wiped her eyes and blew her nose, then twisted her hands in her lap. "Oh, Will," she said, grateful to finally have someone to pour everything out to, "I'm in the most terrible predicament. I've—I've left John Henry, and I can't possibly go back, not after what he's done, but the dreadful thing is that I can't stop loving him, even if he is the most horrible, deceitful man on the face of the earth."

"I see," Will said, not sounding the least bit alarmed, which offended Pip deeply. The least he could have done was to be a *little* sympathetic. "What exactly did John Henry do that upset you so greatly?"

"You won't believe this—you just won't," she replied, marching to the fireplace, taking the poker and digging at the logs, sending sparks flying in every direction. "He thoroughly misrepresented himself to me, lying at every turn. I married him, Will, believing him to be one thing, when he was someone else entirely."

"And who was that?" he said calmly, settling in an armchair opposite the fire and crossing one leg over the other.

"He's not plain old John Henry at all, he's a Knight of the Realm! And on top of that, he has some sort of huge fortune, and he's not just working at Manleigh as a steward, he owns the blasted estate." She shoved the poker back into its stand and turned around, fuming, her hands planted on her hips. "Furthermore, he didn't even bother to tell me any of this fascinating information himself—oh, no. I had to hear it from a complete stranger. John Henry just sat there and couldn't deny a single word."

"Do you know, at this moment you remind me exactly of your mother when she gets into a bait. The resemblance is uncanny," Will said, looking highly amused.

"How can you possibly be so casual and unconcerned when my entire life is falling apart?" she cried, hurt and astonished that Will of all people didn't exhibit any outrage on her behalf. She couldn't believe that he was taking her catastrophe so lightly.

"My dearest girl, I am not the least bit unconcerned, but I do think you might want to take a step back and look at your marriage from a slightly different angle. Are you willing to do that? After all, I did raise you to use logic when emotion overrode your ability to reason."

"I don't see what reason has to do with any of this," she said, seething.

"Come now, Pip. Why don't we work this out together." He gave her a long, hard look. "In the first place, I know for a fact that John Henry loves you too, very much, and he told me so himself."

"He did?" She frowned. "When?"

"At Alconleigh, before you both left. Secondly, he was also under the distinct impression that you didn't care two jots about him. He told me then that he'd bought Manleigh—and before you go flying up into the boughs about that, just listen to me. He hoped that if you could learn to love him for who he truly was and put aside your doubts about why he'd married you, then you would both have a real chance at happiness."

Pip stared at her stepfather in horror. "You *knew* about everything? About the knighthood and the fortune and Manleigh?"

"I knew," he said evenly. "I also believed that you and John Henry had an argument, which is why I said nothing to you." He held up a hand to forestall her before she could take off his head.

"Here is the third point, and, Pip, think about this very carefully. Your father did you no service when he abandoned you and your mother. But why should

John Henry have to pay the price for your father's actions? He's nothing like your father. John Henry made
his success—nothing was given to him just because of
an accident of birth or by making an advantageous
marriage. He has done a fine job of creating a good life
for himself and you and for Peter. I admire him very
much." He leaned back against the cushions, slinging
his arm over the back of the chair. "Given all that, do
you think it's possible you might have overreacted to
learning the truth?"

Pip hadn't considered John Henry in that light, but
she grasped Will's point. She sank down into the armchair next to Will's.

"So you're telling me that it's all right that John
Henry lied, just because *you* think he had good reason?"

"Don't forget that I lied about my position to your
mother when we first met, and in the end she managed to understand. I still regret not telling her the
truth about myself from the beginning, but I don't
think she would have given me the time of day if
had. So you see, I believe I do understand why John
Henry behaved as he did. We all make errors of judgment, but at the same time, we equally deserve for
giveness for those errors."

She nodded, staring down at her hands. "I just
don't know if I can do that," she said, fighting back
tears.

"But you do know you love John Henry. Isn't that
what's important here? We can overcome all sorts of
obstacles, as long as love is in place." Reaching over, h

took one of her hands between his own and squeezed it. "Pip, listen very carefully now. Do you remember when you were a little girl and you hurt yourself jumping from the hayloft? You very nearly bled to death."

"I remember," she whispered with a small shudder. She'd leaped into a pile of hay below, but she'd cut her foot on a scythe. She didn't recall much after that, save for her fear when she'd seen the blood pumping out of her foot in great squirts. "You came for me and you sewed me up."

"Yes. I came for you because John Henry ran like the wind to fetch me. He was as pale as you were. Even then I knew that he loved you, as young as you both were, although I never expected you would grow up to marry each other. But that's not the point. Do you also remember what happened after that?"

"I only remember waking up and seeing you sitting by the side of my bed and knowing that everything was going to be all right."

He stood and slipped his arm around her shoulder. "We haven't talked about this since, but I think now is the time to remind you. You spoke of talking to the angels, of traveling far away and being given a choice of staying with them or coming home to us."

"Oh, yes," she said with a little laugh. "I think I must have been dreaming."

"That was no dream, my dearest. I was there in the room, praying that we weren't going to lose you. I saw their light as they brought you back, and it was one of the most beautiful sights I've ever witnessed. That light filled the room, touched every corner, filled me with a sense of peace that passed all understanding. And then the light faded away and you opened your eyes." He smiled and gently kissed her cheek. "I've never forgotten what you described then about where you'd been and how you were carried home through that same light."

She looked up at him in astonishment. "Do you mean that was *real*?"

"That was very real. And the reason I bring it up now is to remind you that God and His angels are always with you, watching over you, guiding and protecting you, but your life is your own to do with as you will. You can turn love aside, for that is your choice. You can live in fear or anger or resentment, for that is your choice too. But, Pip—all you ever need to do when you're in doubt is to reach out to those very angels who watched over you when you were in need and ask for their help, for they will never forsake you."

She covered her face with her hands, shaken to her core. She *did* remember. Everything came flooding back—the beautiful garden, the waterfalls, the incredible, brilliant light, that overwhelming sense of love surrounding her, filling her with its ineffable beauty and peace.

She hadn't felt such peace since. When had she lost her faith in the divine nature of the universe? When had she forgotten to reach deep within and ask for spiritual guidance? Somehow she had lost her way, putting her faith in her own ability to map out the course of her life, but that hadn't done her much good, her compass pointing her in all the wrong directions.

Maybe the angels had stepped in after all and guided her to John Henry, or him to her, to put her back on the right path.

She didn't know. She was so confused that she couldn't think anymore.

"Thank you," she said, looking up at Will. "If you don't mind, I think I will go see Peter for a bit."

"That sounds like a good idea," he said comfortably. "I've always found that small children have a way of putting things into perspective."

"Will . . ." she said hesitantly, wondering if she wasn't about to make a terrible mistake, then deciding that she owed him the full truth. She couldn't lie to him any longer, especially after what he'd just shared with her about the angels. How could she dissemble in the face of that level of truth? She desperately needed to confess. John Henry might have lied to her, but she had been lying to her parents, and she couldn't carry that burden any longer. She drew a deep breath.

"Will, there's something I've been keeping from you, and I think you have a right to know."

"You can tell me anything, dearest. You should know that by now."

"It's—it's about Peter."

"Yes?"

She stared into the fire, trying to think how to phrase her confession, not knowing how he would react but dreading it all the same. "I haven't been entirely honest with you and Mama. About Peter, I mean." She looked back at Will, hoping he would accept what she had to tell him and not be too disappointed with her.

He looked perplexed. "I don't understand. What could you have been dishonest about?"

"Peter—well, you know how much I love him and he will always be the child of my heart—but the fact is that . . ." She swallowed hard and forced herself to go on. "The fact is that he's not actually my son. That is, I didn't give birth to him."

Will drew back, staring at her. "I beg your pardon? Did I hear you correctly?"

She colored hotly. "Yes. I'm so sorry to have deceived you, but I couldn't think of any other way to handle the situation."

"*What* situation?" he demanded. "If Peter isn't your son, whose is he? Is he John Henry's child by someone else?"

"No," she said quickly. "John Henry just stumbled into the mess by accident." She told the story as succinctly as she could, sparing herself nothing. "So you must understand that I couldn't just abandon this innocent baby," she said, finishing her narrative. "John Henry understood, and that's why he married me."

Will didn't say a word, pressing his palms together and resting his forefingers against his lips. After a few long moments, he spoke.

"That actually explains a great deal. Well, Pip. I wish you'd come to us with the problem sooner, but I see why you felt you couldn't." He half smiled. "I suppose I should be touched by your concern for our reputations, and I do indeed understand why you didn't want to alert Isabel's parents. But you certainly didn't make things easy for yourself."

"Then you really do understand?" she asked, infinitely relieved to have made her confession, feeling as if a huge weight had been lifted from her shoulders.

"Naturally I understand," he replied. "The important fact is that you love Peter, whether you gave birth to him or not, and we will continue to love him, as does John Henry. This only reinforces what I've been trying to tell you. I think you need to see that what John Henry did for you under those extreme circumstances speaks even more strongly of his love for you. He wanted to give you his name as well as give it to the child. His character continues to speak for itself, and I have nothing more to say on the subject."

He stepped back. "I suggest that you go visit Peter in the nursery, then have some dinner. I'm going out on business. You might take the night to think all of this through. I trust you will have reached a sensible conclusion by morning."

Pip pushed herself to her feet. "Thank you for your advice," she said, giving him a quick, hard hug. "You've given me much to think about."

18

Pip took a few moments to collect herself, then went up to the nursery and found Peter busily scooting around, Aafteh just as busily running after him.

After exchanging a few words with Aafteh about the excitement of the day, which involved a walk in the park and Peter's voracious appetite, Pip gathered Peter up into her arms and kissed his head. "Hello, darling boy," she murmured into his dark, curly mop of hair. "You're looking very handsome today."

He gurgled and smoothed his hands over her cheeks, leaving a trail of drool. "Mama," he chortled, using his new word with delight.

"That's right. Mama." She squeezed him tightly, her heart breaking with love. Peter wriggled against her embrace, his little arms flailing as he struggled to be let down.

Pip gently placed him back on the floor, where he quickly crawled back to his toys and began to throw them in every direction.

He was already beginning to exert his independence from her, she realized. How quickly children grew up, she thought sadly. Less than a year ago he'd been a helpless newborn, and now he was a proper little boy in his own right, just as it should be.

She sat down at the window and watched him play, her thoughts wandering back to the day of his birth, when John Henry had appeared out of nowhere and saved his life.

Not only had he saved the little boy's life, but if he hadn't married her so that she could keep Peter with her, she wouldn't be sitting there right now, watching him attempt to tear the nursery to pieces.

Will was right—she'd done John Henry an enormous disservice in discounting what he'd done for her and Peter. At the time she hadn't realized how selfless his motives were, but looking back over everything that had transpired from that time forth, she saw that he had acted out of love for her.

Rubbing her hand over her forehead, she decided that she wasn't doing Peter any good. He was bound to sense her mood, and that would only make him unhappy and tearful.

Quickly kissing her son good night and taking her leave of Aafteh, she went downstairs to her bedroom, wanting nothing more than to go to sleep and find oblivion. Exhausted, she managed to get out of her dress by herself and slipped on her nightdress. Climbing under the covers, she settled her head on the pillow.

But hours passed and sleep refused to come. Instead, her thoughts ran in circles, chasing their own tails, with no answers coming to her mind.

Will's words kept ringing in her ears: *I admire him very much. . . . His character continues to speak for itself. . . . John Henry has earned what he has. . . .*

She rolled over and pulled a pillow over her head, unable to shut out the silent litany.

In her heart of hearts, she knew Will was right. John Henry *had* earned his place in the world. John Henry *had* made his own way. He'd left England to seek his future and fortune elsewhere, and he'd accomplished that by means of hard work and the strength of his inner nature. Because he'd stayed true to himself, he'd met the challenges put before him and become a hero in the process.

She, on the other hand, had stayed in her sheltered, comfortable environment, never having to worry about anything other than fulfilling her own selfish interests. She might have gone off to Egypt to pursue a dream, but where was the merit in that?

Pip abruptly sat up in bed, rubbing her knuckles against her tired eyes as an alarming thought suddenly dawned.

She'd spent so much time blaming John Henry for his supposed trespasses that she'd never once considered that she might have been the person who lacked character and the sort of honesty that had no place for fear.

Lying back down, she stared at the ceiling while looking deep within herself for the real truth of who she was and what she wanted from the life that had been so graciously granted her.

Searching hard, she carefully peeled back the layers of defenses that she'd built up over the years, seeking the young girl she'd once been before fear had touched her soul and made her so careful.

She found only darkness. With a sob, she buried her face in her pillow, clutching it hard against her chest. Surely there had to be more to life than this terrible uncertainty? She'd thought she had experienced love with John Henry, after all, as brief as that had been. Perhaps she'd only been able to accept his love conditionally, waiting and maybe even deep down expecting to be betrayed. At the first sign of trouble she'd run back to her comfortable, familiar world, never giving him a chance to explain.

What did that say about her? Only that she was too proud and arrogant and stubborn to listen to the one man who had continued to love her through the years despite the terrible way she'd treated him.

Pip rolled over again, still holding the pillow against her aching chest. She'd never felt such a sense of loneliness and despondency. The thought came to her that she might very well have lost John Henry forever.

Then gradually she began to realize with despair

that if she didn't heal herself, she might very well lose her own soul to this terrible void.

She lay very still, blankly looking up, silently struggling, finding no solace. And then something else Will had said came quietly into her mind.

"All you ever need to do when you're in doubt is to reach out to those very angels who watched over you when you were in need . . . they will never forsake you."

Her breath caught on a sob. "Oh, please!" she cried. "Please, angels, if you helped me before, please help me now, for I have never been in such need. I put myself in your hands, and in the hands of our Heavenly Father, for I cannot face this alone."

To her amazement, she felt something like a breeze caressing her, but instead of chilling her body, a warmth slowly built in her until she was filled with comfort and love and reassurance. She recognized the embrace, although she hadn't felt it for twenty years. But she knew it for exactly what it was, the embrace of divine love.

At that moment the first light of dawn crept into the room, and Pip, shaking with emotion, shoved back the covers and went to stand at the window, looking out over the square. She caught her breath in awe, her hands clenching the material of her nightdress as she watched the sun make its slow climb, bringing in the day.

Fingers of red and purple streaked the sky, spreading across the vast expanse above, gradually fading into a deep gold as the sun slowly extinguished the last of the stars.

Suddenly she realized that the ancient Egyptians had experienced the same miracle, but had given it a different name—Ra, creator, god of the sun and giver of life, lord of rebirth. She shut her eyes, remembering the old belief. Ra, born anew at every dawn, sailed the skies, slowly flooding them with his energizing rays of penetrating heat and light, giving life where before there had been only darkness.

Pip sank to her knees, her hands resting on the sill of the window, drinking in the peace that flooded through her soul. Whatever name people had called the light throughout the aeons, it came from the same source, and she could only be grateful that she'd been granted a sanctuary within its embrace.

She took one last look at the sun as it crested the trees, then went back to bed and fell into a long, deep, tranquil sleep.

Three days later, Pip finished her Egyptian portfolio. With a deep sigh of satisfaction she pulled the pile of papers together and put them into a folder. She stood and stretched, rubbing her aching back, but feeling a sense of completeness.

She might not be any sort of heroine, but at least she'd met the challenge she'd set for herself. In two hours' time she'd know whether the governors of the British Museum agreed. All she had to do now was to present them with her proposal.

Odd, she thought, as she tucked her watercolors and sketches into a separate folder. Only days before she'd been in such torment, struggling with confusion and despair, and now she felt so calm, so much at peace, as if she'd waged a battle with her demons and won.

She had Will to thank for setting her on this new path, but most of all she owed thanks to God and His angels, into whose hands she'd put her life.

Pip shivered, wondering if John Henry would come for her. He knew where she was—Will had told her that he'd written to John Henry before he left Alconleigh, telling him she and Peter were safe and sound in London. She had been trying for the last three days to write him herself, but had yet to find words that would adequately explain.

Maybe with time he would forgive her, although she knew she couldn't count on that. She could only hope and pray that he would return to her, for she knew now that she would love him until the day she died.

She gathered up her two folders and went out to the waiting carriage. All she could do now was to turn her face to the future and let God's will be done.

Three hours later, Pip stood alone in the huge, musty hall of the British Museum's Egyptian collection. She wandered from exhibit to exhibit, taking in the statues, the stelae, and sarcophagi, but she hardly saw any of it. Her head still spun with amazement and joy that her paper had been accepted. The governors had yet to read the actual pages, but her presentation had been enough to convince them that her work was a worthwhile endeavor. She couldn't believe they'd actually given her a grant to write a second paper.

She passed by a statue of Sekhmet, the lion-headed fire goddess, one of Sethos II, a black granite statue of Amemophis III, and a vast head of Ramses II. Then she stopped abruptly in front of a much smaller bust, her eyes widening in wonder. A small, quartzite sculpture of a head sat in a case, and she immediately recognized it as Nefertari.

Awestruck, she gazed at it, drinking in its delicate beauty. Nefertari had always represented to Pip the finest aspect of romantic love, the deepest commitment of a woman to a man and him to her.

Hot tears welled in her eyes and slowly trickled down her face as she thought of John Henry and what she might have lost. He had offered her that infinite love, that total commitment, and she had turned her back on him.

She could only shake her head at her folly. How could she have been so blind as to take her dream and crush it between her own two hands?

She closed her eyes and tried to remember the light, to let divine will guide her now. She had to trust and believe that it would see her through.

John Henry halted at the door of the Egyptian Hall as he spotted Pip across the room, her back turned to him. She stood very still in front of a small statue, her hands clenched at her sides.

An infinite love swept through him as he watched her, her slender form so dwarfed by the huge room that he felt an overwhelming sense of tenderness and protection. He wanted to go to her, but he was wary of how she would receive him.

For all he knew, she might treat him with the same icy silence of that terrible night ten days before, only this time he didn't intend to let her get away, at least not without forcing her to talk to him.

If he had to pick her up and carry her off over his shoulder, he would, although he doubted that the staff of the British Museum would appreciate that.

He hesitated, not sure how to proceed. Then suddenly Pip turned around. A bright ray of sunlight broke through a high window, piercing the gloom and bathing her in its glow, illuminating her as if she were an ancient goddess. He realized that she'd been crying, and his heart nearly broke.

She stared at him as if she were looking at a ghost, her face paling.

He didn't move. He couldn't have at that moment if he'd tried.

He stood waiting, his heart pounding with a combination of dread and anticipation. This was it, the culmination of all the days and months and years that he'd loved her, the moment of reckoning that might well decide their future. Tension mounted in him until he didn't think he could bear another moment. Still he didn't move, knowing intuitively that Pip would have to take the first step if she was to come to him freely.

And she did. She began to walk very slowly toward

him, then suddenly broke into a run, throwing herself into his arms, her face pressed against his shoulder, her arms fast around his neck.

"Oh, John Henry," she sobbed, "I'm so sorry. Can you ever forgive me for my stupidity? I do love you, so very, very much. I've been a fool, but I've worked everything out now and I can see how much I'm to blame for everything that's happened."

He held her just as fast, his cheek resting on top of her head as he drank in her sweet scent, the feel of her back in his arms. Pip's reaction was the last thing he'd expected, but he had no objections at all.

"There's nothing to forgive," he said. "I am the one who should ask for forgiveness, since it was I who kept the truth from you."

"No," she cried, gazing into his eyes. "If I hadn't behaved as I did, you would never have had reason to dissemble. I understand that now, and I'm ashamed of myself. I've missed you so much." She clutched him more tightly.

"As I have you," he said hoarsely, tenderly running his hands over her cheeks. "Don't you ever do that to me again. I can't have you running off every time we have a disagreement. Honestly, Pip, I don't think I could survive another two weeks the likes of these."

She shook her head vehemently. "I promise. I just want to go home. I have so much to tell you, but this isn't the right place, even if it does represent a little piece of Egypt."

John Henry produced a handkerchief from his coat and gently wiped away her tears. "Just know now that

I love you, Pip, and am deeply sorry for any pain I caused you."

She gave him a watery smile. "I caused my own pain. I know that now. I hurt you too, and you didn't deserve any of it. It's all so complicated, but I think I might be able to explain. At least I hope I can." She pulled slightly away from him. "How did you know where to find me?" she asked, looking puzzled. "I mean here, at the British Museum."

He rubbed his lips against her cheek. "I finally decided to storm Hanover Square. Lady Samantha has held me prisoner for the last two days in Upper Brook Street, determined to sortie with Will and decide what was to be done, but I finally got impatient and escaped. Will was happy enough to tell me that you'd come here. He mentioned a paper you were presenting to the governors?"

She nodded happily. "I wrote a treatise on my experiences in Egypt, working in the ancient history and antiquities, and it's been accepted, John Henry, along with my drawings and watercolors. Can you believe it? They even want another paper and are prepared to pay me to produce it."

His heart swelled with pride for her. He had known that she was working on a project, but he had not given her the opportunity to tell him about it. "I can well believe it, sweetheart. Congratulations."

"Thank you, for I really did want to accomplish something, but I'd very much like you to take me home now."

He chuckled, offering her his arm and leading her

through the museum and out into the street where his carriage waited. Pip was a law unto herself, and he could only be grateful. She would always be a challenge but a worthy consort, and he knew he'd been blessed. Whatever had happened in the ten days since she'd left Manleigh, she'd come to some sort of peace with herself. He imagined she would tell him about it when the time was right.

In the meantime, he had other important things on his mind and no patience to wait.

As soon as they entered the carriage he drew the curtains and pulled Pip straight into his arms, kissing her hard, drinking in the feel of her full mouth, her honeyed taste, the way her tongue danced against his. He felt like a man who'd been starved and was now more than ready to indulge his appetite.

Pulling away abruptly, he looked deeply into her eyes as if to assure himself that she was really there. Then, cupping her head, he kissed again with a fierce passion. His lips never leaving hers, he lifted Pip onto his lap, pushing up her skirts to bare her legs.

She wriggled against his straining member, and with a groan he reached under the layers of her undergarments, his fingers seeking her innermost recesses.

Pip fell against him with a muffled cry, her legs parting, giving him access to her soft, hot folds, thrusting up against his driving fingers as he took her mouth in another frenzied kiss.

"We're only a few streets away from Hanover Square," she gasped. "Even less now." But at the same time she rubbed her breasts against his chest, her hips moving against the rhythm of his fingers, as lost as he was, until she began to climax.

John Henry thought he might completely lose his mind as she reached her release. Her inner muscles contracted against his fingers and her head fell back as she cried out, her hips rocking hard against his hand.

"Wait now. Just wait a few more minutes," he groaned, kissing her quickly as the carriage drew up in front of the house. He lifted her off his lap, where his arousal threatened to explode at any moment. Hastily adjusting her clothing, he somehow managed to assume a neutral expression as the footman opened the door and let the steps down. John Henry very much doubted that they fooled anyone as they alighted, disheveled and with faces flushed.

Deciding he didn't care, he swept Pip up in his arms and carried her up the steps, pushing straight past the butler who opened the door and marching to the stairs that led to the upstairs bedrooms.

"Good afternoon," Will said cheerfully, walking out into the hall just at that moment. "My. May I assume you have worked out your difficulties?"

John Henry shot him a swift smile. "I don't have time for conversation just now," he said, starting up the staircase.

"Indeed not," Will called up to him. "I'll just go tell Lady Samantha that she may cease her campaign. I might have to give her strong drink to get her over the disappointment of such a quick resolution."

Pip smothered a laugh against John Henry's shoulder. "Poor Samantha," she said. "I'm sure she was looking forward to a protracted battle. Second door on the left, and be quick about it."

John Henry wasted not a moment, pushing the door open and locking it behind him with one hand, carefully shifting Pip's weight in the other. He wasn't going to let her go for a minute until he had her exactly where he wanted her, which was in bed with no clothes on.

He didn't waste a moment there either, depositing her on her bed, stripping off every bit of her clothing as he took off his own. He kissed every available inch of skin as he went, trailing his lips over her neck, down to her creamy breasts, adoring those delicious, tantalizing mounds, sucking the lovely, taut peaks of her nipples, then returning to her mouth as she writhed beneath him.

Pip spread her legs beneath him, urging him to come into her, her small hand reaching for his engorged shaft, guiding it to her entrance.

Wild with need, he lifted his hips and slid into her hot, slick flesh, burying himself in her in one full thrust, his heart pounding so hard that he thought he might break apart. He began to move in her, slowly and gently, but the forceful movement of her hips and the insistent, unrelenting tug of her hands on his buttocks told him that she wanted more. Somehow, he knew that she was giving him more of herself than she ever had before.

John Henry wanted to give her what she needed in return. He thrust hard and deep, over and over, watching her face the whole time, seeing her reach for something beyond physical release, her eyes filled with a love and peace that he'd never thought to see there. He realized in one blinding flash that Pip was finally free. In the same moment, he understood that he too was free.

He couldn't hang on to his control for another moment. "Now, my love, my darling," he gasped, lifting her buttocks closer to his hips.

Pip instantly wrapped her legs around his waist and pulled him closer still, her body shaking. "Now," she echoed against his groan, her muscles contracting and releasing against his, drawing him into her fire as she took his seed into her with an abiding love and acceptance.

He collapsed onto his side, breathing hard, not sure what had just happened but knowing that it had been an epiphany of sorts, a giving and taking of love that spoke of forgiveness and healing and something beyond.

Pip lay still and quiet in his arms. When he finally recovered, he lifted himself onto his elbow and gazed down at her, only to find tears streaming down her face.

"Sweetheart? Are you all right?"

She nodded, gulping back a sob, wrapping her arms tight around his back. "I'm fine, John Henry, just—just very, very happy and grateful that we're together again."

"As am I," he murmured, kissing away her tears, smoothing his hand over her hair.

"So much has happened in the last few days," she said, sitting up against the pillows. "I had an experience

hat I want to tell you about. I don't know if you'll
understand, but I want to tell you anyway."

"Then do. I can't imagine that I won't understand."

"This has to do with another realm," Pip said
earnestly.

"Another realm? What sort of other realm?"

"I don't really know how to describe it, but maybe I
should start by telling you about something that happened a long time ago. I'd forgotten all about it, but
Will reminded me. Do you remember the day I cut my
foot so badly, jumping from the hayloft?"

He shuddered, the memory far too clear for comfort, even now—Pip lying ashen, blood everywhere,
and his desperate panic as he ran to find Will, terrified
that she might die. "That's not a day I'm likely to forget. Why do you ask?"

"Something extraordinary happened then that I
never told you about," she said, a little smile hovering
round the corners of her mouth. "When I was uncon-
scious, I had a dream, only it felt entirely real, as real
as you and I are here in this room right now."

"What sort of dream?" He picked up her hand and
kissed her palm.

"I dreamed that I was in the most beautiful place—
a wonderful, magical garden, held safe and close by
angels. I had no fear, only a sense of peace and joy. The
garden was filled with an indescribable light, clear and
bright and perfect. Then the angels carried me home
and I woke up to find Will sitting at my bedside."

"Are you saying you think this really happened?"
he asked, fascinated.

"Yes. I do. Will saw the light too. I didn't know that until he told me the other night when he was trying to make me see sense about our quarrel. He wanted me to know that I wasn't alone, that my life had purpose and meaning and all I needed to do was reach out and ask for guidance to discover what that purpose and meaning was." She squeezed her eyes shut for a moment. "That night I had the darkest hours of my life. I felt completely lost, overwhelmed by despair. And then I remembered what Will had said, and I finally asked for help from above."

"What happened?" he asked, loving her so much at that moment that he thought his heart might crack open.

"I suddenly felt the same light surround me and fill me with love and peace and understanding. It was like a miracle, John Henry, it really was," she said, her eyes shining. "I felt I was no longer alone, that God would guide me and show me my way, that He had taken my burden from me and I was finally free. Do you understand?"

John Henry gazed at her through a mist of tears, so moved he could hardly speak. "I believe I do," he whispered. "I love you Pip. I love you for so many reasons, but most of all I love you for your honesty. Thank you for telling me." He pulled her down to him, holding her close against his chest. "Know that as long as you are on this earth you will never be alone, that will always look after you and love you and do my best to make you happy."

She kissed his shoulder. "Bless you for that," sh

said softly. "And I will love you always and look after you and do my best to make you happy. I give you my vow."

He rolled her over and kissed her gently. "I can no more help loving you than I can help breathing." He smiled down at her. "However, I do ask that you at least *try* to behave yourself."

Pip gurgled with laughter. "I'll do my best, but I can't promise that I'll be entirely successful."

"No, that would be expecting too much. Pip . . . do you think that we might go visit Peter now? I've missed him terribly."

Pip's eyes shot wide open. "Oh! I almost forgot—I hope you don't mind, but I told Will the whole truth about Peter. I told him the truth about everything."

"Did you?" he said, not sure how to react. Still, he didn't think that Will could have been too terribly upset, given that he hadn't said a word when John Henry had seen him earlier that afternoon. "What made you decide to do that after you'd gone to such lengths to keep Peter's parentage a secret?"

"I'd had enough of lying," she replied. "Will won't tell anyone but my mother about Peter, which is how it should be, but from here on out, let us promise to be entirely honest with each other."

"I promise," he said, "and I truly am sorry for having misled you about my standing. But, Pip, tell me this—do you really balk at being Lady Lovell and having an estate and enough money to keep you in comfort for the rest of your days?"

"Don't be absurd," she said. "You could be King of

England for all I care. Or the Ali Khan. Or Emperor of China."

"Don't exaggerate," he said with a laugh. "Come, Pip. Let's get dressed and go see our son."

"Whatever you'd like, your royal highness," she said, jumping out of bed before he could give her a swat on her well-rounded bottom.

Life was truly good, he thought, shrugging on his clothes. As he followed Pip out of the room he sent up a quick prayer of thanks to Pip's angels for bringing her safely back into his arms.

Epilogue

May 10, 1837
Manleigh Park, Dorset

"Spring is finally here to stay," Pip said lazily, leaning against the balustrade of the arched bridge as she gazed out over the lake where the lily pads floated, their delicate white flowers in full bloom. She glanced at John Henry, who stood peacefully next to her, an expression of contentment on his face.

"I think you're right," he said, slipping an arm around her waist and holding her close to his side. "Though I can't complain about all the rain we've had. See how green everything's become."

"Mmm. And next week we move into the main house. I can barely wait."

He chuckled. "Nor can I. I think I've had enough of workmen and the sound of hammering to last a lifetime. My ears are still ringing."

"You've done a wonderful job," she said, standing on tiptoe to kiss his cheek. "I'm so happy. These last few months have been truly wonderful, but I have to admit that I've been impatient to settle in properly."

They turned as a shout of laughter and then a burst of short, high barks came from the lawn behind them on the near side of the lake.

Peter ran in circles, his arms flailing wildly as he chased after the puppy that John Henry had given him for his first birthday, three months before. Aafteh waved merrily at them from where she sat on the grass next to Tobias, her other hand filled with a bunch of daffodils.

"It's a good thing those two have had the banns cried," John Henry said dryly. "Two more weeks and I can stop worrying about whether Tobias is going to drag her off to the nearest hay pile."

Pip grinned. "What Aafteh and Tobias get up to is their own business. They're blissfully happy, and that's all I care about."

"As do I, as long as Aafteh doesn't present Tobias with a child before a suitable amount of time. I'm a squire now and I don't want the local people to think I neglected my responsibilities," he replied, his eyes dancing with humor.

"You, John Henry, have enough responsibility to keep you occupied for a long time to come, and you might as well prepare yourself for another."

He stared at her for one brief moment, then grabbed her hands and held them tightly. "Are you—?

Pip? Are you going to have a child?" His face was filled with hope and excitement.

"I am," she said. "I saw the doctor yesterday while you were busy with the plasterers. He says we can expect a brother or sister for Peter sometime in early October."

John Henry picked her up and swung her around with a whoop of delight, then placed her back down on the ground with a look of alarm. "Oh—I probably shouldn't have done that. Do you need to sit down?"

Pip laughed. "Have you ever seen a cow sit down just because it's with calf? Honestly, John Henry. I'm just going to have a baby. You did start life as a farmer's son after all, no matter what you've become since."

"Yes, but you're not a cow, you're my wife. I don't want to take any risks." He regarded her anxiously. "Are you sure you don't want to sit down or lie down or eat something?"

"The only thing I want," she replied, seeing exactly how the next six months would be, "is for you to furnish the nursery. I thought we might paint it pale yellow, the shade of cowslips—or that lovely soft color that the light has when dawn is just breaking. . . ."

"I love you," he said, gathering her into his arms and kissing her soundly.

Katherine Kingsley is the author of six historical romances for Dell: *Lilies on the Lake*, *In the Presence of Angels*, *The Sound of Snow*, *Call Down the Moon*, *Once Upon a Dream*, and *In the Wake of the Wind*. She has won numerous writing awards, including two career achievement awards from *Romantic Times*.

Katherine lives in the Colorado mountains with two Jack Russell terriers and an Amazon parrot, and spends a few months every year on the Greek island of Mykonos.